J
THE
5/05

Singer

❧ JEAN THESMAN ❧

VIKING

VIKING
Published by Penguin Group
Penguin Young Readers Group, 345 Hudson Street, New York, New York 10014, U.S.A.
Penguin Group (Canada), 10 Alcorn Avenue, Toronto, Ontario, Canada M4V 3B2
(a division of Pearson Penguin Canada Inc.)
Penguin Books Ltd, 80 Strand, London WC2R 0RL, England
Penguin Ireland, 25 St Stephen's Green, Dublin 2, Ireland (a division of Penguin Books Ltd)
Penguin Group (Australia), 250 Camberwell Road, Camberwell, Victoria 3124, Australia
(a division of Pearson Australia Group Pty Ltd)
Penguin Books India Pvt Ltd, 11 Community Centre, Panchsheel Park, New Delhi - 110 017, India
Penguin Group (NZ), Cnr Airborne and Rosedale Roads, Albany, Auckland, New Zealand
(a division of Pearson New Zealand Ltd)
Penguin Books (South Africa) (Pty) Ltd, 24 Sturdee Avenue, Rosebank, Johannesburg 2196, South Africa

Penguin Books Ltd, Registered Offices: 80 Strand, London WC2R 0RL, England

First published in 2005 by Viking, a division of Penguin Young Readers Group

1 3 5 7 9 10 8 6 4 2

Text copyright © Jean Thesman, 2005
All rights reserved

LIBRARY OF CONGRESS CATALOGING-IN-PUBLICATION DATA
Thesman, Jean.
Singer / Jean Thesman.
p. cm.
Summary: Imprisoned by her wicked and power-hungry mother, Lady Rhiannon, Gwenore
escapes to a women's healing community, later changing her name and becoming nursemaid and
protector to the children of the magical king of Lir, who is now married to Rhiannon.
ISBN 0-670-05937-4 (hardcover)
[1. Healers—Fiction. 2. Mothers and daughters—Fiction. 3. Nannies—Fiction. 4. Fantasy.] I. Title.
PZ7.T3525Si 2005   [Fic]—dc22   2004014905

5-4-05
Printed in U.S.A. • Set in Bembo • Book design by Jim Hoover

CONTENTS

Prologue

a strange story has been told about the four motherless children of King Lir. They lived long ago, in a beautiful, secluded place that only occasionally was harried by dragons, a place where King Lir's grandfather had sealed up all of the troll caves and signed a binding treaty with the Lord of the Dwarfs in order to ensure peace. In this kingdom, everyone knew everybody, and not many of them ever quarreled. The people prospered, but when their traders and merchants went out into the world, they were wise enough to keep the prosperity a secret, for fear that strangers would hear of it and travel there, bringing their problems with them.

The king's children were beautiful, pale and blond and dark-eyed, and they were cheerful and generous. They were beloved by all the inhabitants of Lir—all but one, the only stranger to appear for years, and she was the king's new wife. Unknown to him, she was a witch. One day she cursed the children and turned them into swans, and the curse lasted for eight hundred years. When they were finally freed, it was too late, for they soon died.

Or so the old tale is told. But it is not true. The truth is happier—and yet more frightening.

Now begins the story of the girl who rescued the children, she who was born Gwenore of Wales, renamed Mary Blondine of the Abbey, and then, before she disappeared, Singer. She was the daughter of the witch.

Listen carefully. I am that daughter. I am Singer and Mary Blondine and Gwenore, caught up in my mother's plots even before I was born, and trapped by the curse of the birthmark on my wrist.

The true story of the enchantment of the children of Lir did not take eight hundred terrible years to unfold. It began and ended briefly, although they were violent times and people died, including one whom I loved. But the people of Lir would not tell you any of this, for they do not want more strangers to come and disturb their peace. Instead, even if you could find them, they would tell you that the witch still lives on the cliffs over the shore, a danger to everyone.

They would warn you to stay away, tell no one—and forget that you ever had found the kingdom of Lir.

◁ ◁ ◁

1

fLIGHt fROm tHE DaRK wItCH

the boatman, scrawny and bowlegged, picked me up as if
I weighed nothing. "Don't speak, Gwenore," he muttered, and he carried me across the muddy marsh toward the
river as if he were certain of his exact destination, even
though he could not have seen his own boots that night, in
the dense fog. He never looked back, apparently trusting that
Brennan was following—Brennan and the mad old priest,
Father Caddaric. I was too terrified to speak, but the boatman growled, warning me for a second time. "Don't make a
sound."

Somehow he found his coracle, and he dumped me on
the damp bottom of the hide-covered boat, on a sheepskin
that smelled filthy. I stifled a cry, waited for a moment in the
silence until I felt safe enough to take a deep breath, and then
I pushed the foul-smelling fleece away from my face. I still
could see nothing. There was no moon that night—Brennan
had told me that we would not attempt to escape when there
was a moon to betray us—but we had not counted on such
a thick and terrible fog. It was both a blessing and a curse.

Now it protected us, but if we succeeded in reaching the river's mouth, we might not see the vessel waiting for us, and we would miss our only chance for freedom. If Brennan and I were stranded when daylight broke, we would be caught and brought back, and we could not expect anything good. As for the boatman and the priest, who could say? The boatman might have friends who would hide him, for a while, at least. After all, he was a successful smuggler and was well liked along the river. And the priest was practiced in disappearing, sometimes for months on end. No one could be certain that he had friends anywhere, except among the Fair Folk, but there were plenty of people in that part of the world who were afraid enough of him to keep any secret he wanted kept—to their graves, if necessary.

But Brennan and I were distrusted everywhere because we lived in the castle. At twelve, I was not so young that I did not know that anyone who lived under the same roof with the malignant Lady Rhiamon would be hated. And while gifts of gold made good people into spies, threats of torture made better spies. But even in the best of times, if there ever had been any times like that, country people had nothing in common with the aristocracy, with families as arrogant as mine. They were thoroughly sick of the endless wars and pillaging, and they rejoiced in any misfortune that befell us. A noblewoman's young daughter, who had committed murder (or so it was said), and her humble maid, a slave woman who had helped her in her crime, would be turned over to the sheriff, or, better still, simply killed after dark, buried in haste, and forgotten. Life was simpler for those who admitted knowing nothing about the affairs of the people in castles and manor houses along the disputed border between Wales and England.

The boatman had moved away, his footsteps sucking in the mud. Then there was only silence. Were the others lost? I wondered. The darkness seemed complete and final, as if nothing existed anywhere except the almost palpable absence of people and objects. Could the boatman have dropped me over the edge of the world? My terror nearly overwhelmed me. How long should I wait in the bottom of the boat? What if I had been betrayed? What if I had been abandoned? If no one came, should I try to find my way back home?

No. Never. I knew what awaited me there, where my mother's will might still go unchallenged, in spite of everything that had gone wrong in the household.

I widened my eyes to see better and stared into the dark, listening for any faint sound that might indicate that someone was coming. I heard only the almost inaudible whispers of Fair Folk, who always seemed to be curious about my affairs, but I could not make out their words. Perhaps they were using their own language that night, instead of mine.

The coracle's flat bottom rested on mud and dead marsh reeds, in water no more than a few inches deep. Now, when my heart quieted, I heard the nearby river lapping against rocks or a low bank. A mile away on the coast, the tide would be ready to turn, and when it did, the river would rush out to sea. Would the coracle be caught up in it? If it was, what would I do, carried out to sea on the swift current, with no one to help me? I had never been in a boat alone—I was not like the children of the river folk, who grew up in boats and could manage them as well as their fathers. I shifted my weight cautiously, easing myself off one of the bare coracle ribs, then pulled the fleece over my face and inhaled the old, sour smells of damp and mold.

Suddenly I heard the brush of fabric on hide. The coracle heaved to one side, and Brennan climbed in beside me in the dark. I gratefully inhaled Brennan's scent, lavender and clean wool and the salve she massaged into the scar on her face twice a day, the scar my mother gave her with a lead-tipped whip.

"Quiet," Brennan said, as if I needed to be reminded—both of us were fugitives now. If Brennan could stay free for a year, she would no longer be a slave. That was the law. But I, the only child of mad Rhiamon, would never be truly free, God save me. No law protected a daughter from her own mother, especially the daughter who had been cursed from her birth. I would be lucky to avoid burning at the stake.

One more person was coming, besides the boatman. I listened hard, hoping to hear the splash and suck of footsteps in the marsh. The boat tilted again, surprising me. The old priest had not made a sound crossing through the reeds to the coracle. Now he settled into the boat next to me, drew his dark robes around his bony body, and sighed. I heard his wooden beads click. His face was close enough for me barely to see that his eyes were closed. He still believed that praying could help?

We waited. Brennan occasionally patted me, as if to reassure me, but reassurance was wasted. If I had been left to plan the night's frantic activities for myself, I might still be in the cellar room where my mother had thrown me weeks before. I now knew and understood confinement and how it worked. If I cried, I got no food. If I was silent, I was fed twice a day. If I asked questions or wept, I got no food. If I bit my tongue until I tasted blood and never begged for relief, I was fed. Life had become simple and predictable, and I valued predictability. In the end, balancing one kind of life against another, being alone in the predictable dark was better than living above, in the great rooms, where I had never known from one instant to the next what would happen. And probably it had been better than what lay before me.

Despite what Brennan and the old priest had told me, I did not believe that escape was really possible, that freedom was possible, and that I might survive somewhere safe from my mother and punishment for what had been done on the rocky hillside at the end of autumn, when I had tried to run away. Where was Tom tonight? Did he still live? Or had they caught him? Where was my dog?

I had supposed that autumn had turned to winter in the time I had been confined, so I was not surprised by the bone-shattering cold. If my little dog had been curled next to me inside my cloak, I might have stopped shaking. Was he still alive? Oh, little bright-eyed Striker, so brave and loyal. Probably he was dead because of his role in the attack on Sir Richard, the cousin of my long-dead father. I pressed my hands over my mouth so that I could not cry out. I missed Striker so! I would ask Brennan about him, when it was safe to speak.

The boatman returned with an extra paddle. The

coracle sat almost still on the barely moving water. Then I felt a change in the river through the oxhide side of the awkward boat. The water was pulling at it, moving us a little over the reeds. What might happen next? Would we still be alive at dawn?

I heard a rough fluttering, and a crow dropped out of the fog, landing on Father Caddaric's shoulder. "Look sharp," it said, and then it dove into the sleeve of the priest's robe, as if it had found refuge there before.

Brennan and I had drawn back when the crow appeared, and now we sat stunned. Brennan stifled something that sounded almost like the beginning of a shocked laugh. Father Caddaric tucked his wide sleeve protectively around the lump under the fabric that was the crow, then raised his head to scowl at Brennan. Fog had collected on his beard and hood. In the dark he seemed to glimmer. To me, this old, itinerant priest was more frightening than ever, but he had volunteered to help us escape, and we had no other choice.

The boatman had heard the crow, too, but he was not amazed or alarmed, at least not at the crow's behavior. Perhaps the bird's message disturbed him, though, because he stood abruptly and I heard him grunt as he shoved his pole against the muddy marsh bottom. The coracle swung out into the river current suddenly, awkwardly, turning broadside against the water's force. The boatman swore under his breath, sat down again, and lifted a paddle. The old priest, without being asked, took the other paddle. Together, in the dark, they turned the little boat and moved it downstream until it caught firmly in the swift current that flowed to sea. It was as if they had practiced this escape a hundred times. Had they rescued others? That would not have surprised me.

Brennan pulled me upright and whispered, "Look back. Can you see? We're leaving it all behind."

But I saw nothing, for the dark was too deep. I leaned against Brennan's shoulder and the maid pulled me close. "We're leaving," Brennan whispered again. "Praise God."

"God had nothing to do with this night's work," the old priest said, wheezing over his paddle. "Nor with anything that came before. That was the she-devil's work."

"Striker," I whispered to Brennan. "Is he alive?"

"Yes. Now hush."

I sagged against Brennan, crying silently. I wanted to ask more about my dog, but Brennan, sensing the question, placed a warning finger over my lips.

From his place inside the priest's sleeve, the crow muttered something under its breath.

The fog did not lift, but who could expect that in winter? Probably it would still lay heavy on the land in the morning, if we even could tell when morning arrived. Sometimes I caught the scent of the sea, and other times the fog was tainted with the acrid stench of burning peat, and that meant that we were passing a farm. For a miserable lifetime, it seemed, the coracle followed the swift current between invisible banks. Once, a voice came out of the dark. "Who's out there on the river?" a man shouted. "Who is it? Samuel, is that you?"

I held my breath.

"Smugglers," I heard a man say, and someone else laughed and grunted a few unintelligible words. But then the voices were behind us, and Father Caddaric muttered, "They are deserters. No decent human would be out of doors on a night like this." He ignored the boatman's snort of laughter.

It was possible that the men we had heard were deserters, and they might have proven dangerous to those of us in the boat, for deserters from the various armies, small and large, were rampaging through the Marches, where a line of castles and fortified manors separated Wales from England. Looting and burning as they moved about, the deserters expected to profit from anyone they caught. Merchants, farmers, refugees, wanderers, or even adventurous youngsters or runaway wives—any of these might be abused, robbed, or even sold into slavery, bringing a few coins at a wharf on the coast. The slave trade had always been brisk on the coastlines, with English slaves sold in Wales and Welsh slaves sold to the English, and everybody more than glad to buy a slave from Ireland, cheap enough even in island waters, if you had the patience to beat common sense into them.

Cold and miserable, I still found it possible to sleep for a while, but only because I lay curled next to Brennan. When I woke, I found that the fog now overlaid a gray sky instead of a black one. We were nearing the mouth of the river, later than we had intended, and now we were in danger.

The priest and the boatman exchanged whispers. They turned the coracle violently, without warning, and the small boat spun halfway around, then righted itself. Ahead, I saw the dark side of a ship. The coracle bumped gently into it.

The boatman whistled, and I heard an answering whistle from the ship's deck. The end of a rope ladder plopped into the boat, and the boatman grabbed the end of it. "Up," he said. "You." With his free hand, he gestured at Brennan.

She picked up a bundle I had not noticed before. In the dim light, it looked as if it had been wrapped in the curtain from my old bedroom and bound with a cord. Brennan slung the bundle by a cord loop across her back and began climbing the rope ladder as if she had done it before. The priest steadied it while the boatman clung to an iron cleat on the side of the ship to keep them from drifting away.

"You," the boatman said, jerking his head toward me. The priest nodded to me. I began climbing and felt the rope ladder twist beneath me. There was nowhere to go but up, to whatever awaited me there. Once, I banged against the side of the ship, skinning the knuckles of both hands, but I dared not make a sound.

Brennan grabbed me when I was near the top and pulled me up the rest of the way. "Don't talk," she whispered. "Hide your face."

I did my best to pull my head inside the rough hood I wore. It was a man's, and big enough to hide my face, as well as my long brown hair, if that was what Brennan wanted.

Father Caddaric's head appeared over the side and he nearly tumbled to the deck. But he steadied himself stiffly, grunting a little. He pulled the crow from his sleeve and tossed it up, saying, "Go home, Vespers! I will see you in good time." The bird flapped away into the fog.

"Come," Father Caddaric whispered to Brennan and me, and we followed him below, to a dark and narrow passageway. "Duck your heads," he whispered. "We hide in here."

He pushed us through an opening into what might have been a cupboard or an enclosed bed of some kind. As soon as we settled ourselves on a pile of rags, he climbed in behind us and closed the door.

"Don't speak," he whispered. "Pray, if you are foolish enough to believe that anything is listening. Sleep if you can."

Brennan helped me settle myself in one corner and leaned close to me. "Don't be afraid," she whispered. "We're almost free."

I wanted to ask where we were going. And I wanted to know about Striker—and Tom. But I had waited months, and so I could wait even longer.

Tom had been injured by Sir Richard's horse. The horse had reared, and its hooves flew up and would have split Tom's skull, but he had thrown himself to one side, then jumped up and grabbed the bridle. Horse, rider, and Tom all fell hard on the narrow, treacherous trail. The horse jumped up immediately and ran off, and Tom, after a terrible moment of silence when his dark blue eyes stared sightless at the afternoon sky, got to his feet unsteadily, holding one hand against the blood streaming down the side of his face. "Run! Run!" I had cried, and Tom did his best, stumbling among the boulders and brush.

Only Richard had remained behind, not moving, not breathing, lying crooked on the rocks, his head twisted to one side. *Dead?* Dead, praise all the saints! My one fumbling plan to escape had failed, and my tormentor had seen us and ridden after us. But now he was dead, thank God, even though my part in it probably was a sin. Dead, and all of his evil intentions toward me with him! He would never creep into my room again at night and slip his hands under my coverlet. He would never back me into a corner again and push his fat, wet mouth against mine. He would never trap me in the lavatory again. He was dead on the rocky trail below the castle wall, and fate had succeeded where I had failed.

I realized that I was nearly panting from remembered fear, and so I deliberately made myself quiet in the way I had learned so early in my life, breathing slowly while reciting prayers, although, of course, no god or saint or spirit would listen to me now. In a few moments, I knew that Father Caddaric had fallen asleep, for he snored gently. But I would never sleep again, I thought.

But I did. I never heard the wind that blew off the fog and sent the ship on its way.

The ship sailed south on rough seas. No one came to the cupboard. We were hungry and thirsty, and Brennan divided half a loaf of bread and passed a flask of water among us. Sometimes footsteps passed, but no one opened the door. Still, the priest cautioned us again to remain silent, no matter what happened. Voices shouted and cursed, and once someone laughed loudly. The ship plunged and rolled, and I was afraid I would vomit, but after a while the motion seemed comforting. It meant that I was moving farther and farther away from my mother. Crowded in with Brennan and Father Caddaric, almost warm in the dark, I had time to think.

Everything seemed inevitable, dark following day, winter following summer, fright following despair. In all my twelve years, I had never found a way to avoid the seemingly unbreakable pattern. My mother hated me, but she had kept me close for a reason she had never shared. That reason had something to do with the birthmark that looked like a drop of blood on my left wrist, for sometimes my mother would grab my arm, twisting it to show the mark to full advantage, and snarl, "Why me? Why me? I'm trapped with you *forever* because of *that*." But no one explained anything. Brennan probably did not know, for she was only a slave.

But the priest—he was another matter. My mother hated him more than anyone else, even the memory of my noble, hapless father. Might he hold answers? Why was he helping me?

We docked after dark, and two men came for us, escorting us roughly to the rail and nearly tossing us off to the sagging quay below. We made our way between stacked bales and barrels, following the priest, who scuttled ahead of us and never looked back. Rain was falling, a drenching, cold rain that soaked my thick cloak within minutes, leaving me sorry that I did not have the fleece to throw around my shoulders. My throat was sore, and when I coughed, my chest hurt. The priest moved too fast, but I was afraid to ask him to slow down.

We passed several men, who showed little interest in us,

and when we reached a narrow, muddy street, the priest directed us toward a low building where dim lamplight fell from the open top half of a door. I smelled cooking meat and my mouth watered.

"Sit on the bench and wait," Father Caddaric said.

We did, and I leaned against Brennan. What next? Where were we going? My clothes were wet and my cough was growing worse. I knew that I needed to be indoors, in a warm place. Perhaps here, where something good was cooking?

After a long time, the priest came back again, this time with another man. "This is Angus," he said. "He'll shelter you tonight and send you on your way tomorrow morning. I'll leave you now." He put his hand on my head. "We'll meet again. Don't be afraid. Everything that comes to you was written for you long ago."

He drew a cross on my forehead and blessed me. He would have turned away in the direction of the wharf, but I grabbed his sleeve.

"Where are we going?" I asked him hoarsely.

He hesitated for a moment. "I am sorry for my part in your dangerous life," he said.

"What do you mean?" I asked, panicked that he would leave without answering.

He walked away then, and I would have followed, but Angus grabbed me roughly and said, "You will keep up with me, or I will leave you behind. You aren't worth dying for."

His speech was educated, like Father Caddaric's, but he was not dressed like a priest. Or a nobleman. I was so suspi-

cious of him that I drew back and pulled against his hand
gripping my arm, but Brennan said, "Go! Go!" and so I went.

He led us down a dark street to a small house, and in a
sparsely furnished room, he rummaged among sacks and
parcels on a table in a corner until he found bread, cheese,
and a jug of watered wine for us. Except for telling us to stay
in the room until he returned, he remained silent. After he
left, Brennan and I ate hungrily and then made ourselves as
comfortable as possible on a narrow platform covered with
rushes, near a smoldering peat fire. My cough shook my
whole body. Brennan urged me to drink the last of the contents of the jug, but by then my throat hurt too much. I
shook my head and pushed away Brennan's hand.

Before we slept, Brennan told me that she had kept
Striker in her attic room, hidden behind a false wall with
Tom, until the boy had recovered enough to travel. Tom's
head had been injured when the horse fell on him, and
something was still wrong with him. He could not remember anything from one moment to the next and he walked
with a limp, even though his leg had not been hurt. But he
was well enough to leave the attic, and he was more than able
to care for the small white dog that I loved so much.

"And then," Brennan murmured, "Father Caddaric took
Tom and the dog away one night. I never heard more about
them, and I was afraid to learn their whereabouts. Knowing
is dangerous. I feared your mother would ask me—and she
did!—and if she suspected me of lying, she would kill me.
You know that she always could read our minds as easily as
she read her book of wicked spells. And you needed me alive.

Then Father Caddaric came and told me that he knew a way to get you away from her. When night fell, the guard was gone and the cellar door had been left open. And you know the rest."

"I don't know where we're going," I said. "No one has told me."

"You'll know when you're there. We have to trust the people who are helping us." That was all Brennan would say.

The room was barely warmed by the smoking peat fire, and I awoke stiff and shuddering, just before daylight. My cough was so painful that I pressed my arms against my ribs, holding myself against the agony. Angus had brought bread and water, and he waited impatiently while Brennan ate, sitting on the floor and using a low stool for a table. I refused food. Then he took us away on his bony, long-legged brown horse, with me riding before him and Brennan behind, clasping him around his narrow waist. We left the village and traveled through a dripping forest in a thick mist, on a narrow path nearly covered over with dead ferns and straggling yellow grass. Silent tree spirits watched from low branches, but I did not point them out to my companions, because no one ever saw them but me.

Rain fell and stopped again. Once we turned out into a broader path, and ahead of us a party of travelers moved in a long line, armed horsemen leading and following and in between several wagons. The last armed man turned in his saddle to stare, then—finally satisfied that Angus, a woman, and a young girl posed no threat to the travelers—turned back again to hunch his shoulders against the drizzle.

When I was sure that I would die if I had to ride any longer, the horse finally stopped. We had left the road and now waited before a thick wooden gate in a high stone wall. Angus shouted, "Hoy!" and after a while the gate opened a crack. An old nun peered out, hesitated, and opened the gate a little more.

Angus, with one smooth movement, grasped me and swung me down from the horse. Brennan tossed the bundle after me.

"Here she is," Angus said to the nun. "Get inside, girl, before anyone else comes along."

I hesitated, looking back at Brennan for help. "Go," Brennan said. "Hurry." She kept her place on the horse, however.

"Where are you going?" I cried hoarsely. "Don't leave me here!"

Brennan sobbed and turned her face away, covering her mouth with one trembling hand. The nun took my arm and tugged it, hard. "Come inside. You'll be safe here, Mary."

"I'm not—"

"You are Mary now," the nun said. She looked around as if she was afraid we were being watched, and then she grabbed the bundle with her free hand and shoved me ahead of her through the gate. "Welcome, Mary. I am Sister Mark. We'll care for you until your aunt arrives."

"I have no aunt," I tried to say through my violent coughing. Clearly the hunchbacked old nun had mistaken me for someone else. "I have no aunt!" I finally cried.

"You will have one," Sister Mark said. The gate slammed

shut and she let go of my arm long enough to drop a heavy bolt in place.

We stood in a courtyard paved with smooth stone. Low buildings with shuttered windows faced the courtyard on three sides. In the center grew an ancient apple tree with thick limbs and a trunk that looked as if it had been scarred by fire. A gray-striped cat sat on the lowest limb.

"Look sharp, Gwenore," it said in the voice of Father Caddaric's crow, and then it laughed. All around us, a hundred crows called my name. "Gwenore, Gwenore, Gwenore!" Sister Mark did not seem to hear, but I was terrified.

My knees buckled and I fell to the ground.

2

BETRAYED

a fterward, in a small room with tapestry-covered walls, I slept and woke, slept and woke, while nights and days passed and my illness brought me so near to dying that the nuns argued quietly whether a priest should be called. Sister Mark gave me medicine by the spoonful, and although the honey in it could not disguise the bitterness of willow bark and something even worse, I swallowed it obediently. Sometimes, awake and feverish at night, I watched the lamp that burned in a small alcove, and I struggled to remember where I was and why I was here. But it took too much effort, and I would sink into sleep again. During the days, I watched the sky through a small pane of thick, greenish glass high in the wall, while the light outside brightened and faded. Rain fell sometimes, slowly, gently, and drops slid down the small window. Once I saw snowflakes spinning past. Sometimes pale tree spirits peeped in, by twos and threes, and once one tapped on the glass with a thin, transparent finger and smiled at me.

Each evening, when the light faded, Sister Mark lit the

lamp, and so I was never in the dark. I could not have borne the dark again, after my months in the cellar. But Sister Mark did not provide company, for she answered no questions and never stayed more than a few moments. She was the only one I saw.

Several times during each day and night, I heard a gentle, muted bell. It woke me from sleep, sometimes startling me, other times soothing me. At the worst times, when I was awakened from deep sleep, I feared I had been captured and returned to the cellar. But in the cellar, I had not had a bed, nor had I worn a clean nightdress, nor had there been a lamp or window to relieve the darkness. Nor had anyone brought me hot food and helped me sit up to eat. Nor had I heard that strange, soft bell ringing.

But it was too much to worry about while my cough was so painful and I burned with fever. I hoped that my mother could not find me, or if she did, that she would kill me quickly. Sometimes I dreamed of her, terrible dreams that caused me to rise up, screaming. Sometimes Sister Mark came in to reassure me. And sometimes the cat came in, to sit beside me and whisper tales that I did not dare believe. My mother had been forced to leave the castle by Sir Richard's sister? She had taken refuge on the estate of an old Norman nobleman who had hopeless pretensions to the throne? The man's elderly wife had died suddenly of what some thought was poison? I never knew whether I should believe the beast or not. Sometimes I suspected that he was laughing at me.

Several times I asked Sister Mark where I was, but the

woman only smiled and said, "You are in a safe place." When I asked about Brennan, Sister Mark said, "The woman you were with? I never knew her and I do not know where she went. It is better not to ask too many questions."

I asked the cat the same questions, but he said, "The birds have not brought news of that woman."

"Can't you ask the people who tell you about my mother?" I asked.

He laughed. "People? When do people ever know anything? The birds are the messengers, and sometimes the fish in the river know an interesting story or two that I've been able to use to my advantage—after dinner, of course. For instance, the boatman who took you down the river found a sack of gold coins on his doorstep two days after he delivered you to the ship. Wisely, he took his wife and six children away on a long sea voyage, and only yesterday I heard that they live comfortably in a warmer climate. What do you say to that?"

"I am glad he is safe. What of the priest?"

"Oh. Him." The cat's eyes narrowed. "He and his crow are stirring the pot somewhere, you may be sure of it. He has plans."

"Plans for me?"

The cat laughed and jumped down from my bed. "Who can say?" He padded silently from the room.

Once when I woke to find Sister Mark in the room, I suffered a moment of panic. I was beginning to feel better, and so my thinking was clearer—or at least clear enough that I understood that cats probably do not speak or bring messages from birds and fish. I had to find out what I was doing in this place! Was I near home or far away? Was anyone looking for me? I struggled to sit up and cleared my throat in an effort to speak. My questions needed answers. But the nun said, "Lie back. I'll return to feed you, and we'll talk then, but now I must go to the chapel for Prime."

"I heard a bell just now," I said hoarsely.

"It was the call to prayer," Sister Mark said. "Go back to sleep." She pushed aside the curtain hanging across the low, narrow door, and disappeared. I coughed painfully and lay back on the bed. The little room was warm, which surprised me, because there was no fire. But I did not wonder long. I fell asleep again and dreamed of Striker and Tom playing in a shallow stream on a summer day, while in the distance, fierce black horses with silver hooves watched over them. Once it seemed to me that four women stood beside my bed, smiling down on me, and Sister Mark led them away, murmuring unintelligibly to them in a magical language I almost remembered. But then Striker and Tom came for me once more, and we walked through the forest on the highest hill, where no one could find us, and we gathered medicinal plants that only the little dog could name. And all the while, four swans circled overhead, against the brilliant blue sky, and I thought I heard them singing. Or were they weeping?

I woke again, with a start, and found a different nun in the room, one as old as Sister Mark. But this one did not smile. Deep wrinkles nearly hid her small, brown eyes, and her hands were splotched with scabs and sores. I jerked away from her reach, for suddenly I had seen the nun's true face behind the one she wore, a face even uglier, with eyes that burned like red coals.

"Who are you?" the old woman whispered intently, almost angrily, as she bent over me. Her black veil fell around her like soiled wings. She smelled of grease and stale sweat and something else, something sharp and bitter, like a burning poisonous plant. "Tell me who you really are, girl," she urged.

"Sister Bernice!" Sister Mark said from the doorway. "How kind of you to look in on Mary while I was bringing soup to her."

Sister Bernice straightened, her veil falling back into place, covering her arms and even her scabbed hands. She rearranged her expression before she turned to face Sister Mark. "I heard the girl cry out," she lied. "I came in to see if I could help."

"I'm here now," Sister Mark said, firmly shouldering the other nun out of her way. "Are you ready to eat a little, Mary? You need to try."

I struggled to sit up, but fell back weakly. "I'm not hungry." Sister Bernice had not left the room, and I watched her fearfully.

Sister Mark saw. She turned and said, "Sister, you are not needed here. I mean what I say. *You are not needed.*"

Sister Bernice hesitated, then pushed aside the curtain and disappeared.

"Probably she is still listening, Mary," Sister Mark said calmly. "Sister Bernice is the abbey snoop and tale-bearer. Now sit up and taste this soup. You will find it much to your liking."

I took Sister Mark's first comment as a warning, but I had not planned on talking to anyone (except the imaginary cat) in this strange place. I knew I would learn more by listening. I propped myself upright and opened my mouth when Sister Mark held up the spoon.

The soup was thick and hot, not the thin gruel I was usually given, and it tasted better than anything I could remember eating for a long time. I finished the portion gratefully, and when Sister Mark unwrapped a napkin, displaying two slices of bread spread with honey, I reached for them eagerly. Sister Mark smiled, watching me.

"Wait for a little while," I begged. "Please talk to me. I need to know where I am." My left wrist burned suddenly, and I gasped and pushed back my sleeve. My birthmark stung like nettles.

Sister Mark pulled my sleeve down. "Keep your arm covered," she murmured. "Some things are not understood here. Now sleep again. When you wake up next, I'll bring you another meal, perhaps even a sweet pudding. I know you'll live now. For a while I feared you would not."

She moved out of the room soundlessly, leaving me with more questions but no answers at all. I pulled back my sleeve and stared at my birthmark again. It did not hurt now, but it remained bright red, like blood. Yes, it was right to keep it hidden, because it was ugly.

I believed that everything about me was ugly.

During the days of my recuperation, unpleasant Sister Bernice came to see me several times, always asking me who I really was. Once she reached out to snatch away the cloth that Sister Mark had pinned over my hair, hiding it as completely as her own was hidden, but I flinched back and held the cloth firmly to my head. I could not bear the thought of those scabby hands touching my hair. Another time Sister Bernice picked up the lamp and moved toward me, as if wanting to see me better, but Sister Mark whisked into the room then and smoothly took the lamp from the other nun's hand. "We must not expose Mary's eyes to too much light," she said. "The physician warned us that bright light could harm the child."

"Perhaps the abbess should hear of this," Sister Bernice said slyly. "Perhaps she does not know that you are harboring this sick girl at the abbey."

Sister Mark, smoothing and tucking in the thick wool blanket that covered me, said, "We harbor many sick children here. And many sick women. If I recall, your sister's elder daughter is here, recovering from her own distressing condition. Again. And her new babe is in the nursery near the kitchen, with last year's babe. Poor crippled little ones. Who would care for them if the abbey did not? Who would care for any of us?"

Sister Bernice flushed unpleasantly but said nothing.

"However, if you like, run along and tell the Abbess's servant that you want to speak to Abbess," Sister Mark said. She bent over me, smiled, and then straightened up again, as much as she could with her twisted back. "Just tell her that I'll be along promptly to explain everything—after *your* visit," she said.

Sister Bernice left without speaking again.

Sister Mark pulled a stool close to the bed. "Be careful of her," she whispered. "She is dangerous, so tell her nothing. Above all, never tell your real name to her or anyone else. And keep your birthmark hidden, for it is unusual, and if anyone is searching for you, that mark will be a way to identify you. We will send you on to your aunt as soon as you are well again, if the roads are fit for travel. In the meantime, promise yourself that you will not confide in people, no matter how friendly anyone might seem."

The curtain at the door stirred.

"And," Sister Mark said in her normal voice, "avoid Sister Bernice at all costs, because some of us disagree with Sister Paul in the infirmary. We think Sister Bernice's sores *are* leprosy after all."

Quick footsteps hurried away from the door, and Sister Mark smiled. "Nuns are not always good," she murmured. "And my confessor assures me that I am the worst of all."

I learned about the soft, clear bells as the days passed. They summoned the people in the abbey for prayers eight times each day. I would wake in the dark at Lauds and Matins, hearing first the bells and then the scuffing footsteps in the hall, and I knew that everyone was going into the chapel to pray, and I was comforted. The night did not seem so full of danger when the nuns were at prayer. It was easier to drift off to sleep in those times, when I was secure, and it was at those times that I dreamed again of the four women. One, a stocky woman, would step forward and show me a sword with wild roses tied to the hilt. She would touch the blade and I would hear several notes from a harp.

Often, there were pale spirits at my window, and once I thought that I saw four blond children there, too. But perhaps I only dreamed them.

When I was stronger, Sister Mark brought a small padded chair into the room and helped me into it. The floor was warm under my bare feet and I asked about that.

"This part of the abbey was built over the ruins of an old Roman manor," the nun said. "The floors are heated with hot air coming from a great furnace, so there is no need of a fire in here. When you are well, I will take you into the refectory. Then you will see something wonderful." She smiled. "Something that Sister Bernice hates."

Sister Mark asked me once if I could read, and I was ashamed to admit that I could read only a little French and even less Latin. My meager learning had come secretly from Brennan, and she had little time to teach me, for we both feared that my mother would catch us.

"Then you would not enjoy a book, if I brought one to you," Sister Mark said, sounding disappointed.

Humiliated, I looked down. "I wish that I could read," I admitted.

"Well, we shall see what we can do," Sister Mark said. "But you will not be here long enough to become as educated as other girls."

"What other girls?"

"The ones who are not running from anyone," Sister Mark said gently. "The ones who are free to stay."

For a moment, I wished that I could be one of those

girls, but I suspected that I did not know enough about the abbey to choose wisely. And so I only sighed.

As I grew well, Sister Mark took me out of my room sometimes, and I learned that what I first had thought was the whole abbey was only a small wing of it. The abbey itself was enormous, bigger than any castle or estate I had ever seen, and made up of a number of buildings situated around a large church. The small building where I stayed had its own chapel, kitchen, and refectory, and even a small garden, bleak at that time of year, with a little ornamental pond beside an old cherry tree. Once, when Sister Mark was helping me walk in order to strengthen my legs, we went through some of the other buildings, and I was amazed at what I found.

There were three hospital buildings, with bedridden women and children suffering from all manner of diseases and injuries. Each hospital had a pharmacy and a kitchen, and many women worked in those places. There were four residences, each with a scriptorium where rows of nuns sat at tables, working on parchment pages. The walls were lined with full bookcases, and I stepped forward hungrily. But Sister Mark pulled me back and led me away.

In other buildings, women who did not wear nuns' habits worked with needlework or knitting, at tables set with candles, water, and small cakes for their refreshment, and when I looked in, they stared at me in silence. A few of them appeared worried by my presence. In another building, there was another scriptorium where women bent over sheets of parchment, and these were not nuns, either. In the corner near the fire, a young woman played a harp, and she stopped as soon as she noticed me. She leaned away from the fire's light, as if she did not want to be seen.

"Who are they?" I asked when Sister Mark led me away.

"Refugee daughters, runaway brides, wives escaping brutal husbands. They are women who did not find that their homes were safe places. Every stranger who sees them worries them."

I, tired now and suddenly, wanting only to return to my room, said, "This is much like a village, then."

"Yes," Sister Mark said. "Only larger than many villages. There are seven hundred women and girls here."

I stared at her. "So many?"

"All of the land between the rivers belongs to the abbey," Sister Mark said. "But no one can come here without an invitation from the abbess, not even the sheriff. Those who take refuge here have forty days before they have to be turned out."

I held my breath. What did she mean? I glanced at Sister Mark and saw that the old woman's fine blue eyes were watching me.

"Not even the sheriff can take you until then," Sister Mark repeated. "We are chartered by the king himself. But that does not mean that everything here is wonderful. We have our spies and thieves, like any village. We have those who will betray another for a set of gold buttons or even the promise of a single coin."

I stumbled a little on an uneven paving stone and Sister Mark steadied me. "You are Mary to me, and you will be

Mary forever," she whispered. "Forget your other life as soon as you can. You will join your aunt when you can travel. Then you will forget this place, too."

"My aunt," I whispered.

"Why, of course, Mary," Sister Mark said cheerily. "You've forgotten her because you've been so ill."

I almost believed her. But I had a greater concern. "How many days have I been here?"

"Thirty-nine," Sister Mark said. "Tonight we shift you to the other side of the abbey, away from Sister Bernice." She smiled a little. "She grows too curious. You will work with someone very dear to me, until it is time for you to leave. You'll blend in with the servants and probably not be noticed. The safest place for you would be one of the farms, but you are not yet strong enough for that. And perhaps my friend can teach you how to read well before you leave."

Of all the places we saw that day, I had liked the last scriptorium best. But the floor in the refectory fascinated me. It was a large mosaic, made of small bits of colored stone, and every animal I had ever seen was pictured there, along with some that I could never have imagined—great gray beasts with long noses, and tall spotted golden beasts with thin necks that allowed them to eat from the tops of exotic trees bearing blossoms and fruit that I could not identify. There were fish swimming in blue waves at the edges of the floor, and ships sailing above the fish, and birds flying over the ships.

"Who made this?" I had asked.

"Wonderful artists who did not sign their work," Sister

Mark had said. "Sister Bernice thinks the devil made it."

I had laughed then. "No, I think that angels made it."

"More likely it was made by slaves who were brought here to do the work by the Romans, hundreds of years ago."

I looked around the floor again. "Where are we? I mean, where is the abbey? Not in Wales? I don't hear Welsh spoken by the servants, just English, and everyone else speaks the Norman language."

"You are in England now."

"And where will my aunt take me?"

Sister Mark shook her head slowly. "I do not know, and that is the truth. The only people who know are the ones who move the refugees, and they are not known to one another."

I sighed. "I had a friend who helped me—when I was home. His name was Tom. I wish I knew what happened to him—and to my dog."

Sister Mark took my hand. "You may never know. One way or another, they are in God's hands, and that should be enough for all of us."

But it was not enough for me.

That night, Sister Mark brought me to a small kitchen next to one of the hospital wards. It was brightly lighted with dozens of candles and lamps, and a nun wearing a large apron waited behind a table with a bowl of a strange white paste. Sister Mark asked me to sit on the high stool, then pulled off the cloth that hid my brown hair and loosened my robe so that my bare shoulders were exposed. The other nun flapped a cloth around me and picked up a pair of shears from the table.

I clapped my hands to my hair. "Please don't cut my hair!"

"It must be done," the nun said, and Sister Mark pulled my hands away. In a few minutes, my hair lay on the stone floor. It had been cut so short that it barely covered my ears.

"Now!" the other nun said, and she sounded as if she was taking great pleasure in what she was doing. She lifted the bowl with one hand and a small wooden paddle with the other.

"Sister Mortimer once worked as a lady's maid in a palace in London," Sister Mark said. "There is nothing she does not know about making a woman beautiful."

I shut my eyes hard. Sister Mortimer spread the cold paste over my hair with the wooden paddle, occasionally poking me hard enough to make me wince. The paste smelled like lye and stung my scalp. When Sister Mortimer was done, she warned me not to move or touch my hair, and then she said, "I'll recite twenty psalms and your hair will be done." She began reciting the psalms, and after a moment, Sister Mark joined in. I understood then that they were marking a measured amount of time, not praying about the results they expected.

When the last psalm had been recited, the two nuns led me out of the kitchen and into a small walled-in yard where a single torch burned. There was a stone tub full of water, and I was instructed to kneel in front of it. Bucket after bucket of cold water was poured over my head until the nuns were satisfied at last. Then Sister Mortimer wrapped my head in a heavy towel and they brought me back into the small kitchen.

"What do you think of this?" Sister Mortimer asked Sister Mark.

"She looks like a Norse child, especially with those blue eyes," Sister Mark said. "She will pass."

I touched my hair cautiously and found that it was coarse now, and felt thicker than it had been before. "I have pale hair?" I asked.

"It is nearly white," Sister Mortimer said with great satisfaction. "No one would recognize you now."

"But I look like a boy!" I cried, tugging at my short hair.

"Almost," Sister Mark said. "We'll explain that you've been ill—that is the truth, well enough—and tell everyone that we had to cut off your hair. Now rub your head dry and I will take you to the bed where you will sleep tonight."

"I'm not going back to my room?" I asked. The room had become my own, a familiar place in a world I did not yet know.

"Dry your hair," Sister Mark said.

Obedient, I bent and rubbed my hair with the towel. I was almost afraid to breathe. When I was ready, I was dressed in a black gown and my blond hair was covered with a white veil so that only a few wisps around my face showed. After that, they helped me into a sleeveless black coat and a black cloak with a hood. My new shoes were made of soft black leather and lined with red silk. I had never had clothes so beautiful.

◁ ◁ ◁

I was given a trundle bed in the room of a young woman called Lizabeth, and when Sister Mark held up a candle so that I could see Lizabeth's face, I recognized her as the harpist in the scriptorium. Lizabeth did not seem to recognize me, however. She was in her nightdress, with a blanket around her shoulders and her dark hair loose down her back, and she had nothing to say except, "Welcome, Mary." As soon as Sister Mark left, Lizabeth lay down on her bed again, sighing.

"Blow out the candle when you are ready to sleep," she told me.

I stood there uncertainly, and then, realizing that Lizabeth was going to say nothing more, I blew out the candle and felt my way to the trundle bed. In the dark, I thought of removing my outer clothing, but the floor was cold and the blankets on the trundle bed were thin and rough. I almost was sorry that I had recovered enough from my illness to be moved to another room.

But then, that was not why I had been moved. My time was up, the forty days and nights had gone. The sheriff could come for me now. I was in hiding—within my hiding place.

I lay down and wrapped myself as well as I could in the thin blankets.

Each day Lizabeth and I went to the scriptorium, where Lizabeth spent half of her time copying poems and the other half playing the harp that sat by the fire. She taught me to copy simple things on small sheets of parchment, and gradually, day by day, I learned more than Brennan had had time to teach me. The poems and stories copied by the lay-women were in French, the language of the Normans who had conquered England. I learned that only the nuns copied religious books. But I did not mind, since I had not had any great desire to learn more Latin than I already knew.

The poems and stories were wonderful, and I wanted to learn all that I could, as quickly as I could. Long before spring, I could read as well as Lizabeth, but my copying hand was still clumsy, and so I was never given important work or title pages. Instead, I was encouraged to create poems of my own, and I did, poems about the natural world I loved so much, the woods and fields and animals that surrounded us all of our lives. I was praised when I read them aloud, and this filled me with joy. Indeed, I might have felt a certain pride— until I remembered that someone like me, someone respon-sible for the death of another, had little reason in this world to be proud of anything.

Each day, when our work was over, Lizabeth and I ate in a small refectory with the other copyists, and then I learned a little about Lizabeth. The woman's face was badly scarred on one side, and she explained that her husband had thrown a lamp at her and the oil had set her clothing on fire. I cringed, imagining the horror. Lizabeth touched my shoulder and said softly, "I'm safe from him here. He'll never find me. But I wish I could see my children again, if only once before I die."

I did not know what to say. I took a bite of bread and chewed, to delay the necessity of a response.

"I dream of seeing them," Lizabeth went on. "But that cannot happen. If I return, my husband will set fire to me again. He promised me that."

Horrified, I blinked back tears. My own story was not the worst, here in the abbey. Being burned to death—there was nothing worse than that.

As time went by, Lizabeth taught me to play simple tunes on the harp and the smaller psaltery. I was told that I had a pleasant voice, lower than anyone expected from so young a girl. Then, cautiously, I began setting my poems to music, and one day, while the women worked, I sang of waterfalls and rivers and leaping fish. When I finished, I thought that I had disgraced myself, for the scriptorium was silent. But the women put down their work and clapped their hands. I bent my head and brushed away tears of happiness.

Some of the copyists asked me to sing my songs every day, to entertain them during the dreary winter afternoons, and Lizabeth was glad enough for me to sit at the harp and release her to rest. Then she became ill with a lung fever, and before winter broke, she was taken to one of the hospital wards.

Now I was the singer. The women working in the scriptorium began calling me Blondine, after a fabled court musician, and so I became Mary Blondine to everyone. I tried to forget that this was not my real home.

Sister Mark came to see me one day, interrupting my painstaking work on a long poem about a child who ran away from a cruel home, with only a dog as a companion.

"I hear you are the marvel of the age," Sister Mark whispered at my shoulder. "You read, you copy, you play, you sing. What next?"

I smiled, but then I asked, with mingled hope and fear, "How much longer will I stay here?"

"Are you eager to leave?"

"No," I said. "I wish I could stay forever."

"But you cannot," Sister Mark said. "I have received word that your aunt will travel here within the month. We will be sorry to see you leave."

I bent my head. "Who is this 'aunt'?"

But Sister Mark left without answering.

I had been sleeping alone in the small room after Lizabeth became ill, but I never rested well. I had bad dreams, and I woke wishing that my imaginary cat would find me again and tell me I was safe. Then, one night, a hand clutched my arm, startling me, and a dreaded voice said, "Who are you, Mary Blondine?"

Sister Bernice was twisting my arm around so that she could see the birthmark by the light of the lamp she held. But, almost as if she had been guarding my room, Sister Mark was there, and she yanked Sister Bernice away.

"You'll be sorry you let her stay," Sister Bernice hissed at Sister Mark.

"I'll make *you* sorry if you talk too much," Sister Mark said. "Remember your sister's daughter and her bastards."

Sister Bernice scuttled away. Sister Mark did not speak until the other nun was gone, and then she bent over me and said, "Hurry and dress. You have to leave now. *Now!*"

"What has happened?" I cried.

"Lizabeth betrayed you. She told a cook's helper whose brother serves the sheriff that a Welsh girl with a birthmark was hiding here, and in return, the sheriff has taken her home to die. She was promised that her husband would allow this, in exchange for a sum of gold. She'll see her children once more, but she has sold you to your enemies. They must hate you very much. Everyone involved in this sin is richer tonight."

While the nun spoke, I struggled into my clothes, fumbling with stockings and lacings, tying knots where there should have been bows, and pulling my coat on wrong-side out. Was everything for nothing after all? Had I been safe for a while, only to be betrayed into my mother's hands?

"How did you learn of this?" I gasped as I tied my hood snugly over my stiff blond hair.

"I have more spies than Sister Bernice," Sister Mark said. "Are you ready? We have no more time."

Sister Mark hobbled out, leading the way with a candle. We turned half a dozen corners in the halls of the old stone building, and at last we came out into a small side yard where a bundled figure sat on a horse.

Sister Mark embraced me and whispered, "Mary Blondine, God has blessed you in some strange way. I see the light that shines around you. And those who hate you have seen it, too. Now mount up. Good-bye."

The thick figure on the horse bent down and snatched me up by one arm, so that I could sit before the saddle. Sister

Mark opened a gate in the wall and we rode through. Somewhere, a deep-voiced dog began barking. The rider urged the horse into a gallop, and we rode into a wood, along a path that was barely visible in the dark.

"Who are you?" I asked, when I could no longer hear the dog barking.

The rider did not answer.

Near dawn, behind an inn-yard wall, I was transferred from one horse to another. The bulky man rode away without looking back. The new rider leaned forward and said, "Greetings, Mary. Your aunt is eager to see you."

I turned to look up at the speaker and saw a middle-aged woman with gray hair showing under a fur-lined hood.

"Who are you?" I asked.

"Margarite, physician of Blessingwood." She urged the horse into a canter. "What luck that I was nearby when you needed a ride home."

"Home!" I cried. Home to my mother? I tried to turn sideways, in order to slide off the horse, even though it was moving swiftly through the forest.

"Home to your aunt!" Margarite said. "Sit still or the horse will think you are dangerous and toss both of us into the mud."

I sat still, but I was afraid. I had no aunt, not in all the world. I did not know where I was being taken, and I was not sure that I was better off riding to an unknown place with this stranger than I would have been if I had remained in the abbey. It had been so large! Surely there would have been some place where I could have hidden.

"No one will find you in Blessingwood," Margarite, the physician, said. "We live a lifetime and a world away from everywhere else. You'll see." She leaned over me and embraced me with one arm. "Stop trembling, Mary. Wait until you see who waits for you—at home."

She meant my aunt, of course. But I had no aunt.

In the East, pale light spread across the gray sky, and a cold wind rattled the trees over us. Half a dozen crows took sudden, noisy flight from one of the trees, and I heard my name shouted across the land. "Gwenore! Gwenore! Gwenore!"

Did the physician hear? She gave no hint of it. But I would never be safe.

3

Lessons in poison

the sky was dark with clouds all day, and the sharp wind that stung us smelled of snow, but neither snow nor rain fell, for which I was grateful. But I was tired and frightened, and it seemed to me that there was a mocking crow in every tree we passed.

Most of the day we traveled on muddy roads, usually trailing a party of men, women, and children. They were the safest traveling companions, Margarite told me, unless we fell into the company of people who had armed guards.

Margarite, physician of Blessingwood, was nearly six feet tall, so she stood a head taller than everyone else, even most of the men. Wherever we went, people stared, but once they saw that Margarite wore the scarlet gown of a physician under her dark cloak, their expressions softened and changed from suspicion to respect. In that part of the country, most physicians were women, and one who looked so impressive—the fine wool gown; the fur-lined cloak, gloves, and shoes—and spoke with such authority must, indeed, be a healer of great importance. Furthermore, there was no telling who her sponsor might be. Having an insignificant priest as a sponsor was one thing; having a member of the aristocracy was another, especially if he had the king's favor and was maintaining a small army in his compound, as so many did. Most observers apparently decided that it was better to smile as sincerely as possible and keep their hands in plain view, so that this physician with her scrawny little helper took no offense—and did not suspect them of plotting a robbery.

We spent the first night at an inn in a prosperous village, where I was not introduced by name. Margarite warned me that she would treat me as a servant, in order to prevent questions. No one so much as glanced at me twice, because all attention was centered on her. As we ate in the common room, several people smiled ingratiatingly at the physician, and by the time we had finished supper and climbed the stairs to our room, a line of people had formed in the dim hall.

"Do not worry," Margarite whispered to me. "They know I am a physician by my robe. They want treatment of one kind or another. It is always this way."

First was a woman with a sick baby, and next was a man with a swollen eye, and so on, down the line, one prospective patient after another. Margarite hurried me into the room and settled me on a stool in a corner between the shuttered window and the fire. "Keep your hood pulled down and sleep if you can," she said. "But if you can't, say nothing. Try to avoid attracting anyone's attention."

I leaned against the wall and did my best to sink inside my cloak. The room, which smelled faintly of wool and burning oil, was square and pleasantly furnished, with a wide bed, a small table and two benches, two candles and two lamps. The floor was covered with clean straw and the bed with several blankets. I longed to lie down, but I obeyed Margarite.

Margarite let the sick people in the hall into the room, one by one, and ministered to them from the contents of a bag made of red and black carpet braced with a sturdy wood bottom. I stayed in the corner where I had been sent and dozed part of the time, in spite of my efforts to remain alert. My eyes did snap open once, however, when I heard a man say belligerently, "Why should I believe that you are a physician? Can you prove it?"

He sat on a stool facing Margarite, and she leaned in toward him in a way that was quite threatening, I thought with mingled fear and enjoyment. "I am licensed by the bishop," she said coldly. "If you need proof of that before you will accept treatment for whatever ails you tonight, then send a message to him. Or better yet, go to see him in his palace and complain all you like."

A man standing outside the open door and holding a moaning child, cursed the other man and said, "If you don't trust her, get out. My son needs help and I don't need a bishop to tell me that I can get it here."

The arguing man did not look around. "Where is your license?" he asked Margarite. "Show us this license that the bishop gave you—if he did."

Margarite pulled at a cord concealed inside the neckline of her gown and retrieved a flat leather envelope. Out of it she took a folded page of fine parchment. Eyes on the man, she unfolded it slowly and held it out to him.

I could tell by the way he looked at the parchment that he could not read, and I hoped that Margarite knew that, too.

Finally the man looked up at the physician. "Maybe I'd better take that along with me when I go to the bishop," he said, and even from across the room I could see his smirk.

Quick as lightning, Margarite snatched back the parchment. "Do not dare threaten me!" she said sharply. She leaned even closer to him, sitting higher than he did because she was so tall, and the muscles in her jaw visibly tightened. "If you doubt me, send the landlord for the sheriff. Do it now! Or else, if you need treatment, speak up—or get out of the line and let the next person have a turn."

The man hesitated a moment, then pulled a rag away from his neck and showed her a boil as large as an egg. I closed my eyes in disgust. The man and Margarite spoke in low voices, and my mind drifted back to Brennan, who was not a physician, but she knew a little of the healing arts and was generous with her skills. She was different from Margarite, a slave instead of a free woman, and not well educated. But she was loving and comfortable, and I could have wept, knowing that I might never see her again.

Life with my mother in the castle had been frightening and tense, but I could remember brief times that were comfortable and happy, when I had been out of her sight. I had spent hours every day with Brennan in the main kitchen building in the keep, while Brennan prepared special trays for my mother or helped the kitchen maids because she was good-hearted and generous. I had shadowed her and became nearly invisible, so that the maids would gossip in my presence—even about my mother. And about Sir Richard's wife.

"The witch is poisoning her," the cook's second helper had said once. "Every time she quickens, the child dies within her and is cast off in a lake of blood. It is the drink the witch prepares for Lady Barbara, the one she swears will strengthen her."

"No," Brennan had said. "Sir Richard made Lady Rhiamon drink from the cup once, before his wife could accept anything from her hand again. It did not sicken her, and he and Lady Barbara came to trust her again. No, the poison was in something else."

"Who says she was poisoned at all?" the head cook had scoffed. "Perhaps she has a cursed womb."

"The babes were all poisoned," Brennan whispered emphatically. "The chambermaid said she had seen it before, babes born with that terrible black-and-blue stain under their skin, because they had been murdered even before they drew their first breaths. Lady Rhiamon wants to be Sir Richard's wife, and she will be, too, once she has bled out Lady Barbara. The lady is too weak to try again to give that pig husband an heir. But he will not listen to her doctors, not as long as she still breathes. And the witch is standing by, whispering to him that she has many babes waiting in her."

"They can't marry!" several voices had said at once. "She's his cousin, perhaps just thrice removed!"

"Ten links chopped from a gold chain for payment, and

she will no longer be his cousin in the eyes of the church," Brennan had said.

No one had argued with that. At the time I had understood only part of what was said, but, young as I had been, I understood that my mother was poisoning Lady Barbara, whose fingers were like dry, peeling sticks and who trembled when she left her bed and tried to walk. Always pregnant—or grieving—or sick—Lady Barbara had been pitied by everyone except her husband. And my mother, the woman who was called a witch even in my hearing.

But Tom, the slave boy who worked in the bakery, had once told me that the baker's first helper had given birth to Sir Richard's child one night in the granary and had disappeared the next day, along with her baby. And Tom never lied.

Lady Barbara died screaming one night. The next night, Sir Richard had come for me, and I had run from him, down the narrow, twisting stairs, stumbling against the stone wall, gasping, weeping, only suddenly to be yanked sideways into a narrow crevice by Brennan, my savior, Brennan, the slave, Brennan, the woman with no rights, not even the right to save a child.

Where was Brennan now? Where was Tom? I owed my life to two slaves, both now lost in the vast country, while I journeyed to stay with a stranger—an aunt I did not know and did not believe existed.

After a while the door to our room closed and I woke with a start, to see everyone gone except for Margarite, who was rubbing an ointment on her hands and wiping them on a cloth.

She saw me watching her. "Many of us believe that some conditions are transferred from one person to another, like dirt, and this ointment cleans and coats the hands and may prevent this transfer."

I could only stare. Margarite's hood had been pushed back and I saw that the woman's gray hair was fastened into one thick braid that fell to her knees. Because of her hair and the delicate skin on her hands, I judged her to be very old, but her face was not lined. For one who cared for the sick, she had remained very healthy.

"How are you feeling, Mary?"

I blinked. "I am well," I said. "Will we leave here tomorrow?"

Margarite was replacing small bottles and boxes in her bag. "We leave before dawn and go straight to Blessingwood—to home."

"But I heard you tell that man with the boil that we were going to London, to the house of the deputy mayor," I said, alarmed.

"Ah. So you weren't asleep all the time," Margarite said. She closed the bag and set it in a corner. "The man was curious about me—too curious—and looking for a way to browbeat me, or rob me. Or perhaps he is one of those cowards who spy on people for rewards. I did my best to convince him that I am expected by someone important in London very soon." She began unfastening her red gown, unlacing the bodice and unhooking the girdle. "I hate

inventing tales like that to protect myself, but being caught
in an argument with a bully is a sure way for a woman to end
up in prison. Or in the fire. Some men are resentful of inde-
pendent women, and there are many ways a spiteful man can
harm a woman." She inspected the bed, looking under the
linen and pillows and picking through the straw. "This is
fairly clean. I don't see any fleas or signs of rats. Get in—yes,
keep your cloak on because it will be cold tonight!—and try
not to worry. I'm going to sit up in the dark for a while. I
need to be sure that our friend with the boil is not hanging
about outside."

"You think he might?" I asked fearfully. What if the man
was a spy, looking for me? Did Margarite know who I really was?

"I think he would enjoy frightening—or robbing—an
old woman and a child if he could. So I'll be on guard for a
while. But I gave him a generous amount of a certain salve
that I make myself, and I encouraged him to rub it into his
boil while I watched, to make certain that he did it properly. He liked the sensation, and so he will apply even more,
and soon it will cause him to fall asleep for a long time.
When he awakes late tomorrow afternoon, we will be gone.
Now close your eyes and think of pleasant things.
Blessingwood waits for you, and you will be safe there."

Margarite had a salve that could make someone sleep?
Oh, if only I had had such a salve to put on Sir Richard—or
on my mother—before everything went so wrong, before
that afternoon on the rocky slope when she and Tom and
Brennan—and brave Striker!—caused the man's horse to fall.

If only Sir Richard could have slept soundly instead of creeping about in my little room, reaching under the covers, touching . . . I turned over on my side and sighed. My plans to escape from my mother and him had been so hasty and clumsy that it was no wonder everything had gone wrong.

I wanted to believe Margarite's assurances that I would be safe. Whatever Blessingwood was, it sounded like paradise. My eyes closed and I dreamed, once again, of Tom and Striker, but this time they sat in a large, handsome room with the four women I had seen before, and now one of them was Margarite. All looked at me. "Where have you been?" Tom asked. "We've been waiting."

Before first light, the innkeeper brought up a pan of coals to start our fire again, and his wife followed with a plate of bread and cold meat and a pitcher of water. Margarite paid them, apparently with a larger coin than they had expected, because both of them offered other help—more water to wash, more bread and meat, extra grain for Margarite's horse—but Margarite accepted only the grain.

"Have him ready and standing at your back door," she said. "I cannot take time to see more sick people before I leave. I am wanted desperately by my lord in London."

The innkeeper's wife stepped back and pressed her hands against her mouth.

Instantly Margarite's imperious manner softened. "What is it?" she asked.

"Our son. His illness turned for the worse last night and we had hoped that you might look at him." Her eyes had filled with tears and she cleared her throat. "But we understand . . ."

"I'll see him while my servant breaks her fast," Margarite said, and the three of them hurried out of the room. I sat at the small table and ate quickly, watching the door. Margarite did not come for a long time, not until I heard a bird calling forlornly outside.

She whisked into the room and snatched up the saddlebags. "Come. Hurry. He has the horse in back, and we must be away from the village before many people are about. Hurry!"

I followed her down the rickety back steps and into a muddy yard where the innkeeper held Margarite's horse by the bridle. Margarite boosted me into my place and then mounted without help.

"Innkeeper, I left medicines with your wife. Your son will live. Now help us by telling no one that you saw us this morning."

"I swear it," the innkeeper said eagerly, his voice husky with relief, and Margarite urged the horse forward. Before dawn broke on that cold winter day, we were out of sight of the village. "We attracted too many people last night," she said. "We are safer if they forget we were there."

Early in the morning, during a light rain, four men stepped out from the trees that lined the road, two on each side, and they attempted to block the horse from moving on. "Give us the horse and what you carry, and we will let you go free!" the tallest one shouted. Another man attempted to grab the horse's bridle, but the horse sidestepped neatly and suddenly rose on his back legs, nearly unseating me, and struck at the man with his front hooves. The man went down, screaming and writhing. The other man backed away, but not quickly enough, because the horse charged him wildly and trampled him into the muddy road.

"Now go, go!" Margarite cried, and the horse broke into a gallop. I hung onto his mane with both hands, afraid to look back to see what happened to the men.

When, at last, Margarite allowed the horse to resume a quick walk, she said, "We must find traveling companions. The countryside is too dangerous for solitary riders, even with a horse as courageous as mine."

I was too terrified to respond.

Halfway through the morning, we joined a group traveling south, after Margarite had a low conversation with the armed men that guarded the people in the wagons. I heard her mention Bishop William, Sir Edward LeClerq, and the mayor of Canterbury. The armed men grunted their approval and invited her to ride in the midst of the group, where she would be safest. I whispered, "We are lucky that you know those important men."

"I am licensed by both Bishop William and the mayor," Margarite said. "And Sir Edward sponsored me after my husband was killed in his service. But do not be impressed by this, because all these favors can disappear as quickly as a spring snow, depending upon the fancies of others. We, at Blessingwood, are careful, because we know that no one will risk themselves for us."

"Who is 'we'?" I asked.

"Why, your aunt Hildegard, my sister Sarah, and our dear friend Julienne," Margarite answered. Then she added, "Let us keep silent while we ride. It saves our strength and bores our companions. Then they have less to wonder about."

The travelers stopped twice near running water, to share bread with one another and feed the horses. I, mindful of Margarite's request, remained huddled inside my cloak and avoided making eye contact with anyone.

When daylight began to fail, the group stopped at an inn, and Margarite and I spent an uncomfortable night in a long, narrow room with six other women and a weeping child. The food had been filling, nothing more, and the landlord asked for more money to provide fuel for the night. Margarite paid for it, but only after an argument. I had seen the full purse fastened inside her girdle, but now she displayed only a flat one with less than a dozen small coins. The landlord took half of them and brought up a bucket of wood chips and dried clumps of grass. Before anyone could complain, he left, slamming the door behind him.

We slept two to each small bed, on bags filled with straw that smelled as if it had come from the stable. The shutter on the small window sagged, allowing a cold, damp wind to blow in all night. The single lamp smoked and finally went out, and meanwhile, through everything, the child cried on and on fretfully, begging to "go home to Da." Morning could not come too soon for me.

The next day we learned some of the travelers planned to take a path along the edge of the forest that morning, in spite of the warnings of the guards. But that way was shorter, the people claimed, and so they left. The child, no longer weeping, waved happily at me from his seat in the back of a wagon piled with sacks of winter vegetables. I waved back— but gooseflesh rose on my arms and the birthmark burned. I rubbed my wrist and winced. Then, suddenly, I knew with terrible certainty that the travelers would be attacked and robbed!

But how could I know this? It was almost as if the crime had already been committed, in my sight, and now I was remembering it!

"Don't think about it," Margarite said, reading my mind. "You can't change anything."

I turned to look at her. "How did you know what I was thinking?"

"The same way you sometimes know what I am thinking," Margarite said. "Or you will, when you are a little older."

In late afternoon, Margarite gave coins to the guards and said good-bye to them. "We have only a short way to go to my sponsor's house," she said loudly.

Then she urged the tired horse into a quick canter and we rode away on a narrow, rocky path that plunged suddenly into a sodden wood. The path was difficult to see, covered with a thick layer of wet, decaying leaves. Thick brush encroached on both sides. Branches hung so low that Margarite had to duck her head to avoid them. We crossed flooded brooks where brown water rushed over the grassy verge, and then we climbed a steep hill. "Where are we going?" I asked.

"Far away from our new friends," Margarite said. "We'll

take up with someone else before long, when we reach a road. There are always travelers, even this time of year."

"But why could we not stay with the last people?"

"Because we cannot make friends or become too familiar with anyone, especially near home," Margarite said. "It's best if they forget us as soon as possible."

At a small, clean inn, Margarite struck up a conversation with a plump and smiling woman whose right foot was wrapped in a clean towel. The woman, who seemed to know Margarite, protested that she could not afford to pay her, but Margarite bargained treatment for company on the following day. The woman, her young daughter, and her brother were traveling to a village not far from Blessingwood. The brother, gray-haired and somber, took no part in the conversation. He sat on the other side of the room stuffing himself with thick chunks of bread smeared with bacon fat. But the woman's daughter sat close to her, watching and listening to everything, safe inside the curve of her mother's arm.

"Do you remember me?" the woman asked Margarite. "I'm Agatha. You attended my elder daughter when her son was born. He was turned the wrong way, rump first."

Margarite, busy rubbing an ointment that smelled of leeks into the woman's foot, looked up and said, "A baby with red hair. I remember. How is he?"

"He's healthy, and he's walking now," Agatha said. Her young daughter smiled and nodded—and got a hug from her mother.

"Good. You know what they say about boys born backside first," Margarite said.

"What?" Agatha said, clearly ready to laugh.

"They were made to be kings, because listening is always the last thing they do."

She and Agatha laughed, and Agatha said, "So then his father also was made to be a king. He never listens. Ah, my foot feels better now. What did you put on it?"

Margarite snapped the lid back on the jar. "It's made of leeks, chamomile, and arsenic. I'll give you the jar, but only use it sparingly, no more than twice a day. It's poisonous."

"Poisonous!" Agatha gasped, and she jerked her foot away from Margarite's hands. Her daughter cried out in dismay.

"Don't be afraid." Margarite reached for Agatha's foot again and began winding a long, narrow cloth around it. "It can't hurt you if you use no more than I did. Things that hurt us in large amounts can sometimes help in small amounts."

"Or the other way around," Agatha said quietly. "You are a wise woman, Doctor Margarite. We only have one guard with us, but you're welcome to ride all the way home with us."

Margarite fastened her red-and-black bag shut and glanced sideways at me. Then she said to Agatha, "That would suit us very well. But tell me, friend. Have you heard any interesting gossip in the last day or so?"

Agatha shook her head. "I heard nothing of interest, either going to the market in Barrelhill or starting home again."

Margarite sighed and straightened her shoulders. "It's good for all of us when there is no news."

"True enough. I'm glad that I live far enough from the

main roads to attract little attention from the troops and the foragers—and the sheriff. Only the tax collector finds me."

"Ah, well," Margarite said, laughing. "Crows and tax collectors always know where there are bright shiny objects." She looked back over her shoulder, to where Agatha's brother was now bent over a plate of meat and turnips. "Is your brother staying with you for very long?"

Agatha shook her head. "No. He is accompanying me home, and then he journeys on to the West."

"Ah," Margarite said quietly, and she crossed herself.

The women did not speak again, and after a while Margarite and I went to our tiny room. "Is something wrong?" I asked. Margarite had been quiet for a long time.

"Agatha's brother is a hangman," she said.

I shook with a sudden chill. One day he might hang me, I thought. One day.

But I fell asleep thinking of the girl, whose mother so obviously loved her.

The following morning, we left before dawn again, riding swiftly along a narrow path between fields. Fog lay heavily around us, and I marveled that the horses could see sometimes, for I could not. We moved through hollows where the fog was as thick as a blanket. But other times it thinned and I saw looming forms close to us, forms that turned out to be trees or hedges.

When we reached a fork in the road, Agatha, her daughter, and her brother turned left and, after bidding us farewell, vanished into the fog quickly. Margarite and I took the other road in silence. The horse's hooves clopped noisily on the road, and sometimes we passed farm cottages where dogs barked at us. Once, another horse and rider rode behind us for a short time, the rider whistling the same simple tune over and over. I felt Margarite stiffen apprehensively. But the horseman turned off at a farm, to be greeted by a shout and a laugh from a man we had not seen as we passed.

The fog thinned and blew away, finally, and as we approached another crossroads, I saw another horse and rider waiting by a bare oak tree.

Margarite broke out laughing and urged the horse forward. "Here's your aunt! She came out to meet us!"

I watched the stranger ride toward us. Aunt? Who was she? Could she be trusted? Or would she turn out to be someone who would hand me over to my mother for a reward?

Margarite leaned from her saddle and held out a welcoming hand to the other woman, who was younger, smiling, and showed strands of curly red hair from beneath her hood. "How did you know we were on the road this morning?" Margarite asked.

"I had a feeling in my bones," the other woman said. "And we were worried because we had heard that there were soldiers on the roads in some places, and you know what that means."

"Nothing that matters to us now," Margarite said. "Blessingwood is safe. Here, let me show you Mary, your niece. Mary! Here's your aunt Hildegard."

I had never seen the woman before. Could she be related

to my dead father? How could I never have known I had an aunt?

Hildegard smiled at me. "Welcome, Mary. We received many wonderful messages about you, and we've been eager to have you make your home with us."

I could only nod. Everything sounded believable, and I was tired enough to want to believe anything, as long as the journey could end at last, and end safely.

The two women turned their horses to the south road, and ahead, I saw a church tower built of pale golden stones. As we grew closer, I saw a tidy village surrounding the church, and gently sloping fields surrounding everything.

"It's market day," Hildegard told Margarite. "No one will pay much attention to us. Sarah probably already has customers waiting for her at the forge, so we'll go in through the orchard and not attract attention. Or collect any questions."

"I'm tired enough to fall off my horse," Margarite said.

"You can't rest yet," Hildegard said. "I'm sorry, but you know what market day is like—you'll have sick people lined up for you. And we can't let on that anything too unusual has happened."

"Like the sudden appearance of a niece?" Margarite said.

I said nothing. I knew I could learn more by listening.

"Sarah and I mentioned to a few gossips yesterday that you were bringing my orphaned niece home with you," Hildegard said. "After the death of her widowed mother. We did our best to make it sound uninteresting and ordinary."

Margarite sighed. "I hope you chose a death for this poor imaginary mother that would not send everyone into a panic. This is the time of year for lung fever."

"I said she died from a fall out of a hayloft," Hildegard said. "We'll keep Mary in the house for a few days, and then let her help Julienne."

Had there ever been a Mary, niece of Hildegard? Was I taking someone else's place?

Hildegard reached one hand out to me. "Don't be afraid," she murmured. "You'll soon see how safe you are now."

I wanted to believe her, but how could I? Who *were* these people?

4

m a n y   r o o m s   f o r
a   c a t   a n d   a   s p y

t he horses seemed to know their way now, for they
   quickly threaded through a large orchard, where the
trees were showing the first signs of spring in spite of the bad
weather. Margarite's big horse nickered anxiously, dancing
sideways a little and tossing his head.

A curious brown cow appeared abruptly from behind a
barn at the edge of the orchard. She stared at the horses and
us, and she mooed inquiringly, her breath steaming in the
cold air. Amazed, I saw that a large yellow cat was sitting on
the cow's back, and both animals seemed comfortable with
the arrangement.

Ahead, a squat man waited at the open door of a large,
well-maintained stable, and he was nodding and rubbing his
gnarled hands together as he watched us approach. He had
the demeanor of a servant or a slave, but he wore a good
tunic over a wool shirt, thick leggings, and sturdy boots that
looked almost new. Margarite and Hildegard greeted him,
calling him Umma, and he smiled and tugged the fringe of
rough gray hair that hung over his creased forehead. I saw,

with horror, that he had no tongue. His mouth was only a dark hole. I cringed and looked away.

Margarite asked Umma questions about someone named Jenna. Had her cough cleared up? Was she eating better? I could not understand his mumbled answers, but Margarite did, and she said, "Good news, then, Umma. Thank you for looking out for her. We'll need that calf she is carrying." I knew then that they were talking about the sociable cow.

Umma helped me down from the horse and Margarite introduced me to him as Mary Blondine. Umma grunted and smiled, and I steadied myself not to look away from his face, for fear of hurting his feelings again. He had not only lost his tongue, but his face was crisscrossed with old scars that looked like healed-over knife wounds. The yellow cat that had been riding the cow's back suddenly appeared in the stable dooryard and leaped to the man's shoulders, purring. Umma rubbed his face affectionately against it and said something to me that I could not understand.

"He wants you to know that the cat's name is King Harry," Margarite said. She handed the horse's reins to Umma and pulled the saddlebags down. "Come, ladies. Let us go in and surprise the others."

"You know your homecomings are never really a surprise," Hildegard said as she slid off her horse. "The cooks have been busy since dawn, so there is a fine feast waiting for us. Please hurry inside. I'm hungry."

King Harry jumped from Umma's shoulders to Hildegard's and rode inside with the women. He leaned forward a little, and his green eyes watched me intently, without blinking even once. Then he said distinctly, "I have heard of you, *Gwenore*. My cousin at the abbey sent word through the birds—and the crows here at Blessingwood never tire of talking about you, you and your evil little white dog. And that boy called Tom. And Brennan."

The others did not appear to have heard him, but I, feeling a prickle of terror run up the back of my neck, looked behind me and saw Umma grinning in a satisfied and knowing way. He had heard the cat! I knew he did! Now he knew my real name. And he knew about Tom and Brennan.

My birthmark burned, and I closed my other hand around my wrist.

"Gwenore, do not make trouble here," King Harry said. "If you are cautious and obedient, I will bring news of the ones you love, even that wretched dog. If you misbehave, I will punish you."

I yanked my hood as far down over my face as I could. This is all wrong, I thought. I am not safe here. But still—if this yellow cat has news of Striker and Tom . . .

"Ignore his threats," Hildegard said. She looked back at me and smiled. "But he does know all of the gossip, and sometimes he is amusing."

Speechless, I followed the woman into the house. The cat smirked as cats will, when, one way or another, they have had the last word in an argument.

We passed through a thick wooden gate set in a high stone wall and entered a paved courtyard. To the right, there was a squat stone building with a slate roof and a large chimney, and from the wonderful smells coming through the open

door, I knew that it was a kitchen. A fat red face peeped out
at us and someone inside giggled. Beyond it sat a smaller
building, and a young man hurried through the door, carrying a wooden tray with two loaves of bread. These women
had a separate bakery to reduce the risk of fire, so they must
be very wealthy—and important. People would notice anything they did—and anyone who came to stay with them. A
runaway girl might be caught, even if her appearance had
been changed. Someone had paid a reward for news of me
to the musician at the abbey, that woman I had lived with for
months and trusted. That same someone might be offering
more money, all over the land. I followed Hildegard reluc-
tantly.

To my left, there was a long building with a row of windows made of scraped and oiled parchment, allowing light
inside. The double doors were closed, and the building was
silent and mysterious.

Ahead, in what appeared to be the main building, a
woman almost as tall as Margarite opened a door and called
out, "Here she is!" and laughed with delight. The sleeves of
her gray wool gown were rolled up to her elbows, and her
arms looked strong. Her dark hair was bound back with a
green kerchief, more to keep it away from her face than serve
as an ornament, I suspected. Then, I saw with surprise, that
the woman was wearing a man's heavy boots.

"This is Sarah," Margarite said. "She is a blacksmith, and
later today, I'll take you through to the other side of our
home, so that you can see her shop."

"Margarite, I'm sorry that I don't have time to sit at the

table with you, no matter how much I want to hear of your journey," Sarah said. "I only came in for bread and cheese. It's market day and we have customers waiting. But Mary, I am so glad to see you! We have waited for you for months, and now that you are here, all of us can give thanks to God. When you are ready, I'll show you the shop and introduce you to Simon, my apprentice."

Sarah seemed honest and friendly, but I could not trust anyone, so I only nodded. Sarah hurried away and took the tray of bread from the baker's helper as she passed him.

"She and her apprentice are always busy," Hildegard told me. "Simon is not much older than you, but he has been working here for years. Our Sarah makes sturdy horseshoes and farm tools, but Simon is already a fine artist. He could be apprenticed to an ornamental metalworker in a city. You'll see his work all through our house. He made the hanging lamps, most of the frames for the window glass in the great room, and the metal hardware on the doors."

We walked through more rooms, including a storeroom filled with bolts of cloth and weaving supplies, where Margarite placed her saddlebags on a wide shelf; then we passed through what appeared to be a small sitting room that was more luxurious than anything in Sir Richard's castle, with tapestries on the walls, cushioned chairs with silk tassels, and half a dozen small hanging lamps; then we crossed a larger room furnished with a long table and many elaborately carved chairs under a large colored glass and metal lamp; and then we arrived in a room meant for dining, where a fine table laden with food waited for us. My mouth watered

when I saw what was there—several kinds of bread, a great
bowl of thick stew, bowls of vegetables, a large platter
crowded with cooked chickens, a leg of mutton covered
with onions, and several plates of cheese. There was a side
table with a dozen small plates heaped with sweets.

"Take off your cloak," Margarite told me as she shed her
own cloak and gloves and tossed them on a bench shoved
against one wall. "Here, sit at the table next to me."

I pulled back my hood—and Hildegard drew in a sharp
breath. "Your hair! It's been cut off—it's nearly white."

Margarite, helping me out of my cloak, said, "The nuns
did it, hoping that it would make her more difficult to recognize. But a Norse youngster would always attract stares—
and questions—so I fear the old innocents are not as good at
disguises as they thought. We'll take care of her hair before
anyone outside the household sees her. I thought that we
might match her to you, Hildegard. Red hair does follow
family lines."

Hildegard smiled at me. "Then you'll see how fine we
make you. But not so fine that anyone asks too many questions. We have already laid out a story for you for everyone
who might be curious, and we'll teach it to you before we
let you meet the neighbors. First, though, you must eat and
then, before you rest, we will take you in to meet our
Julienne. She has not been well this winter, so she spends
most of the time in her room, but she will want to see you
on your first day here."

"Who is Julienne?" I asked. I accepted the bread that
Margarite gave me and watched while the woman ladled
stew into the small pottery bowl that sat before me. I was still

afraid, but I was so hungry that I thought I might faint.

"She is the Blessingwood singer," Hildegard said. "She is the one who makes wonderful music and poetry here. And we have heard that you, too, are a singer and that you play both the harp and the psaltery—"

"And don't forget that our Mary can read and write, too," Margarite interrupted.

I suddenly lost my appetite. My throat tightened in panic. "How did you learn all of this about me?" I asked in a small, tense voice.

In the instant before Hildegard answered my question, I remembered what King Harry had said. "The birds never tire of talking of you." And I remembered Father Caddaric's pet bird. In my imagination, I saw birds carrying messages from Wales to England, gossiping in trees and bramble thickets, while cats eavesdropped along the way. Were there spies everywhere?

"We received regular reports about you," Hildegard said, busy with a roasted chicken and a knife. She did not look up to notice my distressed gaze.

I swallowed hard and forced myself to ask, "But why? No one ever explained why I was taken away from . . . from . . . taken away, then sent to the abbey, and then brought here."

"Push up your sleeve, my dear," Margarite said.

I knew what she wanted to see, but I hesitated for a moment, then showed the birthmark under the edge of my sleeve. "There it is," Margarite murmured. "The sign of enchantment, of magical blessings. We, who know of such things, are always glad to give shelter to someone like you."

"You might not be Hildegard's true niece," Margarite said. "But we are filled with happiness at having you here— even for the rest of your life."

Hildegard nodded. "Now eat. Then we'll take you to see Julienne, and afterward you can rest all you like."

But I barely tasted the food. How could I have magical blessings? "Magical" meant that I must have mysterious pow- ers. But if I had these powers, then why had my life at the castle been so hard? I could have changed many things—and not just for myself.

Oh, yes, I would have found a way to have dealt with Sir Richard, a way that would have stopped him from trying to harm me but somehow stopped short of bringing him to his death. But first, I would have found a way to have pleased my mother long ago, even while my father was still alive. Then my mother would have loved me, just as the mother in the inn had loved her daughter.

So I believed, then, that I had no special powers, and these women would discover this, and then what would hap- pen to me?

After the meal, Margarite and Hildegard took me down a twisting passage to another room, a small, warm one where an elderly woman with delicate features and graying light brown hair sat propped up on a lounge chair, her legs cov- ered by an embroidered silk robe, a small book open across her lap. King Harry, curled at her feet, opened his eyes and stared indignantly at me.

Margarite presented me to Julienne, and Julienne held out a frail hand to touch my wrist. So she wanted to see the mark, too. I pushed up my sleeve and showed the birthmark.

There did not seem to be any reason to hide it.

"Ah," Julienne said, tipping her head to one side and smiling. "It's true, then. I dreamed of you, even before you were born. Sit at my feet—yes, push King Harry off on the floor. He thinks the world exists only to serve him. Mary, we're glad you are here at last, because we have so much to tell you, so much to share with you."

I sat down cautiously, because the cat's ears had flattened and the tip of his tail was twitching. I did my best to smile at Julienne, but the old woman's claim to have dreamed about me before I was born worried me.

"You are wondering about your birthmark," Julienne said. "I am not the one to explain it—that is for priests and warlocks—except to say that it can be both a gift and a curse. In time you will learn to use the gift—and avoid the curse. But your own enchanter is the only one who can tell you the reasons why you have the mark on your wrist, for he is the one who called it to you."

"What do you mean?" I asked. I did not believe any of this. "What 'enchanter'?"

Julienne folded her hands over the book that lay on her lap. "I do not know who enchanted you, Mary, and that is the truth. If he did not offer you the information, then you must seek him out, even force him to give it to you." She sighed. "I once knew someone else who carried the mark that meant she had been enchanted before her birth. Her enchanter was sorry for what he had done to her, and it took her years to persuade him that he owed her the reason."

Julienne fell quiet then, and her eyes closed, as if she were shutting out a painful sight. But then she looked up and smiled. "But that is another story, my dear. You will discover your own story as you grow older. In the meantime, I have a small gift for you."

She lifted a folded piece of blue silk from the table next to her lounge and unwrapped a round, flat piece of silver, not much larger than her palm. She handed it to me and said, "Look at both sides carefully."

It was a curious silver medallion of some kind, engraved lightly with a pattern of leaves and flowers surrounding a small animal I could not identify. I turned it over to see what was on the other side—and nearly dropped it. A face stared back at me.

"What is it?" I cried. "*Who* is it?"

"It's called a looking glass, and that is your face," Julienne said. "Have you never seen a looking glass before?"

I shook my head, and in the looking glass I saw the strange, coarse white hair stir. "My mother had a silver mirror, but the image was not so clear as this."

"So you know what you looked like," Julienne said. "Before the nuns bleached your hair."

"Yes," I said slowly, not understanding. "I saw myself several times when I was in my mother's room. But not so well. Not so clearly."

"This looking glass holds a secret," Julienne said. "And you will learn more about it as the years pass. Now I know you are tired, so let Margarite and Hildegard show you where you will sleep. The day after tomorrow, we will begin our lessons."

"Lessons," I said, nodding. I was too tired to be curious, but I tried to be polite.

But Julienne lay back on the lounge, as if she were exhausted. "Thank you for coming to see me," she said, and she closed her eyes. I knew I had been dismissed.

I followed the other two women out of the room, down another twisting hall, and through a door into a small room with greenish glass in the window, so that there was light in the place. A small bed took up one corner, a small table and bench took up another, and a padded chair and footstool sat near the window. The walls had been hung with colorful tapestries woven to look like gardens and woodlands, and they made the room seem much larger than it was.

"Rest for a while," Margarite said. "I'll come back for you later."

I put the silk package containing the looking glass on the table and then lay down, not intending to fall asleep— but I did. Then, abruptly, I woke, certain that something was in the room. Had I been dreaming?

No, I saw something in the doorway, a small figure. A girl!

I sat up, alarmed. "Who are you?" I cried.

"Hush, hush," the girl said, as she stepped into the room on bare feet. "Don't scream so! I just came to see if there was anything you needed, anything I could do for you."

"Who are you?" I demanded again.

The girl drew closer, smiling and showing rather pointed teeth, but she did not tell her name. She was short and her body was thick. Under her veil, bits of rough dark hair showed here and there. She seemed to have no neck, and her eyes were small and dark, sunken under colorless brows. The hands she held folded against her wide waist were small and fat—and far from clean—and she smelled unpleasantly of greasy food. She did not seem like someone who would be a servant in a household like this. She reminded me unpleasantly of a spider.

"Are you warm enough?" the girl asked. "Do you want another blanket? I could bring a heated stone from the kitchen, wrapped in fleece." Her ingratiating tone did not disguise her malice. She drew closer. "What is your name?"

"Get out!" I shouted suddenly, pulling back as far away from the girl as I could get. "Stay away from me!"

Suddenly King Harry jumped up on the bed, growling, his tail whipping back and forth.

The girl backed up to the door, hesitated a moment by the table with her hand outstretched over the silk package, but then she turned and ran out. Her bare feet slapped on the stone floor outside.

"So," King Harry said, sitting down and wrapping his tail around his front feet. "What did we learn from that?"

I was speechless. I pulled my blanket up to my neck.

"We learned," King Harry said patiently, "never to fall asleep without locking our door first. This is a very large house. Actually, it consists of several houses joined together, with many nooks and crannies that only I know about."

"Who was that girl?" I asked. My heart was still pounding.

"No one important," King Harry said. "Just an ignorant *spy*, looking for a chance to earn a coin or two by turning you in to the sheriff. Who knows, you might be a runaway princess. Or a witch. Or a bride who deserted her ugly old husband on her wedding day. Or a thief. Or a murderer.

Anybody who doesn't want to be found is worth turning in. Anybody with hair as ugly as yours must surely be up to something that could be worth a reward to someone else."

"But who was she?" I insisted.

"A nasty little gardener's helper," King Harry said. "She will be gone tomorrow. Hildegard has been watching her, and when I tell her what the girl has done, Hildegard will send her back to the county where she is wanted by a sheriff for stealing a sheep that was worth more than she was."

I pushed my stiff white hair away from my forehead. "Hildegard knew she was a thief?"

"She believed she was falsely accused," King Harry said. "But Hildegard believes almost anything, even the encouraging tales we've heard about you."

"What does she believe about me?" I asked hesitatingly.

The cat snickered. "She believes that you are talented and magical, and that's enough for her. I don't care about your supposed talent, and we'll see how magical you are, Gwenore. We'll see. I have yet to be impressed with your powers. I don't even believe that you know how to read, although I met a crow who knew a dove who swears that she saw you reading once."

He jumped off the bed and ran to the door. "Lock up after me," he said, and then he was gone.

I got up and padded across the room. There was an ornate key in a lock that resembled the face of a lion. I turned the key and heard the gratifying click. Then, just to be even safer, I took the key from the lock and put it under my pillow. As I was making myself comfortable, I thought I heard the distant sound of harp music, but it was very far away. I fell asleep again. When I awoke later in the day, it was to a polite knock on the door, and Sarah calling to me to come and visit the blacksmith shop.

Should I tell her about the visit from the dreadful, dirty girl who had come into my room? No, perhaps it was best not to say anything at all. The story seemed scarcely believable. And I was not so sure that I could trust anybody in this place. A few days before, I had never heard of them.

I dressed hurriedly, unlocked the door, and stepped out.

Sarah handed me a heavy woolen cloak and a black scarf for my head. "Here, wrap up, because it's cold this afternoon. Market day is over and nearly everyone has gone home, so this is a good time to see where I work. And to meet Simon, of course. You and he will be great friends, and Julienne will be teaching the two of you together now."

Sarah walked rapidly ahead and I had to run to keep up. "What do you mean by 'teaching'? Teaching what?"

"Why, everything, of course," Sarah said in such an off-hand way that I wondered if I had missed part of a conversation, when all of this had been explained completely and somehow I had agreed with it. "Here, we'll leave by this side door and go into the shop through the back, where we won't be seen."

We left the house through a low door and made our way along a stone path around a corner and into the back of a blacksmith shop. It was hot inside, for the coals in the forge were still glowing red. A family stood in the open side of the shop, a man and wife with their young daughter, talking to a boy near my age. He must be Simon. I pulled the scarf lower on my forehead and hunched my shoulders, trying to make myself smaller.

We waited in the back of the shop while Simon finished his conversation with the man, apparently regarding repairs to be made to a plow. The woman stood with her arm around the girl while the girl gawked at Simon, whose black hair was rumpled and untidy and whose hands were dirty. The girl seemed tired. She leaned her head against her mother.

Mother and daughter. It made a pretty scene.

The man thanked Simon, told him good-bye, and then led his family away. Simon turned and greeted Sarah. "I can have the plow ready for him tomorrow morning, if I build up the fire again," he told her.

"No, leave it for today. He won't mind waiting until noon tomorrow. Come and meet Mary Blondine. She's living with us now, and she will be studying with you. It will be nice for you to have someone your own age in the household."

Simon's eyes were as dark as his hair, and his jaw was stubborn. He looked straight into my face for too long a time, and then he shrugged. "I hope she can keep up," he said.

I opened my mouth and shut it again. I had no way of knowing what Simon knew—or what he had been studying. But I was not sure I liked him.

"I'm glad to know you, Simon," I lied.

"And I am glad to know you, girl," he said. But he was not looking at me anymore. He was hanging tools on hooks.

"Come in when you're done," Sarah told him. "We'll have supper and all of us will get to know Mary better."

"Good," Simon said, but I doubted that he meant it. And then to make his position clear, he added, "I'm hungry."

I sighed. So this was to be my home, for an unknown time—and for an unknown reason. That I had needed to escape from Wales was obvious. But why I had been sent here was a mystery. I was certain that Father Caddaric was somehow responsible for my being with these particular women in this particular place, but did they know why?

I followed Sarah back into the main house, passing King Harry as I went. He trailed behind us. "I have messages," he said.

I whirled around. "What?"

He sat down neatly, curling his tail over his paws. "Striker and Tom are well and content enough where they are, for today. But their home is not permanent, and they know it. Brennan fancies herself in love with a carpenter, but she still remembers to pray for you every night. And your mother still wants you dead, but only after she cuts off your wrist. She has offered a very large and tempting reward. I may have to look into it myself."

He leaped up and ran off, disappearing around a corner into a dark part of the house.

I bit back an angry retort. Then I made myself walk again, following the oblivious Sarah to another part of the house, where we would have supper. I could hear harp music again, soothing and sweet, echoing through the twisted halls.

But I wondered about the spider girl. Was she a spy? Did she know enough about me to turn me in?

5

BIRtH of tHe wHIte woLf

Days passed uneventfully in calm Blessingwood, and fear began to lose its cutting power over me. Summer ripened into autumn, and winter returned once more. I was part of the household then, taken for granted by the women, Umma, and Simon; I was assigned tasks and lessons. I grew taller, and my hair, once brown and then bleached blond and then dyed red to match Hildegard's, was then showing gray at the roots unless the dye was applied frequently. Margarite blamed this strange condition on my long illness and, she said, the poor care I probably had received as a child. But women's hair was kept almost completely covered by veils or headdresses when they were out of doors, so no one in the village had any reason to remark on my changing appearance.

Most of the time I felt almost safe. Sometimes I dreamed again of whispering to Tom that I could escape with his help, down the narrow trail carved into the rocky hill below the north castle wall. We had been caught, of course.

We had been children, and my plan had been foolish.

In the end, we had panicked and committed murder (at least in my mother's eyes), and Brennan had helped us run away. But now, was I not safe? And King Harry assured me that Tom and Striker prospered, too. Was this not what we had wanted—except for our separation?

But still, in the early mornings and late in the afternoons, I heard the crows gathering in the trees, shouting my name. *Gwenore. Gwenore.* Were they calling it out with the hope that someone would recognize it and send word to my mother? Or was I the only one who understood them? And were they letting me know they were watching over me? I did not know whether to fear them or be glad for them.

During my first two years there, the Blessingwood women took in three other refugee girls. One, Anna, replaced the ugly spider girl; she learned quickly and was sent off to marry a farmer's son in another village. One, called Sophia, came already gifted with healing arts and left for London in a few months, even more skilled, thanks to her work with Margarite. King Harry, whose art for causing me pain never faded, told me that she lived in a household not far from Brennan, and even knew Brennan, and often stopped to chat with her, even mentioning my name, Mary of Blessingwood.

Of all the girls, I was closest to tall, pale Elaine, who had been there six months when winter came around again, and who shared most of my gifts and possessed one that was new to everyone in Blessingwood. She embroidered tapestries, then wrote music and poetry to tell the story of the scene she had created, and her skill was so great that she was famed

all over the countryside, so much that whenever she
appeared at a fair or festival with her newest tapestry and her
lute, people crowded around to see and hear her. All her
tapestries were purchased eagerly, and sometimes she was
invited to entertain at elaborate dinners given in the manor
houses in the countryside. And those times, Umma and
Simon accompanied her and stood guard over her.

One afternoon, Elaine and I were preparing for a special evening in the great dining room, when the village eld-
ers, three priests, and another physician would be present for
dinner. We would play and sing for the guests, and Julienne,
our music teacher, had given me the key to the big cupboard
behind the small stage, where her most valuable and rare
instruments were kept. Elaine had not seen them yet, for they
were Julienne's special treasures. I pulled open the cupboard
door, and Elaine gasped, "Mary! All those fine instruments!
I've never seen so many."

I had spent months learning to play them, and Elaine
was more than ready to begin. "You will learn to play them
all. Julienne wants me to help you at first, and then she will
take over your training."

Tall, pale Elaine shook her head, disbelieving her good
fortune. "Here is a pipe and tabor. And a psaltery. And so
many different flutes and pipes! But what is this strange
thing?"

I picked up the instrument and rubbed the beautiful
wood with my fingers. "It's called a rebec, and Umma
brought it back with him from the Holy War. Here's the bow.
This is human hair on it. And the rebec strings are silk

threads wrapped with silver. We'll ask Umma to play for you—he's much better than anyone—"

Through the windows we heard a loud cry, followed by a long, deep groan and the weeping of children. The sounds came from Margarite's surgery, only twenty steps across the courtyard. I was accustomed to hearing occasional cries of distress when the physician was seeing patients, and I no longer panicked at the sounds. But Elaine had never become used to them—she had no healing gifts. Her face had turned white and she put down the rebec and bow and turned, as if she wanted to hide.

"Stay here and wait until I return," I said, touching Elaine's arm, trying to reassure her.

At that moment, the youngest of the maids burst into the room, shouting, "Mary, Mary! Come quick! They want you in the surgery!"

Without hesitating, I ran after the maid. While I spent two hours every day with the physician, learning her healing arts, I rarely was called to help in emergencies. Umma was the one Margarite preferred, for he had worked with her physician husband in the Holy Land, and there was nothing that Margarite knew that he did not know. His appearance and his inability to speak were what prevented him from the practice of medicine. But patients, if they were ill enough, or severely injured, did not object to his scars and his strange, mumbling talk.

The maid held open the doors for me, and I ran outside, across the courtyard, and into the surgery, while the cries and weeping of children drew Blessingwood servants to the windows on both floors. Simon and Sarah were holding a frantic woman down on a table while Margarite cut through her skirt with a short, curved knife. Blood pumped from a long, deep gash above her knee, arcing into the air, spraying and splashing everywhere, even though Umma was pressing his hands against the wound. A heavy trail of blood led from the door that opened to the street outside the walls of Blessingwood. A boy younger than Simon and three little girls waited by the door, all four drenched with blood. The girls wept "Mama! Mama!" between horrified shrieks.

"Mary, I need you to find the blood vessel and tie it off," Margarite said as soon as she saw me. "Quickly! She has not much blood left in her, and Umma's eyes are not sharp enough."

Umma moved his fingers and I looked down into the gaping wound. It was impossible to see the severed ends of the blood vessel, and so, without hesitating, I pressed my thin fingers inside the wound and felt for what I hoped I would find quickly. No, the flesh had swollen too much. I could not sense the pulsing end of the vessel that carried the woman's life from her torso down into her leg.

"Umma, can you hold it open farther?"

Umma's thick fingers pulled apart the wound, the woman moaned, and I saw the severed vessel clearly between spurts of bright blood. "Here it is!" I murmured, and I reached in and pinched the vessel closed. The blood no longer arced high into the air, but oozed out instead. "Umma, hand me the thread."

He did, with a loop already made at the end. I worked it over the severed blood vessel and pulled it tight. "There," I said. "It stopped."

But it was too late. Even while we worked over the woman, pressing small rolls of cloth into the wound to sop up the blood and close off the smaller vessels, she drew a deep breath, then several shallow ones, and then she shuddered and died.

The boy at the door cried, "No! She can't die! She didn't do anything wrong! She only wanted to cross the bridge, but we have no money for the toll until we sell her cloth, and the knight would not let her pass. He was drunk and he used his sword on her. He laughed when he did it!"

Margarite closed the woman's eyes and spread a clean napkin over her face. Her own expression was set and grim. This was not her first patient attacked by the knights who held the two bridges over the river that skirted the village. No one could control the violent men, and the sheriff would not investigate, probably because they shared what they stole with him. I knew he was corrupt, and I had reasons of my own for avoiding him. But this poor woman had been murdered in front of her children, and in broad daylight! I looked imploringly at Margarite. She would know the right thing to say.

Margarite turned to the children and said, "I am sorry that your mother died. But even if she had received this wound right outside my door, I could not have saved her, not without a miracle. By the time she first felt the pain, she was already dying. But you were right to bring her here, for she died knowing how much you loved her and how hard we were trying to save her."

I was disappointed. That could not have been much consolation to the children. Their mother had been killed by the louts who demanded money illegally from every person who wanted to cross the bridges, and now what would happen to them? The physician was a powerful woman in the village, surely powerful enough to challenge the sheriff over an outrage like this. The young mother was dead because of a drunken knight!

A maid came and took the children out of the surgery, and I heard her saying, "Come along. I'll clean you up and give you hot soup to drink. And then we'll decide what to do next. No, don't look back. Let the doctors take care of your mother until the priest comes. Later you can see her."

I looked around the bloody room and bit my lip. If only the children could have had a better memory of their mother's last hour. But when had anything been different? All of my life, women and children paid the price for the presence of warriors, in between their wars.

Everyone in the room was soaked with the woman's blood. Margarite gestured to Simon, Sarah, and me to leave, and we hurried away through the door that led to the courtyard.

Elaine stood there, not ten steps away, and when she saw us, she gasped and took a step backward.

"Well, *she* will not be helping Margarite anytime soon," Simon said, scowling. "Those pale ones always puke when they see blood."

Sarah pinched his arm until he yelped. "Hush. Go wash up, and change into clean clothes! You can finish the work at the forge while I bathe with the women. And don't speak again unless I give you permission." She leveled a stern look at Elaine then, and said, "That cannot be the worst thing you have seen in your life. Straighten up and behave like a woman."

"It was not the worst thing," Elaine said, her voice shaking. Tears spilled out of her eyes. "The worst was when my brother was dying." She turned away toward the stairs that led to the second floor over the dining room, where she had a small room.

I followed Sarah through the courtyard without speaking. There was only one place where we could clean ourselves completely after the bath of blood we had received. We passed through an old hall, then a newer one, then into a small private courtyard where the men of Blessingwood were never allowed. There was a well on one side, and Sarah pulled up a leather bucket and poured cold water over me. Then I pulled up water to pour over her. We left our stained clothing in a heap on the paving stones outside the entrance of the bathhouse and went inside, passing the closed and locked door that led, I had been told, to a ruined underground bath that had not been used for centuries.

The weather was warm for winter, and the great furnace that heated the water in the large ground-floor baths had no fire in it that day. A small amount of water, heated by pipes that ran through the bakery ovens next door, steamed in a small tub set in the middle of a white marble floor, and Sarah rinsed me with warm water until no more blood ran from me. "Take a blanket from the shelf and hurry back to your room," Sarah said. "But keep your hair covered so that Elaine does not see it. The color needs refreshing at the roots."

I, still shaken from the morning's experience, tried to smile. "I looked red enough a while ago," I said. "I'll stay until you are done and refill the tub for Margarite. Poor Umma. He—and Simon, too—might like a warm wash in the bathhouse after what they have been through."

Sarah snorted. "Let them use the tub in their lavatory. If the men want a bathhouse, let them build one. Or dig one up, as we did. I doubt that the Romans who made this ever intended it to be for women only, but we found it and rebuilt it with our own hands, while our husbands were off killing heathens and getting themselves killed in turn. There's little enough comfort for women in this world, and I doubt if there is any at all in the next."

I, huddling inside a rough blanket, laughed suddenly and made myself stop just as suddenly. "Don't let the priest hear you say anything like that."

Sarah shook her head. "The priest thinks I am a duffart," she said. "A dullard. So I am fortunate, am I not? He does not expect anything of me as long as he thinks I am too dim to do anything except pump a bellows at the forge. Run along. I'll refill the tub for Margarite."

I clutched the blanket around me, and ran back across the courtyard and upstairs to my room. Usually there would be two maids upstairs cleaning at that time of day, but they were gone, probably called to the surgery to help clean away the blood. The priest would be there by now, with some of the village men who would carry the dead woman home to her own house, the house where her children would no longer be welcome as soon as her grave was covered. Their landlord would put them out on the road.

Someone should demand that the sheriff arrest the knights who made the villagers' lives so miserable. For more than a year, both bridges had been guarded day and night by them, and the crossing tolls had grown higher and higher. The village had been successfully cut in half by them. And now they had murdered someone.

Later, when I went downstairs, I learned the rest of the story. The woman had been widowed the year before, and now the children were orphans. The priest, not an especially kind man himself, would help them find homes, if possible. The boy would be easy to place because he looked strong, and he was old enough to do nearly as much work as a grown man. But the little girls might be turned out on the roads and left to beg.

We Blessingwood women had gathered in Julienne's small room for a simple meal. Everyone looked to Hildegard for comment, for she was head of the household. Blessingwood had been her husband's land, which she had inherited when he had been killed in the Holy Land war, along with Margarite's physician husband and Sarah's husband, the blacksmith. Hildegard made all the final decisions.

"Margarite and I have discussed this, and I agree with her," she said. "This has been a tragedy—an outrage!—but we risk a great deal if we challenge the sheriff to arrest the knight who did this. We know who it was. The men in the village may decide to take matters into their own hands."

"It's about time!" Sarah cried, her callused hands clenched into hard fists.

"Or they may not," Hildegard went on. "The risk is great. Unless the villagers have help from the sheriff, the knights can take revenge whenever they wish. They still have their battle weapons. The men here have little more than farming tools. We do not have many choices now."

"I know that boy," Simon said. "He worked hard with his father, but the land belongs to the lord, and now the children will have nothing. The knight should pay for what he has done."

"Simon," Sarah said warningly. "This is a dangerous time for all of us." She leaned across the table and stared into his face. "Do you understand me? You know that you cannot do anything that causes the sheriff to look too closely at any of us."

Next to me, Elaine gasped a little. Her face grew so white that I thought she might faint. Why had she come here? No one had explained about her, any more than anyone had explained about me. Elaine had arrived late one evening, in the company of a strange man who left immediately after delivering her to the main door.

Simon, Elaine, and I put the women in danger. Some of the hot anger I had felt at the young mother's murder died away, even while I was ashamed at my willingness to save myself before fighting for whatever justice was available under the sheriff.

But Simon was still scowling. He glared down at his callused fingers and shook his head. "It's wrong," he said.

"The world is full of wrongs," Julienne said quietly. She had not spoken during the meal, but now everyone turned to her. Her thin hands trembled a little and she folded them in her lap. "Blessingwood has been a refuge for certain children, children who are important to this world. We have to protect Blessingwood, for as long as we can."

It was as if a cold wind blew into the room. No one spoke. Everyone knew who those "certain children" were.

That evening Elaine and I played for the guests in the large dining room, and we smiled as we sang, for the duty of a true singer is to make music and take everyone into a different place and time, where blood, if shed, is washed away by angels, and no child wanders the roads hungry. That is the magic of music.

The dead mother was buried on a bright day when the hedgerows and grasses glistened with frost. Her children sold all of the household belongings, few that there were, in order to pay for the burial. They could not afford the price of a gravestone, so the Blessingwood women paid for it. Umma sent the boy to another village to work with an old Holy War companion, and the three girls moved in with a widow who wove rough woolen cloth in her cottage. The girls were already able to spin. They would be of use for a while—until they began eating too much.

The knights at the bridges grew bolder. No girl or woman was safe from rape now, unless she traveled with at least four men. That spring, Martha LeBaker's daughter hanged herself after they caught her fishing alone and left her barely able to walk. The sheriff would not help. The priest called for prayer and fasting, even after Lent was over, but he had done nothing more, except to chastise the girl and tell her that perhaps evil had befallen her because of the evil in herself. The lord who owned more than half of the land in the area had gone to London for the month of May. The bakers, the ale makers, the shoemaker, the tailor—all suffered from the lack of business. Early vegetables could not be carted across the bridges without the farmers giving up half their loads. The old man who made the finest harnesses, even though he was nearly blind, attempted to cross the bridge with only two coppers for the toll, and the knights cut off his right hand and hung it around his neck on a cord. The following day the old man killed himself with his favorite awl, and the priest refused to bury him, so Umma and Simon put him to rest in the woods. Half of Tom Shepherd's sheep were driven into the river and drowned, and the knights laughed, watching them struggle while their thick wool soaked up water and carried them under.

The village was not on a common road, but the tales of the knights were told for a day's walk in all directions, and so no one went there. But then, who can wonder at that? Nearly every village had its own vandal knights now, not interested in working and too fond of violence. Women everywhere whispered prayers for another war on foreign soil, to lure the knights away with hopes of spoils.

One day, while I was working in the small, crowded

room where Margarite prepared her medicines from the herbs that Hildegard grew or gathered, Simon appeared silently in the doorway. When I looked up, he put his finger to his lips and came in, silent on bare feet, and closed the door behind him.

"You know poisons," he stated.

I stared at him. "Why are you asking?" I knew many poisons, but Margarite had sworn me to silence about them long before.

"What if a traveler feared that he would be robbed? What if he wanted to put something on his coins that would punish a thief if he did not know it was there? A liquid of some kind, something that would dry and not show on silver, but would poison through the skin somehow. I have heard of such things."

"Who is this traveler?" I asked slowly, suspiciously.

"Any traveler," he said impatiently. "What if I were going on a journey and did not want a thief to get away with his crime? Would you want me to be robbed of my only coin?"

I read Simon's mind easily, for he had a pure spirit, and he must have known that I could. In his imagination, he approached one of the bridges carrying a load of firewood and holding out his worn wallet, with only one small silver coin in it.

I blinked away the vision. "You are sure about this thief?"

"He is the kind to brag and laugh about his crimes when he is drunk."

Outside, a crow shrieked angrily. I thought that I saw King Harry in a corner, watching and judging me, but when I turned to look, the cat was not there. But, still, I felt his presence.

"If there were such a thing as a poison like that," I said quietly, opening my mind to Simon and hoping that he could see what I wanted him to see, "someone might find it to be dangerous to touch." I concentrated on a small black stone vial that contained the poison, and the red wax that sealed it. I knew this was wrong, but Martha LeBaker's daughter, younger even than I, had come to the surgery once to have an ugly splinter pulled from her foot, and I had sat with her while the wound was cleaned. She had been a plain, cheerful child with freckled skin and large gray eyes. So patient. So uncomplaining.

Simon nodded. He did not read minds as well as I, but he could sort true sight from dreams. "Is this poison quick?" he asked.

"On the skin, it will kill within three breaths," I said. "In the mouth, the first breath will be stopped."

"Is it painful?"

I nodded slowly. Would Simon take pleasure in this?

"Can it be stopped?"

"Not by anyone, not even Margarite."

King Harry leaped to the table close to Simon. "Use it, then," he told the boy. "Someone has to help." He turned his head to glare at me. "You owe a debt."

King Harry was right. Without allowing myself to think, I turned and reached behind a row of jars on a shelf, feeling blindly for what I knew was there. The small stone bottle. I took it out and handed it to Simon.

"Do not let the poison touch your skin. Remove the wax and let one drop fall on your coin. Then, after it dries, slide the coin into your wallet *without touching it*. Reseal the bottle and return it to the shelf."

He was going to turn away, but I said, "You can use it only once. There is an acrid odor that will linger. People will be suspicious. Remember who has cared for you—and me—all these years, and be grateful."

I expected to hear the next day that one of the knights was dead, but the first death did not occur for four days. His drunkenness was blamed, for his habit was well known. The second, on the other bridge, came about in another four days, after that particular knight developed a griping of the guts. He did not come to Margarite, who was known widely to refuse treatment to anyone who bore arms. Instead, he consulted the physician on the other side of the village, Hiram, who dosed him with a thick brown liquid that caused him to vomit for hours. The knight returned to the bridge, shaky but improved, he told his companion. But the griping came back upon him suddenly that afternoon, so suddenly that he collapsed with his hand still in the purse of an old fellow with a badly scarred face. Or so his companion said as he was leaving the village in haste. The remaining knight from the other bridge joined him, and they were not seen again.

The bottle was in its usual place when I checked on it. Simon had taken a dangerous chance, using the poison twice.

Everyone's life returned to normal except for Hiram's, whose reputation was damaged. "He never did know anything about griping of the guts," the carter told the shepherd. "It's best to see a woman about pains in the guts." Hiram the physician probably bore a grudge against Blessingwood now. Simon repeated the story to me with a sober face.

That night I sat for a long time on a bench with King Harry, in the small courtyard outside the bathhouse, watching the moon slipping across the night sky. I am a murderer, I thought. Someday I will pay for these sins. But I am not sorry. I cannot be sorry.

"You are like a wolf," King Harry said. "A white wolf. They do only what is necessary, and they don't waste a good moon with whining over nothing. Look at that moon, Gwenore. Someday a man will stand on it and look down at our earth."

"Never," I said, getting to my feet. "I think you have been drinking Umma's cider." But I looked up once more and wondered, and for a moment I thought I saw something small and bright springing up from our world and flashing out—and out—into the blackness.

A week later, I held my head low over a basin, longing to push Hildegard's hands away from my hair, but I knew better. For more than two years Hildegard had dyed my graying hair red every ten weeks, as an important part of my disguise. The people in the village knew me as Hildegard's niece, and Hildegard's hair was red.

Only the four women at Blessingwood knew of the

dye—the women and King Harry, the cat, who never missed one of the ordeals in the small room connected to Hildegard's workroom, where she preserved the products from her vegetable, fruit, and herb gardens, where she invented the creams and ointments—and dyes—that she sold in her little nook of a shop to the village women and the strangers who occasionally traveled through the remote village. Her hair dyes were popular, but only I (and Hildegard herself) knew about and used red.

"I'm almost finished, Mary," Hildegard said. "It takes more dye now, because most of your hair is white! I never saw such a thing on one so young." She poured another cup of the dye over my head and massaged it into my hair. "How different you look now from the way you looked when you came to us. Your hair is long and thick. You're taller. The sad, frightened, pale girl is gone, and here you are, a strong and happy young woman. No one from your past would ever recognize you."

"Perhaps," I said, thinking of the time I had spent holding up my looking glass and deliberately changing my expression, turning up the corners of my mouth until the small half smile became habit and my worried frown disappeared. Julienne had taught me to do that. "No one wants to listen to a scowling singer," she had told me. "And the wrong people might remember her, wonder why, and talk too much."

Hildegard poured a bowl of warm water over my head, then wrapped a heavy towel around it. "Go sit outside while you're drying your hair. The sun will warm you."

"Our hair is always covered, so what does it matter what color mine is, red or white?" I offered the mild complaint cautiously, because I was deeply grateful to the women who had given me, a stranger, shelter for so long. But I hated the dyeing process, because it stung my scalp until my eyes watered. Surely no one was looking for me, not after all this time. Sometimes I wanted to ask the women if they had heard anything of a widow in Wales, looking for her runaway daughter who had killed a nobleman. But I had been warned never to tell anyone about my past, and so, no matter how much I wanted to confide in the people who took such good care of me—and be reassured by them—I had kept my silence.

"I know the dye stings and this takes so long. But all it would take is a chance wind, or a branch that snagged your headdress, and someone would see and wonder why my niece's hair had changed color. There would be gossip and questions, and word could get back to the people who were looking for you. Perhaps they no longer search for you, but we can't take chances. The one who sent you here said that you had to hide for the rest of your life." She hesitated, then added, "We gave our word, and if that means that I will dye your hair until it falls out, then I will."

I nodded, did my best to smile, and went to sit by the door to the yard where the bright sunlight reflected off the wall of the house. King Harry sat across from me on a stack of clay pots, blinking in the light. "Once I heard a traveler tell a tale of the ugly women he had seen on his pilgrimage to the Holy Land," he said. He curled his tail around his feet and smiled. "He saw heathen women whose eyelids had been slashed at the corners so that their eyes would seem larger, but the cuts had turned rotten and the flesh fell away, so that their eyeballs appeared to hang out of their heads."

"Be quiet," I said, combing my wet hair—and pretending that he had not horrified me.

"And Christian women," the cat went on, "whose skin had burned in the desert sun and fell away in great, blackened sheets as they died. And my friend described heathen women whose noses and ears had been pierced for gold rings, but the holes stretched and grew maggots—"

I threw a pebble at him, missed, and went back to combing.

"You're talking about Umma, aren't you?" I said. "He's the friend. But he can't talk. How do you know what he saw when he was in the Holy Land?"

"He tells me in his nightmares," King Harry said smugly. "He has terrible dreams, even worse than yours, *Gwenore*."

King Harry enjoyed panicking me by using my real name, which no one else knew. "Someday," I said. "Someday, cat, I will give you a good reason to be silent."

"You'll give me *what*?" King Harry asked. "Now that I have your attention, shall I tell you about Tom and Striker?"

"You've heard something new?" I cried. The cat's reports of my friend and my dog did not come often, over this long, long time.

"I hear *everything* that is new," he said. "They are traveling in this direction, with a troupe of players and musicians who are on their way to Canterbury for the festivals. They will pass within a mile of the village, on the old Roman road. You could see for yourself—soon."

I clenched my hands together so tightly that they hurt. "Is this the truth?"

"Have I ever lied?"

"Probably. But I want to know if *this* is the truth."

King Harry stood up, stretched, and looked around. "My spies tell me that the players expect to pass the cross-roads on the same day that Margarite plans to bring medicines to the midwives at Upper Willows. She doesn't intend to take you. But isn't it time that you began paying these good women back for what they have done for you?"

"I could serve as her assistant now," I said thoughtfully. "I know I am ready. Hildegard won't need me in the gardens for a few days. Julienne will excuse me from my class. I'll ask Margarite if I can go with her."

"Do better than ask like a child," King Harry said. "Find three good reasons why she would want your tiresome company. For myself, I can't think of one." He left then, jumping to the top of the stone wall surrounding the yard, and disappearing.

I braided my hair slowly, thinking. By the time the noon church bell rang, I had invented several reasons why Margarite should want me with her on her journey to Upper Willows.

I found Margarite in her room, sitting at the table under the shelves that held her books and records. I knocked on the open door, and she looked up from the sheets of drawings of human eyes.

Immediately, I forgot my errand. "Are you going to remove someone's cataracts?" I asked eagerly. I had wanted to watch Margarite perform this surgery for a long time.

"I know I promised you that I would let you watch next time, but it's in another village. . . ."

"I can go!" I cried, remembering Tom and Striker, and Upper Willows.

"The man is in Upper Willows," Margarite began.

"I'll go!" I almost shouted, scarcely able to believe my good fortune.

"It's a long ride, and I'll have to spend the night there."

"I don't care," I babbled. "I'll sleep on the floor, if you'll let me go. I can carry half of our supplies on my horse, and you'll be more comfortable." I was beginning to remember all my reasons for going with Margarite now. "And I'm ready to start training as your assistant. And I'll have to work as your assistant before I can be licensed as your apprentice, so the sooner we begin, the better."

Margarite studied my face. "All good reasons. I had been thinking of taking you around with me regularly. Soon you'll have to decide what you want to do. You've had experience with Julienne, singing, although she says you need more work creating your own songs. But even now, you could find work as a singer and storyteller. Hildegard tells me that you can keep more plants alive than you kill, so you would be a worthy gardener. You did not seem to enjoy your lessons with Sarah at the forge, so perhaps you've decided against becoming a blacksmith." She narrowed her eyes. "Ah. Are you eager to go with me—or just eager to visit a new place?"

I took a step forward. "Yes, to both. I want to go with you. I have been wondering how long it would be before you would take me. But King Harry told me that my friend and my dog will be passing over the Roman road at the same time you will be passing by, and if I could just see them once more . . ." I began to weep suddenly, unable to stop. "If I could see them once."

Margarite drew a deep breath. "Your friend and his dog."

"*My* dog!" I cried. "And Tom. They saved my life. They escaped, and I want to see them and let them know that I am alive and safe."

Margarite brushed one hand over her eyes, as if she could make the problem vanish. "I'll have to speak to the others. The risk is very great."

"Tom would never betray me!"

But she shook her head. "I'll have to ask the others. If you are betrayed, then so are we. And my friends have done nothing to deserve what would happen to them."

I would have said more, but Margarite sent me to my room to await the decision. I sat on the edge of my bed for what seemed to be a long time, my door open, listening for footsteps coming my way. Suddenly, I picked up the looking glass, and I stared into the reflection of my eyes.

The loneliness in my eyes was terrible to see, even for me. The smile I had thought was now habit had disappeared. Young Gwenore looked back at me. Sometimes I saw visions in the glass, events from the past, and events I could not identify, but what I thought might be the future. Dimly I saw a

cave deep underground, and a wild sea—and Tom—before
the mirror cleared again. I turned it over and looked down
at the ornate back. The small animal engraved there, impossible to identify before, seemed more definite now. Surprised,
I looked closer while my birthmark burned. The animal was
a wolf. I blinked. The wolf raised its head, and through the
polished silver I saw it standing on a high hill at the edge of
a forest. She was white, the same color as my hair. She looked
toward me. . . .

I put the looking glass down in my lap suddenly and
drew several deep breaths. When I looked again, the small
animal was once more impossible to identify.

Just then, Margarite and Julienne came into my room. I
could not read their expressions, and so I said, "Did you
decide?"

"You may go with me," Margarite said. "We will wait
for a part of the day for your friend and the dog. If they pass
by, you are to say nothing and not show in any way that you
have ever seen them before. If they recognize you, then we
will know that your disguise is not good enough, and you are
in danger here anyway and could be recognized by someone
else. We will have to make new plans for you. But if they do
not recognize you, we will know that we have changed you
enough to keep you safe."

"May I speak to them?" I begged.

"No," Julienne said. "Not if they do not know you. If
they do, then it won't matter, because we will know we have
failed. In that case, you may speak to the boy—for a few
minutes. Then Margarite will take you away, to meet some-

one who will move you to another place where you will be safer than here, and we will not see you again."

I could not speak for a long moment. Finally I said, "Never again?"

"It is for your sake," Julienne said. "If a boy from your past knows you, then anyone from your past would know you. You will have to move on."

Everything that had happened in the last two years flooded into my mind—the care and the teaching and the kindness, the hundreds of meals in the small dining room, the many festive meals in the big room with neighbors and shopkeepers. Could it be worth it, just talking to Tom for a few minutes?

"Perhaps I could just see him," I said numbly. "He wouldn't notice me. I could stay hidden, or cover my face. If I could just see him and Striker . . ."

"If he doesn't recognize you, and you don't talk to him, then I don't see what harm could be done," Margarite said. "But you cannot speak one word, or indicate by any means who you are, because if he recognizes you, then you will never return to Blessingwood. Are you sure you understand?"

My eyes flooded with tears. So I would not be able to ask Tom about Brennan. King Harry's news had never been satisfactory or consoling, and I could not see her in my mirror, not ever. Finally I nodded. "I agree," I said.

They left me, not unkindly but with nods and gentle smiles, but I was devastated beyond bearing. King Harry slipped in.

"Lock your door," he said as he jumped up to the bed. "How many times do I have to tell you? No one else has enemies like yours."

"Maybe I don't have enemies anymore," I said. "Maybe everyone has forgotten me."

"The reward for your capture—or your dead body—has increased tenfold in these two years. The evil one is sure that you live, but she cannot find you. She sends out questions with rats and with vultures, but she receives no answers, because they are held to silence by the old priest. Her spies question the innkeepers and travelers. All that saves you is that she is hated more than *you* are wanted. She has been cast off by the old duke. He married his neighbor's thirteen-year-old daughter, and she is already pregnant. Rhiamon's hunger has grown, not faded. She wants a husband, a son, and a castle, before it is too late."

"Have you told the women here?" I asked, afraid to hear the answer.

"Never." The cat was very firm. "They deserve better than learning about someone so evil. But listen, if you betray them on the journey, do not think of returning here, because it will not be me who kills you. It will be Umma. I will set him on you, because he values them more than himself, and that is a rare thing in this world."

I sat abruptly on the bed. "I should not go," I said. "But . . ."

"But. But. But," King Harry said. "The world would be a better place if not for the 'buts' of lunatics like you. Open the door. I want out before I am tempted to scratch out your eyes and put an end to talk of journeys, now or ever."

I rose unsteadily and let him out, then locked the door again and curled up on the bed in misery. I would not go on the journey.

But was this not a test of my strength? I wondered. And a test of the success of the Blessingwood women in making me into a different person? What if my presence was discovered here, when they least expected it? The penalty for hiding a murderer was death. And they, being women, would likely not meet the hangman, but instead they would be burned.

Was I recognizable? Would someone come to the forge one day, or to Hildegard's shop? Would someone be in the audience when Elaine, Julienne, and I were singing at a festival? Would that someone send a message to Rhiamon, collect the reward, and be miles away before men came for my protectors and me?

A true test would be to pass by Tom. If he did not know me, then all of us were safe. If he did, then I must run away again, for the good of the people I loved.

6

the dagger and the sword

In the nights that followed, I slept poorly. It was true that I was full of hope that I might see Tom and Striker again, and I lay awake anticipating the event, as well as dreading the possibility of great problems. But what little sleep I got was devastated by terrible dreams of frightened children and swans circling a black lake in a foreign land. Who were these children, that I dreamed of them so often? I did not know them, but I always woke expecting to see them standing by my bed, begging for help. If Brennan had been there, I would have told my dreams to her, because she loved speculating on the meanings of dreams and nightmares, even though she had been warned once by a priest (not Father Caddaric) that they came from the devil.

I had never trusted dreams to foretell my future, any more than I trusted the fortune-tellers who set up shop at the fairs. Both Hildegard and Julienne had assured me that, as I grew older, I would see the ways ahead without needing the help of others or using devices such as coins, or crystals, or the curious ornamental decks of cards that travelers had brought back from the desert countries. They had not explained how this would happen, telling me only that it was different for everyone. When I asked them about my looking glass, they smiled and assured me that looking glasses sometimes provided "views" of other worlds and times, but these views often required study in order to understand. That had not been much help.

So now I became preoccupied with my terrible nightmares, wondering which might be warnings and which might be prophecy. I also dreamed of being killed. I dreamed of killing. Were these events I could avoid, or was I destined to die fleeing ahead of men on horseback who wanted to murder me—or wanted me because I had been responsible for the death of someone else? Sometimes they were men I recognized. And sometimes the spider girl was there in some of my dreams, watching, smirking, beckoning me with a crooked finger to follow her into a dark wood, as if she represented all the evil in the world. And I dreamed of endless caves I entered but never left, caves occupied by mystical creatures—and danger.

And several times I dreamed of four swans circling over my head, calling my name urgently. Why did I dream of swans? What did they want from me?

The days passed slowly, marked by only one extraordinary event. Simon came to my room late one afternoon and gave me a small, sharp dagger. It was concealed in an ornate belt made of long silver links, decorated with dangling silver tabs. The vicious little steel blade was concealed among the tabs.

"You made this?" I asked as I examined the ornate flowers and leaves engraved on the links. "It is beautiful—but is the knife only part of the decoration?"

He took back the belt and flicked out the knife, holding it an inch away from my throat. I sat very still, and then I said, "Is this a lesson, Simon? You are not a good teacher. You are frightening me."

He slid the knife back into its silver scabbard and handed it to me. "That was a perfect lesson, Mary Singer, for this is a knife to use to kill someone secretly, and not for clanging awkwardly about on a road somewhere like a drunken knight with a sword he never learned to use properly. This is the knife you use in the dark, after being shown how only once."

And then he was gone. Simon had a way of disappearing quickly and silently in the halls and back rooms of the house, reminding me of a thief. Or worse. I had been at Blessingwood for more than two years, and I still knew almost nothing about him, but I suspected many things. Sometimes, when he was tired, I caught the hint of a foreign accent in his speech, as if he had spoken a different language when he was a small child. He was darker than most people, except some of the Welsh who were descended from the ancient families. But Simon was not Welsh. And once I had thought I had heard him speaking to Umma in a foreign tongue, and Umma was nodding seriously, as if he understood every word.

I had discussed this mystery with King Harry, who told me I had gone mad from having my hair dyed so many times—and then he warned me to keep my mouth shut regarding the personal business of Simon and Umma. Forever. He had told me that Simon was not the only one who knew how to make—and use—sharp knives.

I put away the belt Simon gave me, with the things I would be taking on the journey, but several times I took it out again and pulled the knife from its sheath and wondered at it. Would I ever use it? Would I have the courage?

Every morning for an hour, in a corner of the large dining room, I helped Elaine with her music lessons, and I spent the afternoons helping Hildegard in the gardens. But one afternoon, she told me that I was preventing the plants from growing.

"The back of your mind is cluttered with fear," she said. "The plants hear you, and they are afraid to reach up, because your fear is as scorching as a drought. Fear stunts the good growth and feeds the evil growth. You have a great gift for raising all kinds of plants, but if I let you stay here—and you do not correct your thinking—the root crops will bear tumors by harvest."

I was horrified. "I'm sorry!" I cried.

"Fear is what kills everything in the end," she said sadly. "Without it, we would be immortal. And we would not harm anyone else." She sighed, and then asked, "What bothers you so, Mary?"

"I'm afraid that I won't see Tom and Striker, and I'm afraid that I will," I confessed as I got up from my knees beside a row of radishes.

She nodded. "But you have duties on this trip, serious duties as a physician's assistant. Which comes first, your personal concerns or your duty to your work?"

The answer was clear. "I've been selfish," I acknowledged, "worrying about what might happen to me. I should be concerned about what will happen to our patients." .

"The only way to God is through service," she said. "And we are all on our way to God, whether we like it or not. The truth is simple—nothing matters except service. God sets our tasks and gives us the skills to perform them. Mary, this is the beginning and end of it all."

Umma came up then, with King Harry riding his shoulder, to gesture a question to Hildegard. "Not today, Umma," she said. Umma nodded to both of us and marched away, with the cat smirking back at me.

"He wanted to fill the water tank for me again," she said. "But it's going to rain this evening."

I looked up at a dazzling blue sky. There would be no rain, not that I could see, not on this day.

"You could feel it coming on your skin, if you would stop thinking so much," she told me, laughing.

Stop thinking? How could anyone stop thinking? But I nodded and knelt down to finish weeding the row. My worries came back like insects, buzzing and stinging. Would I even be alive in a week? Should I abandon my desire to look for Tom and Striker?

But then I sat back on my heels and changed my thoughts deliberately. Would the patients we would see do well at our hands? Would we be wise and steady? Yes, we would help, not hurt. I knew that.

And then I felt the promise of the rain brush cool fingers quickly over my face, before it fluttered away. How could I not smile at what I had just learned?

I dreamed better dreams that night, of walking through a mountain pass with my friends, of discovering a carved rock that held the good secrets of my life, of swans on a calm lake, of singing a new song in a new land with friends at my side and Striker in my arms.

On the morning of the journey, I was in my room, packing a saddlebag with what I would need. I had been concentrating on my concerns, unable to stop myself right then from hoping that I would see Tom and Striker—and still not cause harm—and so when I heard a sound in my open doorway, I was startled.

It was Elaine, who apologized for surprising me. "Can I help you with anything?" she asked. "Umma has brought the horses around, and Margarite sent me to make myself useful to you."

I wrapped my looking glass in a small shawl, packed it, then closed the flap on the saddlebag. "I'm done now, but thank you." I looped the strings of my small wallet around my neck, then tucked it inside my gown. "I'm sure I've remembered everything," I said. "We'll only be gone two days, so I don't need much." I fastened my new belt under my loose, short tunic, and I was grateful that Elaine did not comment on it.

"I almost wish I could go with you," Elaine said. "But I'm still so grateful to have a home that I dread the thought of leaving it, if only to go to the cobbler with Hildegard for new shoes."

"You'll feel better as time passes," I said, smiling to cover my own apprehension. I had never asked Elaine where she had come from or what she had been doing before she arrived at Blessingwood. Elaine was not the first girl to arrive after me, and I knew she would not be the last. But each one had been given an invented reason for coming, for the sake of curious villagers. As I was called Hildegard's orphaned "niece," Elaine was called a third cousin of Julienne's, in training to be a companion, and eventually to be placed with a country family.

No one in the household asked questions of anyone else. The refugees seldom visited the village, and they left Blessingwood as they had arrived, unseen, at night or at dawn. I knew that they were like me, in danger and consequently endangering these good women. Some, I knew, had certain powers, like mine, the beginnings of magical abilities. One had also spoken to King Harry, and I had seen her several times with a hawk close by, apparently deep in conversation. Elaine seemed to have a gift I could not clearly describe to myself. Her embroidered tapestries seemed to be ... *alive*. I could have sworn that I had seen the flowers on one small tapestry stir and flutter. And the wings of a white dove on another had raised up once, then settled down again when I exclaimed. I had thought of asking Elaine about these marvels, but remembering my own need for secrecy, I did not.

So I smiled at Elaine now, and said, "I hope we'll always stay good friends. As soon as I get back, we can begin working on a new song together." For a moment I wondered what Elaine would think—what they all would think!—if I did not return from this journey. It was possible, if Tom recognized me. If that happened, Blessingwood would be lost to me, and I might have no other safe place anywhere.

Elaine walked with me to the yard where Margarite and Umma were loading the packhorse with the last of the supplies she would be bringing to the midwives. In the distance, the bell at the village church rang once. It was the sixth hour after midnight, the sun was already above the hills, and my heart beat quickly. By the time the sun set that evening, I might have seen Tom and Striker. And I might know whether or not I would leave Blessingwood.

"Good-bye!" Elaine called out from the doorway. "Have a safe journey."

I caught Umma's level look, perhaps centered on me a moment too long. King Harry sat on his shoulder, and who knew what the cat had told him? That cat who knew everything.

As Margarite and I rode toward the bridge we would have to cross, a disheveled man in a soiled tunic stepped forward from under a low-spreading tree. He wore a sword, and he kept a dirty hand on the hilt as he approached us.

Margarite reined up. She already had coins in her hand, and she held them out. "Good morning to you," she said. "We are two riders with three horses." She nudged her horse, and he danced forward nervously.

"Hold on," the knight said. He grabbed for the bridle on my horse, but the horse sidestepped. I felt the animal shiver. Even the horses hated these men. I slipped the tips of three fingers under the hem of my tunic, barely touching the dangling scabbard. I could have the knife out in an instant, if I needed it.

Margarite flipped back her cloak so that her red gown showed. "I paid for my assistant, too," she called out sharply, boldly. "Count the coins in your hand."

The man stepped back, mumbling something. I thought it was profanity, and I wondered if the man could even count, but I urged my horse ahead quickly, anxious to cross the bridge.

The knight on the other side barred our path. "There'll be a toll to ride off this bridge," he said, grinning, showing blackened and broken teeth.

Margarite was ready again with more coins, and before the man could count or argue, she nudged her horse into a canter, leading the packhorse. I followed, glad to get out of reach.

"Only one more bridge before we reach the Roman road," Margarite called back. "Umma said there are no guards there, not since the Green Riders drove them off."

Everyone had heard of the Green Riders, illegally armed men who lived in the forest and had begun driving the toll-taking knights out of the county. No one knew for certain who they were, but some said that they, too, were knights, good men who had dedicated themselves to God, and to protecting villagers and travelers who could not afford bodyguards.

The morning was ideal for traveling, windless and pleasantly cool, so there were others on the road, even though it was early yet. We passed a dozen people on foot, wisely guarded by men ahead and behind who carried stout poles, excellent weapons even against swords and pikes. But Margarite was looking for mounted travelers with guards, and at last we saw a group ahead, what seemed to be a family of four, riding with men with swords. Margarite asked for permission to ride with them, and after we were inspected by the elderly man who seemed to be in charge, we were given permission to ride along.

Margarite began a conversation with a handsomely dressed young woman who carried a curly-haired child ahead of her on her horse. She complimented the woman on her child's apparent health, something mothers always wanted to hear, especially from a red-gowned physician. Then she asked where they were going.

"We are going to my aunt's house in Canterbury, for the festival," she said. "This is my son's first journey. Where are you going?"

"We have friends in Upper Willows," Margarite said. "We can only stay for a day or so. Alas, we do not have time this year for the festival at Canterbury. It is a wonderful place."

"It is a *holy* place," the elderly man corrected, scowling at Margarite.

The young woman dropped her gaze to her son's head and said nothing else. But a woman close to the man's age said to him sharply, "Do not drive people away with your arguments. There is a *festival* in Canterbury. Daughter and I are going to enjoy every moment of it. You may spend your days on your knees on the stone floor in the cathedral for all of me."

The man said nothing more, and I, amused, thought that it was clear who ruled that household. A younger man caught up with the mother, stroked the boy's head, and rode on ahead to talk to the forward guard. The husband and father, I thought.

Would I ever have a family such as that? Probably not. My past, and the red birthmark, and the magic that was growing in me every day—all those things made it unlikely. And my hair grew whiter every month. What young man would want a bride who could be mistaken for a crone from the back, unless she dyed her hair? My face was still young and unlined, and my eyes were bright and good, but the color of my hair might hold the secret of my fate.

Mother and daughter talked quietly about the queen, who had been imprisoned in a convent in Canterbury by the king. They hoped to see her, for it was said that she often walked around the walls, in clear view of everyone.

"See what happens to women who know too much?" the mother asked her daughter. "Do not ask for another book at the market, until *they* are busy somewhere else." I knew that her "they" meant their husbands. There was another reason why I was certain I would never marry. I did not have easy obedience in me, only the obedience that results from inflicted pain and fear, and that was a very dangerous kind. It could explode into rage. And it had.

We reached the Roman road early in the afternoon, and

the party stopped at the largest public house at the crossing, where the well-traveled dirt road crossed over the old and sunken stone road. That public house seemed in the best repair, and the boys who stood ready to help people dismount were clean and smiling.

"We'll stop here for a while," Margarite told me quietly. "I'll find a place where we can rest unobserved, and then we shall see if your friend comes."

But I was worried. "If our party leaves, will you want to leave, too?"

"It would be better, but I promised you a chance to wait for your friend. We can find another group of travelers. There are many people here, and more coming all the time."

We cared for our horses ourselves, watering and feeding them after we pulled off the baggage. We had found a discreet spot behind a cherry tree, and Margarite laid out our noon meal on a woolen robe. While we ate, we watched the passersby, and I thought that all of England must be on the roads that day. There were large families and couples, groups of men in good clothes on horseback and ragged men on foot, farmers with carts loaded with bundles of firewood, a caravan of merchants with wagons covered with heavy canvas, an elegant woman borne on a tasseled litter carried by four men dressed in black and silver, and a long parade of pilgrims led by a priest and a boy carrying a crucifix.

And then came a bright red cart small enough for a child, pulled by a large white goat wearing a red hat and a collar of bells and flowers. A white dog, not much larger than a good-sized cat, sat in the cart, while a thin young man limped alongside. The young man wore a loose green tunic over a white shirt, and his green hat sported a black feather stuck through a twisted red-and-gold cord. Clearly he was a part of a group of players, traveling actors or acrobats, on their way to the festival.

And he was my Tom. And the little white dog was Striker.

I started to get to my feet, but Margarite yanked me back down. "Be still," she said. "Do not call out to them."

The cart passed, and my heart broke.

The cart was followed by a dozen players on foot, dressed in fantastic, wildly colorful costumes, some with masks, some with musical instruments. Then came three large, brightly painted closed wagons. The company stopped farther down the road, in front of a public house where they seemed to be known, because a man and woman ran out, shouting enthusiastic greetings.

I blinked hard to keep tears from my eyes. I had not really believed that this day would ever come. Now I knew that Tom and Striker were alive. They looked well. Older, but well. Tom limped a little, but not as much as he had when I had seen him last. He had been too far away for me to see his face. Perhaps his affliction was healed, and one side of his face was no longer frozen with that condition Margarite called *paralusis*, when she saw it in others.

I have seen them alive, I thought. I have no right to ask for anything else.

"I don't want to draw attention to us," Margarite said. "So I think we'll ride on as soon as the players go inside, even if our party is not yet ready."

We loaded the horses quickly and mounted. There was no sign now of the players. Their wagons and horses waited at the side of the building. The goat, taken out of harness, was tethered to a tree, and he munched grass. Striker was nowhere in sight. I longed to run inside through the door, shouting Tom's name. I wanted nothing more than to grab up Striker and hold him close again. But I blinked away my tears and steadied my trembling mouth. I had had everything I had wanted, a sight of them alive and well. They were safe; I was safe. What else could matter?

But as we passed the public house, a white blur streaked out into the road. It was Striker, barking hysterically, and I, without thinking, slid down from my horse and picked him up. The dog, shaking all over, wailed and licked my face.

"He remembers me," I said, my voice breaking. I kissed the dog's head and hugged him to my chest.

"God save us," Margarite whispered. "Mary! Leave the dog and mount up! We must not attract attention. Here, let me help you! We must go." She turned her horse so that she could reach out to me and help me up on my saddle.

But I was helpless. I could not put down the dog, even though I knew people were beginning to stare at us. I pressed my face against his sleek white coat and wept even harder.

"Mistress, my dog seems to have taken a strong fancy to you," someone said.

Tom! His voice had changed. He was a young man, not a boy. He stood back several feet, smiling politely as if I were a stranger. He seemed strong, but his smile was lopsided. His face had not recovered completely after all. I nearly called him by name and asked him how he fared, but Margarite said briskly, "The dog is charming, friend, but we have far to go and cannot buy him. Please take him away. *Now.*"

"He's not for sale," Tom said, and he smiled up at Margarite. "But the little fellow is weary of the player's life, and I have been looking for a good home for him, one with a lady who knows the ways of a small dog. He is content enough on horseback and he doesn't eat much. I'll pass him on to this young lady and say good-bye to both of you now. I am needed inside."

And he turned and was gone. Striker looked after him, tensed his muscles as if he would jump from my arms, but then he tucked his head under my cloak and pressed against me.

"Mary!" Margarite said warningly. "You must not . . ."

"I need a place to mount," I said, and I led my horse along the road to a stone where I could climb up and then slip onto my horse. I never let go of Striker for a moment. "A dog such as this will keep guard over us when we sleep tonight," I said. My voice was firm, but my heart thudded in my chest. I was determined to keep the little dog, no matter what Margarite said. If necessary, I would turn back and find Tom. My worst fears might be realized, but I would not give up the dog who pressed against me, trembling, trusting me to keep him. In this hard world, we must not abandon the creatures who trust us.

"Did your friend know you?" Margarite asked. There was a harsh note in her voice and I understood why. All of Blessingwood depended on no one ever finding me, and I had broken my promise.

"If he recognized me, he has chosen to deny it." I spoke

more calmly than I thought I could. "I trusted him when I was a child and I'll trust him now. He has always been in as much danger as I have, because of me, and if he has not betrayed me by now, he will never do it. And I will not betray him. Some things do not need to be spoken aloud. I know his heart and he knows mine."

Margarite sighed. "Let us hurry on, then, out of sight of this crossroads and the Roman road. And out of the memories of anyone who witnessed this scene."

In a short time we found a congenial party whose tall, husky leader invited us to ride along, and while the sun was still far above the horizon, we reached Upper Willows. Most of the time, Striker had slept across my lap, his head resting in the crook of my elbow. But whenever he woke, his tail wagged wildly and he rolled his eyes up to meet my gaze.

Anyone could find a dog during a journey and decide to take him home, I told myself. Anyone. And England had many such dogs, small and white with foxy faces. I bent and kissed his head. "I found you, boy," I whispered. "I will never let you go again."

Margarite led us to a two-story farmhouse, and when we reined up before it, a stout woman ran out, calling excitedly. Several other women came out then, and they helped us down, unloaded the horses, and one woman led us away to a thatched barn behind the house. The large farm dog barked once at Striker, was rewarded with a display of Striker's small, sharp teeth, and strolled away as if he had no further interest in that little interloper with his ridiculous, curly tail.

A meal was waiting for us, on a long table set under fruit

trees. A smiling maid with a clay jug poured water over our hands while a small girl in an embroidered apron caught the water in a shallow basin. The woman who greeted us, another Mary, handed each of us a soft towel.

"Sit down now," she said. "Yes, bring the little dog. He looks hungry, too. Before we eat, we'll ask for a blessing on our food and give thanks that Margarite and her assistant have come so far to help us."

It was a peaceful scene, and I relaxed for the first time since I had left Blessingwood. Surely this place was safe enough. The women quickly began talk of healing and medicines, and I did my best to listen, but I was weary. Striker, sleeping in my lap, openly snored, and the woman sitting next to me laughed.

"You and your companion need a long rest in a cool room," she said. She called over the smiling maid and asked her to take "young Mary" to the room that would be mine that night. I followed, and found that my saddlebag had been unpacked and the contents laid out on the coverlet over the bed. My looking glass lay on a small bench next to the bed. I wondered if the maid had stolen a glance in it—and I wondered what she might have seen. Something wonderful? Something terrible?

The maid saw my quick look, and she said, "I confess that I looked in it. I'm sorry. But I have only seen myself in water basins and the pond."

I laughed without meaning to do it, for she was so sincere—and so innocent. "And how did you find yourself?" I asked.

The maid looked down at her feet and her blush faded. "Fair enough to be a good nun, I hope. I desire to enter the convent where my sister lives, after I have earned my dowry."

I, thinking of the convent where I had taken shelter, said, "It can be a good life for a woman."

The maid smiled. "My sister is happy. It is a large place, larger than most villages, built on the site of a Roman town between two rivers, and the women have a great library, famous everywhere."

I could not help but smile back at her. She had described a place that could have been the abbey that had sheltered me, but I knew I should not talk about it. "It sounds fine indeed."

Striker moaned impatiently and struggled out of my arms, to leap to the bed. The maid laughed to see him curl up on my pillow. "There's a little fellow who knows he is loved," the maid said.

"Always," I responded.

I shared the pillow with my little dog and fell asleep quickly.

Later, I sat with Margarite and the women in the kitchen while Margarite told them of herbs she had found that could ease the pain of childbirth without impeding it. The women were attentive, and they passed the small pot of crushed herbs around while Margarite explained how to distill them.

Then she unwrapped the tools she used to perform eye surgery. The women scarcely breathed. "I will show you how to cut out the cataract with this," she said, holding up a small, curved knife. "But you cannot begin the surgery unless the man or woman is heavily drugged and then tied down." She put down the knife and picked up a small jug. "Here is poppy juice. I have only a small amount left from last year's crop, but I brought this much to use on the man with the cataract tomorrow. And I brought seeds for you to sow. But you must have a place to sow them where no one will notice. Plant them along a fence, among the grasses where your animals will not graze, or in a hedgerow. Many people have heard of opium now, and they will steal the plants if they can. And many priests do not want it used at all, because they believe that pain is inflicted by God as payment for sins and should be endured—especially by women in childbirth."

"We have a place near the garden ready," Mary said. "We are growing nettles there, for hot drinks. I doubt anyone will look too closely."

Then Margarite brought out her greatest treat, a small bag of tea. "My friend Umma found this in a market far from our village. The seller thought it was a poultice for boils. He and my husband grew fond of the drink on their travels, and you will like it, too."

She sprinkled the dried leaves on the bottom of a bowl and poured boiling water over them. The women exclaimed at the fragrance as they waited for the leaves to steep.

"Is it a restorative?" one asked.

"Yes," Margarite said. "And a sedative. And a stimulant. And it is pleasant to the taste. Umma believes that people who drink this instead of plain cool water do not suffer from as many stomach ailments. He doesn't know why this is true. It could be that hot water itself is good. Who knows?"

We drank tea from small cups and smiled at one another. Whether this tea was a restorative or a sedative or a stimulant did not matter. It warmed friendship. The sun was going down, and long shadows stretched across the dooryard. I leaned forward on my elbows, causing Striker to protest with a little squeak. The women laughed.

"He is a man," one said. "They always protest when women talk too long."

In the morning, shortly after dawn, an old man came to the house with his wife and two sons. He was a weaver, and his sight had failed so much that he was unable to work. Mary explained to him what Margarite would be doing, and he consented to being drugged and tied down to the kitchen table with his head resting on a bag of sand, cupped to hold his head.

When he was asleep, Margarite slipped a gold ring into his eye to hold open his eyelids. The wife and sons left, to wait outside. The wife had begun to weep, and I did not blame her for her apprehension.

Two of the women held the man's shoulders, in case he should stir. And he did stir, at the first cut of the knife. He made an odd squealing sound and attempted to turn his head to the side. A strong woman held it in place on the bag of sand.

Margarite leaned over and said, "Friend, you must lie still now, if you want your sight returned. Think of being able to see clearly again. Think of the joy of it. Think only of seeing again."

The man lay still and Margarite completed the surgery

in a few minutes. The man slept deeply while his head was being bandaged, and when he woke enough to walk, his sons helped him away.

"Will he really see out of that eye again?" one woman asked Margarite.

"Half of the people do," she said. "Half do not, because the eye becomes inflamed. But they never come back to have the other eye repaired." She laughed a little, wryly. "The cure is not certain, and it is surely more painful than the disease. The only people who are willing to go through it are the ones who are desperate to see. I would be, too."

In a little while, several other people came to the house, villagers who had health problems they wanted to discuss with the visiting physician. Most were women. Not many men trusted female physicians. And most of the women brought children, who, if they did not ail them-selves, were fascinated watching their mothers being treated. Margarite and I, with her supervision, drew infected splinters, pulled teeth, lanced boils, treated several cases of joint inflammation, and, in the last moments, set a leg that had been broken only an hour before. A few paid us with coins. Most paid with lengths of cloth or food. One, after hearing that we had a small dog with us, paid with a bit of fleece for Striker's bed.

Margarite and I left after the midday meal, riding quick-ly along the road until we caught up with a farmer who was traveling to the crossroads with his sons. They were willing to have traveling companions, and Margarite seemed relieved. I had asked her if she was more nervous now than on the journey to the village, but all she said was, "Perhaps."

But I had seen someone watching us when we stopped to talk to the farmer. A woman, or perhaps a short and gnarled man, had stood behind a thin stand of hazel trees watching. I bent my head and let my headdress shield my face. Striker whimpered inquiringly and I patted him to silence him.

But in a few minutes we rode out of sight and the ugly spy was a part of the past, I told myself. Now we had blended into the traffic heading toward the crossroads at the Roman road. Soon we would be lost to anyone who might be curious about us.

We were safe.

But a crow dropped down to a branch at my eye level and said distinctly, "Look sharp."

I had heard that warning before. Striker stirred in my lap and bared his teeth at the bird.

The rain that began later in the day was no surprise, for I had felt it on my skin and heard the first thunder in my mind. We reached Blessingwood in a howling storm, but they were ready for us, standing ready with blankets and hot drinks. Umma and Simon led the horses away quickly, and Elaine, laughing, held her arms out for Striker, who jumped into them willingly.

"You found a little dog!" Elaine exclaimed. "He is wonderful. Look at that sweet face! Was he a stray?"

"He belonged to a group of players," Margarite said, looking straight at Hildegard. "But they wanted a good home for him, and Mary was willing to take him. He is a pleasant fellow and seems to want to be a watchdog, in spite of his size."

Everyone laughed at that. But I knew how fierce Striker could be.

Hildegard helped me out of my wet cloak. "I felt the rain before it came," I told her.

"And I hope you learn to feel trouble before it comes to you," she murmured. "But I like your little dog. He carries blessings with him, given to him to bring to you by someone who is wise."

"Tom," I murmured. "My friend."

"No, someone old—and very holy."

I shook my head. I knew of no one like that except here at Blessingwood.

Striker and King Harry met in the back courtyard. I held the dog, and the cat was riding Umma's shoulder again. Striker did not bark or even tense.

"Dogs actually can speak, you know," King Harry told me. "But they want you to pity them, and so they only make annoying racket."

Striker tensed then, and I clutched him to my chest to keep him from leaping on the cat. Umma laughed, shook his head, and carried King Harry away.

"Is that true?" I asked Striker. "Can you talk?"

But his bright little dark eyes only studied my face the way they always did, when he was trying to understand me.

Simon came to my room early the next morning, and Striker greeted him as a friend. "Your journey went well?" he asked.

"I had no need of the knife, if that's what you mean," I said, laughing.

His gaze was level and unblinking. "You will," he said. "Have you been listening to the birds?"

I stared at him. Could he hear them, too? "What birds?" I asked, pretending innocence until I could gather my thoughts.

"The messengers," he said impatiently. "The crows. They never stop calling now. Trouble will be on the roads by autumn. I don't know if someone is coming for me, but I know I must go."

"Have you told the others?" My heart thudded uncomfortably. Trouble was coming. Now even I could feel it, without hearing the messenger crows.

"I told Umma. He is teaching me to use a sword."

"But he can't!" I was astonished. Ordinary people were not allowed to own swords. I would have asked him more, but he left. I locked the door behind him and sat down on the bed for a moment while I quieted my thoughts. Then I reached for my looking glass. "Tell me," I whispered. "For once, tell me so that I can understand." My birthmark burned.

In the glass, I first saw my face, and then I saw a long road, and then I saw the cave that haunted my dreams, and then I saw the four swans circling over the black lake. But I did not see Simon.

"Will I be alone?" I whispered. I did not want to be alone!

The glass showed me nothing more but a wide gray sky streaming with black clouds.

Striker whined and pawed my leg. "What is it?" I asked.

But he did not speak. My little dog could not talk. Cats lie, I thought, and now I must wait to see if looking glasses also lie.

I would not wait long.

7

tHe SCORCHING

On one single day at high summer, my life began unraveling in my hands, like a ruined scarf.

The morning was too hot for traveling, but that was the appointed time for Elaine to leave us. The young lord of Shalott had sent servants to accompany her to his island home, where she would be a companion to his beloved sister, a young woman said by many to have been enchanted. The servants had spent the night in the orchard, where it was cool, and they were up and about at sunrise, with Umma helping them with their horses and Simon carrying out Elaine's possessions, her clothes and books, and the musical instruments Julienne was sending with her.

The courtyard was busy with comings and goings, and Elaine and I stood to one side, searching for words to use to say good-bye, for it was unlikely we would ever see each other again.

"You can change your mind and stay here," I told her, for she had not smiled once all morning. "You know you can."

"No, I am glad to go to the island. It sounds better than anything I could have hoped for. But I am worried about you and the ladies. There is something in the air, something that bothers me. . . ."

"What?" I asked, alarmed, for I was aware of nothing more than an unusual gathering of birds in the orchard, and if they carried messages, I did not understand them. There were several tree spirits in the orchard that day, too, but they seemed serene and placid, and I had thought that they were there out of curiosity about the visitors. I had seen no shivering in the grasses that meant the Fair Folk were nearby again.

Elaine shook her head. "Pay no attention to me. I don't know what's wrong with me this morning." She took a small square of material from her pocket and handed it to me. "Don't look at this tapestry now," she whispered. "I made it for you. . . . I don't know why. It almost created itself, and you are on it, so I knew it must be for you. It tells a tale. . . ." Her voice trailed off. But then she said, "Show it to no one."

Before I could say anything more, she strode toward her horse and let Umma help her up. She called out good-byes to all of us, and the party left, cantering out into the dusty road.

"I hate to see her go," Julienne said wistfully. "Her voice could melt stone."

Striker yipped once as the travelers disappeared beyond the trees. Umma looked at me and smiled. But King Harry, never one to allow a gentle moment to go unchallenged, said, "Before the year is out, she will weep and she will marry—and she will forget she ever knew you, *Gwenore*."

Umma shrugged the cat off his shoulder and Striker sent him on his way with frenzied barking. Simon glanced at me out of the corner of his eye and then went back to the forge. I could not be sure if he was able to hear the cat. But everyone who was not deaf could hear my indignant little dog.

I took Elaine's gift back to my room, and after I had locked the door, I spread the small tapestry over my lap. It was beautiful, and yet it was terrible. There I was, holding my dog in my arms, looking up at four swans circling overhead, their white bodies gleaming against a stormy sky. My head was uncovered, and my windblown hair was long and white. How had Elaine known? The dyeing process had been kept secret from her, too.

I looked closer at the embroidered picture. My birthmark, created by no more than three stitches of bright red silk, showed clearly on my wrist. It looked more than ever like a drop of blood.

My feet were bare. I was standing on a dark stone slab, and nearby there was an opening in a rock, the entrance to the cave I had dreamed of a hundred times.

Then, as I watched, the swans soared away into a setting sun and the small dog in the tapestry turned his head and looked out at me.

Striker whined suddenly and pressed against me.

I folded the tapestry and put it in my trunk, under everything else. One day I would look at it again, I promised myself. But not soon. I knew that it was prophetic, and I was afraid.

◀ ◀ ◀

Before that day was over, Striker had reason again to raise a racket, but this time in joy, for our Tom appeared without warning.

Umma and I were carrying water to the scorched garden, determined to save the vegetables, when Striker suddenly barked. Umma dropped his bucket and had his long dagger out of his belt in an instant. A man came through the orchard, a man dressed in plain brown, carrying a pack, and using a staff for support. He limped badly.

Tom.

Striker tore toward him, yelping, and Tom dropped his staff in order to catch the dog as he flew through the air into his arms.

Umma looked inquiringly at me. "He's my friend," I said as I started forward, stumbling in my hurry. Umma grabbed my arm to keep me from falling with one hand while he put his knife away with the other. But his expression told me that he was uncertain about this intruder.

"Tom, why are you here?" I cried. "What's happened?" My joy was mixed with terror, for if he was here, then Blessingwood might be in danger, and I owed this place everything.

Tom was exhausted, his face streaked with sweat and dirt. He held Striker out to me and said, "I have news that will not wait. I must talk to you alone."

Umma withdrew out of earshot and turned his back courteously.

"They know me as Mary here," I whispered. "What is your news?"

"Your mother has left Wales, traveling slowly with a large party of attendants and guards. By late autumn she will be in London—and Brennan is there. She must not find Brennan."

My knees almost gave way. "Mother left Wales. Why?"

"She has been invited to the house of a noble family who knew your father. She hopes to find a husband."

"The king hates her," I whispered. "My father built a castle without a license—my mother was responsible for that—and the castle was torn down. The king will not forget that she cursed him. She won't be accepted anywhere."

"The old priest says she has a new plan to get the castle she wants—and the army she wants to raise against the king."

I shook my head, unbelieving. "Mad dreams. She was always mad." And then I realized what he had said. "You have seen Father Caddaric?"

"He found me and sent me out on the road. It is time, he said. You, Brennan, and I must leave the country. We are not safe anywhere."

I could not take all of this in at once. My life here was to be over so soon? A hundred years would be too soon! I struggled to speak before I finally made my voice heard. "Where will we go?"

"Ireland," he said.

Suddenly I was filled with rage. "Why? Why? What did I ever do that I should be hounded this way? Why?"

Tom shrugged, as he had so many times before when I had asked those questions.

"The priest knows!" I said angrily. "I know he does! He

even told me he was sorry that he had given me such a *dangerous life*."

Tom's mouth tightened. "Then let us find him and make him tell," he said. "You, Brennan, and I will *make* him tell— and if we believe him, we will decide then if we must go to Ireland."

I knew my path, then. I was sure of it. "I will go with you to London—"

"No!" he said. "It is too dangerous. Your mother will have spies everywhere, looking for you. If your people can give me a chance to rest for a few days, then I will go to London, find Brennan, and bring her back. And then, if we must, we will leave for Ireland together."

And so it was to be, I decided. I left him in the orchard, drinking the cool water Umma brought for him, while I hurried into the house to tell the Blessingwood women that I must give Tom shelter until he felt better—and that I would be leaving them when he returned from London.

My words left them in silence. We sat together in the small dining room and looked at one another. Finally Margarite said, "I think we always knew it would come to this. Do you want to tell us why you are being pursued?"

"Never," I said. "You must never know. Will you let Tom rest here for a few days before we go?"

"Of course," Hildegard said. "And when he leaves, he'll leave with good horses—and Umma for a companion."

"Umma!" I exclaimed.

"Umma is a warrior," she said. "You and your Tom need a warrior now."

Umma gave Tom a small room next to his own and introduced him to Simon, who treated him better than I had expected. Simon was not a friendly fellow. He and Tom rested in the shade and spoke in low voices, but I knew that Tom would not betray me.

Then, later, I saw Simon measuring Tom's weak leg with a marked stick, and I walked over to ask why.

"I can make him a sturdy brace," Simon told me. "One with a hinge. He will be able to walk and even run."

I was so grateful to Simon that I nearly cried, and I told Margarite about it while I was helping her prepare medicines for the travelers to take with them to London.

"He does not need a brace as much as he needs to be cured," Margarite said. "Simon's heart is good, but your friend needs more than a clever invention. He needs his health restored."

"Do you know of a concoction that can mend his leg?"

"I know of a ceremony that can," she said. My face must have informed her of my skepticism, because she frowned for a moment, and then said, "There are bathing ceremonies that we have not shown you. I don't like the idea of letting a man into our secrets, but I think we can make an exception for Tom, for this is an unusual time. You will need your friend well and healthy for all that comes next."

"What comes next?" I asked quickly. "What have you seen? What do you know?"

She shook her head. "Not much at all, and none of it useful to you or to us. I do not dream true now, so what is coming must be terrible. That is the way of it. We do not see

the worst things we must face, because we might turn back
from our destinies and destroy the plan of this world."

"What plan?" I cried. "What evil plan am I a part of that
has now involved you? Surely not God's plan."

"Who can say?" she said quietly, resigned. "We take one
moment at a time when we are called to stand up against the
darkness of this world. If we could see the next moment,
fright would conquer us, and thus the darkness would be the
victor."

I did not understand her—then. But I accepted it.

The healing rituals in the underground bath at Blessingwood
were secret. Not even the servants had ever been present.
None of the refugee girls had been included, and I do not
know if I would have been, ever, if it had not been for Tom.
I had been told of them, told how Julienne had been healed
there of a terrible lung fever many years before, and I had
wondered many times why she had not been given another
healing ceremony, now that she was so old and ill. But questions about the underground bath were not encouraged. The
secrets were too deep and ancient.

Why would they let Tom into the women's place, that
great, warm, steaming bath under the building, the bath that
was a thousand years old and yet somehow still new? I was
filled with doubts and misgivings. For two years, I had studied healing with Margarite. I had learned about the human
body. Even while I learned skills with a scalpel, I had also
learned how music can speed healing and how certain
words, said in certain ways, can bring on restful sleep and

even stop bleeding. But Tom's affliction had something to do with the blow to his head. It would make more sense to open his skull, if he were willing, and let out the pressure. Margarite had done surgery like that; I had witnessed it several times.

"I don't see how a bath can cure him," I said. "He is my friend, but I will not experiment with him. And—the bath—" I stopped and bit my lip, then went on. "I would not want him to think that his affliction was considered a curse—or imaginary. I *saw* him injured. I know that it was real."

"Of course it was real," Margarite said, smiling. "As real as any injury. But you will see how a certain kind of bath can cure."

And so, that night, when the moon rose, we took Tom down the narrow steps under the ground floor of the old building, and through the stone portals, and into the great room where the water in the pool, Margarite explained, was always fresh and always warm, heated somewhere deep beneath the earth. We brought heaps of towels with us, and baskets of flowers and ferns that Hildegard had grown in a secret place in the shade on the north side of the building, and a flask containing a drink especially prepared by Margarite, as taught to her by Umma. The drink would induce dreams in Tom—and in us.

Tom, lured into the building by Margarite's promise that he would leave whole, appeared ashamed when he saw me. "You will see," I said. "You will be well again." But I was not completely convinced.

I sat with Julienne and Hildegard, in a far corner on an

old marble bench, while Margarite led Tom into the shallow end of the pool. Tall white candles burned all around, their flickering lights reflecting off the polished marble walls. The air was sweet with the scent of flowers and ferns, and with the spices Margarite had sprinkled into the warm water as she waded out into it.

Margarite, clad in a dark linen robe, stood waist-deep in the water, while Tom, wearing nothing but a breechcloth, stood before her. She rubbed his face with oil of cinnamon and then gave him the vial, from which the rest of us had already sipped. Soon after he finished it, his face resumed its normal shape, as if some constricting muscle had let go its grip, but I could tell from his movements that his leg was still bad.

Margarite began singing softly, and the women with me began singing, too, in a language I did not know, but one that seemed familiar, as if I had heard it in my dreams.

I realized then that I was singing, too. Gently, Margarite pushed Tom's head below the water.

I wondered if the water had the strong, unpleasant, mineral taste of a holy well I had seen in Wales, and I expected Tom to pop up again, sputtering. But he stayed below the surface.

And still he stayed.

And still he stayed.

I sat forward, alarmed. Hildegard pushed me back, shaking her head at me, warning me.

The water in the pool slowly began to move, ruffling a little on the surface, then sweeping in a lazy circle, then moving faster, then splashing out on the mosaic tiles. A pale, tall woman, a stranger, rose abruptly out of the water. Her long, straight hair was gray as iron, but she was young, younger than I. Her eyes were the color of ice. She said one word, and the moment I heard it, I forgot it. But the echo of it rang through the chamber.

And then she faded gradually, as if she had been made of mist, or dreams, and then she was gone.

Margarite raised her arms, and Tom stood up. His face was smooth and relaxed, and his eyes were closed. The water quieted. The magic was finished.

Tom opened his eyes and asked, "What is this place?" He sounded marveling, astonished.

"It is a place you can only come once," Margarite said. "The goddess at this well will heal someone one time, that is all. If you are injured again, you cannot return. Will you remember that?"

Tom nodded.

But he need not have agreed to anything. Blessing-wood's blessings were ending.

Tom and Umma left for London the next day, and they could not have gone far when a woman, Angela, known to us all came to the door, weeping. Her sister, Emmaline, married to Hiram, the village's other physician, had been in hard labor for more than a day, and Hiram had not helped her. Emmaline was dying, and Hiram, Angela said, had stood over her, smiling.

Smiling, she said. Smiling because he wanted her dead.

There was a girl in a nearby village he desired, and Emmaline was in the way.

"He has done nothing for her?" Margarite asked.

"Nothing," Angela said. "He has not even given her a potion for pain."

Margarite frowned. "You want me to help? I will, if he lets me in the door. If he refuses, I can do nothing. You know that. The sheriff will take me away."

"Hiram has gone to the farm beyond the moors, where the farmer has fallen on a hayfork. If you hurry . . ."

Margarite grabbed several packets and vials and put them into her red bag. "I'll come, too," I said, gathering up a bundle of towels.

"No, it's too dangerous," Margarite said. "If Hiram sees you . . ."

"Then he'll see both of us," I said. "I'm coming."

We ran across the village and pushed through a crowd of women standing outside the door of Hiram's house. From upstairs, we heard his wife's exhausted moans. "No more. No more. No more."

"Help her, Margarite!" one woman cried. "Not even a beast should suffer like this."

We ran up the narrow steps, into a small room that was stifling under the hot thatched roof. The cot where Emmaline lay was soaked with blood. Her eyes had rolled back. But still she had the strength to cry out when the next spasm clutched her.

Margarite felt Emmaline's swollen abdomen with quick, clever fingers. "The baby is turned the wrong way," she said.

"Rump first?" I said. Those births were always difficult.

"Worse," she said. "He is facing the same direction his mother faces, which means that the back of his skull is caught in the curve of her tailbone. He cannot be born this way, and Hiram knew it."

I closed my eyes for a moment. "Then what can be done?" I whispered. "Will you open her stomach?" I had seen that procedure only once, and only the babe had lived.

"It's too late for that," Margarite said, her voice crisp with anger. "The babe's head is stuck in her pelvis. We could not pull it out before she bled to death."

"What, then?" I asked, desperate for the dying woman.

"First, we put her to sleep," Margarite said. "Give me the green flask. We can't hurt her babe now, no matter what we give her. The babe will die, if he is not dead already."

I took the green flask out of Margarite's bag. It contained distilled poppy juice, so strong that only three drops would put a man into a deep sleep. Margarite tapped two drops into the suffering woman's mouth, and then when she screamed again, she dropped a third onto her finger and rubbed it inside the woman's lower lip, careful to avoid her gnashing teeth. Then we called for cool water and clean bedclothes, and we made Emmaline as comfortable as we could while she thrashed and cried until the drops took over and she sank into a deep sleep, barely breathing.

"What will we do about the child?" I whispered.

I saw that Margarite was coating her hands with fat. "I will get him out," she said. "I want you to go downstairs now, and tell the women waiting outside that the child is dead, but

I might be able to save Emmaline. Don't let anyone come up here. And if you see that priest coming, run up to warn me. And stop him if you can."

I wanted to ask why, but as I turned to go out of the room, I saw Margarite withdraw a forceps and something else from her bag. I ran downstairs, afraid to even wonder what would happen next.

Margarite came down later, and sent Angela upstairs to sit with her sleeping sister. "The baby was a boy," she told the waiting women. "He was facing the wrong way, which is why the birth took so long. But his spine was not formed into a closed column, so he could not have lived, even if he had survived his birth."

"Hiram will blame Emmaline," one woman said bitterly.

"It was his seed that was crooked!" Margarite said, and the women nodded. None of them used Hiram as a physician, for he was known far and wide for the smile he could not repress when he saw a woman in pain.

We left then, and returned home in silence. I knew that Margarite was thinking what I was thinking. Hiram would be enraged that she had intervened. He had wanted his wife dead. Surely he knew that the baby was in the wrong position, and he could have moved it early in her labor or just before it began.

"What will happen?" I asked her, before we entered our door.

"I don't know," she said. "Perhaps I will be fined. Perhaps I will lose my license."

"Her husband was not home," I argued. "Angela had a right to ask for help."

"Not from me," she said. "Not in Hiram's eyes."

The worst was yet to come. In the next days, we heard from many people that Hiram was furious to discover that his son was dead, even though the boy, had he managed to live through the first weeks of his life, would never have been able to sit up by himself, much less walk. And we all suspected that Hiram was even more furious that his wife was still alive. She not only lived, but she was already on her feet and working about the house.

And then Emmaline died, screaming all one night. He declared the next morning that she had died because of injuries she received from Margarite's evil instruments. As if that was not enough, he added another accusation: Margarite had stolen the afterbirth, to use in magic spells.

Margarite, he said, was a witch.

On the following morning, shortly before cockcrow, the sheriff and three men came for Margarite. She was taken away and locked in the small cellar under the armory where the sheriff's men stored their weapons. It was all over in a few moments. I was barely awake when the miracle that was Blessingwood ended.

I stood in my nightdress in the courtyard, with Striker in my arms and King Harry perched on my shoulder. "This could not have happened if Umma had been here," I said. "This is my fault."

"I have put out the word," King Harry said. "Umma is riding this way even now, with your two friends."

"*Two!*" I exclaimed.

"The woman with the scarred face rides with them," King Harry said.

"Brennan!"

King Harry jumped down, and as he walked away, he looked back over his shoulder. "Prepare to leave," he said. "You are next for the cellar, *Gwenore.*"

"What? I can't leave. Not until Tom and Brennan are here."

But King Harry had nothing more to say to me.

Before I dressed, I took up my looking glass. "What good are you if you do not tell me the future?" I said.

My reflection looked back at me. I saw my hair wrapped close around my head and concealed with a boy's cap. I saw my chest bound flat with linen bands under a boy's tunic. I watched while I walked through deep woods at dawn, with Striker following close behind. We were alone.

Alone.

The glass cleared, and I saw only myself again. "Where was Tom?" I asked the glass. "Where was Brennan?"

I turned over the glass and watched while four small swans circled in the silver.

I could have thrown the glass against the wall, for all the good it was doing me. But when Hildegard came to my room later, I had packed a few garments into a small backpack, along with the cursed looking glass, Elaine's tapestry with the embroidered picture that moved but never changed, several surgical instruments wrapped in a soft cloth, and an assortment of potions and medicines. I was wearing the belt that Simon had made for me, the belt with the concealed dagger.

"I am going to meet Umma on the road," I said. "We will make a plan to free Margarite."

"No," she said. "You will hide in the forest in a place that Simon will show you, and you will never return here. Never. Hiram knows you attended his wife. He is only waiting for the magistrate's order to come here with the sheriff and take you away. You will burn with Margarite, Mary. You must leave now."

"She will not burn!" I cried. "Umma will not let her burn!"

But Hildegard was bundling me into a sleeveless coat and pulling a hood over my hair. "When you reach the hut, use wood ash to remove the red color from your hair and do your best to hide it. You could still pass as a boy, dressed in Simon's old clothes. But I wish you would leave the dog behind with us—"

"No!"

"I knew you would not. So keep him quiet, at least."

"I will keep him quiet," I said. "Which horse will Sarah give me?"

"None. You must go on foot. There is no place to keep a horse where Simon is taking you. Now hurry. Your time at Blessingwood has ended."

Weeping, I embraced them all at the gate, while Simon sighed and paced. "I wish I could stay," I said. "You won't forget to tell Tom and Brennan where I am?"

"Simon will meet them a league from the village and take them there on foot," Sarah said. "God bless you, girl. We won't see you again, but we will never forget you."

I ran off then, with Simon and my dog, and I dared not look back. My journey into the dark had begun.

The hut was a miserable, almost roofless little pile of stones, deep in the forest, far beyond any path or road. Simon had brought a sack of food for me, and a roll of clothing and bedding, from which he extracted a short sword.

"Do you have any idea how to use this?" he asked, disgusted even before I answered.

"No."

"Does Tom?"

I did not know. "He might have learned when he was with the players. They often stage mock sword fights."

Simon rolled his eyes. "Mock sword fights. Yes, that would keep him alive. Give him this sword when you see him and assure him that I will pray for all of you."

"What will happen now?" I asked.

His level look told me that my fears were correct. "Sarah is moving the stock to a nearby farm where the animals will be cared for, before the sheriff takes everything away. The farmer will take our tools, too. Julienne said she will invite the village women to take what they want from the rooms. We hope that by nightfall we'll be on the road."

"You are abandoning Margarite?" I cried. "Will no one stay to fight for her?"

Simon glared at me. "If we stay, we will all end up in the cellar with her. If we leave, we will have a chance to come back to help her escape. Umma will know what to do. He escaped from a prison in the Holy Land. He can do anything."

I watched him slip away into the forest silently, leaving me to clear the fallen leaves and twigs from the small hut and make what repairs I could to the roof. With every sound in the forest, I looked around, hoping to see my friends. Late in the afternoon I smelled smoke, and that worried me, but the smell was faint.

I could not know yet that what I smelled was Blessingwood burning.

In early twilight, Striker barked once, softly, and there, from between the trees, I saw Brennan hurrying toward me, her arms held out. "It's you, it's you!" she wept. "So tall now, so strong."

Behind her, Tom stood awkwardly, smiling. But his smile was strained.

"Where is Simon? Didn't he bring you? What about the others?"

That was when Tom told me about Blessingwood—and Umma. "Umma sent the others fleeing on the last of the horses, in spite of Hildegard's pleading with him, and he sent us here, on foot, to you. But we watched from the trees, and we saw him arm himself and stand at the gate. Oh, you should have seen him! He wore the armor that belonged to Hildegard's husband, and the Holy Warrior's cross, and he struck out at them, shouting like a whole army. But, the cowards, they sent three men behind him to cut him down. And then, listen to this, his cat attacked the one who plunged the knife into the back of Umma's neck, and I swear to you that he blinded the bastard."

"King Harry!" I breathed.

"Simon and the women are riding the back roads," he said. "They have a plan to rescue the physician, but they did not tell us what it was. They said to tell you that she will be free by tomorrow, and that all of us would meet in that place that Father Caddaric has chosen."

"Ireland," I whispered.

"Ireland," Brennan said, and she smiled even as she wept. "I'm going home at last."

My friends and I spent only one night in the hut in the woods, long enough to rest and for Brennan to help me change my appearance, so that I looked like a boy. Again. Then, in the morning, we walked east, into the sunrise, keeping to the footpaths that crossed fields. Tom carried Simon's sword in a rolled blanket, for a young man of his station was not allowed to own a sword. I hoped he could use it. My hand often strayed to my concealed dagger.

Once a crow fluttered down beside us and said to me, "King Harry sends greetings and says that your mother has been told that you died in a fire."

"Does she believe it?" I asked.

"No, but she can hope, can she not?" the crow said. "Look sharp, Gwenore. And obey the priest when you find him along the way."

"When will that be?"

But the bird cackled and flapped away.

"You talk to birds?" Brennan asked. She looked amazed. But Tom was past amazement, after his night in the bath.

"The crows bring messages sometimes, from Father Caddaric and others."

"I remember that pet crow of his," Brennan said uneasily. "He kept it in his sleeve. So what did this one tell you, Gwenore?"

"To obey the priest," I said.

"So he can get us into more trouble?" Tom asked. "I'll go to Ireland, because that makes great sense. I've heard that there are places there where everyone has escaped from England. Perhaps the Blessingwood women might make their way there. But after I reach the island, I hope never to see Father Caddaric again. I have long suspected that he is a wizard, not a priest."

Brennan nodded. "I have had enough of him, too," she said. "Somehow he is responsible for all of this. I do not know how, but that is what I believe."

And I did, too. All of this was the fault of the priest. If only I knew why.

We walked on. I did not take out my looking glass to see what my future might be, because it played games with me, pushing me toward seeing my future myself. And I was afraid of the mystical tapestry Elaine had made for me.

But now I can admit to myself that I knew that day that I would not yet be going to Ireland with my friends. Not yet. The priest and I had something to resolve.

My birthmark stung like a nettle's touch.

8

OBSESSION

We three traveled early in the morning and late in the afternoon, using the ancient and narrow paths that crossed fields and circled villages, paths so old that I could almost hear the quiet feet of people who lived and died long before the Normans invaded, even long before the Romans came. During the day, we hid in hedgerows or at the edges of small woods where we were not likely to be found by gamekeepers. We slept anywhere we could at night, in sheds with cows, tucked into haystacks, or in the shells of abandoned cottages. We were strong, so we traveled quickly, and we reached Canterbury in a few days.

The fair was over and the pilgrims had gone home. We were hungry for cooked meals and wanted to sleep in beds, so we found a small inn with an empty room, and Brennan paid a reasonable sum for herself and her "two sons." The long, narrow room contained two beds, stuffed with fragrant heather instead of straw, a table and benches, and a small glass window that overlooked the street. It was clean, and the reeds on the floor were fresh. We left our bundles on the table, then went back down the narrow stairs. Below, in the common room, we shared one of the long tables with two old men. Striker made friends with them immediately, even sitting in the lap of the stout fellow and begging for bits of bread.

Brennan introduced herself as Alice, a farmer's widow, and she dismissed Tom and me as her lazy sons, louts who dawdled on the road and wanted only puddings for their suppers. The men laughed, and after that they ignored us, spending their time at the table telling Brennan of their adventures during the Holy War. But I was worried, so I kept my face lowered, and I was grateful that neither of the men spoke to me.

They did not speak to Tom, either. He ate quickly, and then he said to the man who held Striker, "I'll take the dog outside for a while." His leaving gave me an excuse to push away the last of my food and follow him out of the inn. I found him standing out of sight behind a tree on the south side, with Striker lying at his feet. Striker jumped up when he saw me.

"Why did you leave?" I asked Tom.

"We're supposed to be good-for-nothing sons, so I thought we should act the part. And I didn't want them asking us questions if they grew tired of talking about themselves. Let Brennan tell the story *she* wants to tell. We will be more convincing louts if we cannot be cornered anywhere."

We lingered outside while dusk fell, and when we saw candlelight in the window of our room upstairs, we went inside, grateful that the men were gone from the common room. Brennan was waiting in our room.

"Did they ask about Tom and me?" I asked as I let Striker jump from my arms to the bed.

"No, and I didn't give them a chance to even think about you. I kept them telling and retelling their war stories. They won't remember us after we leave." She seemed confident, and I had learned years before to trust her judgment.

We were on our way at dawn the next morning, carrying with us our breakfast of bread and cheese. Just as the sun rose, we passed a tower, and Brennan murmured, "The queen is imprisoned there, at the convent. And look! A woman is standing on the wall!"

The woman was very tall, as the queen was said to be. Slender and erect, she stood facing the sunrise, her white veil outlining her thin face. Suddenly I wanted her to look down and see me there. I knew she had never heard of me, never heard of the daughter of the man who foolishly built a castle without a license from her husband, the king.

And then I thought again of my mother—and Father Caddaric.

When we found him, I would demand that he tell me everything he knew about my mother and my birth. I must have my way in this, I thought. I had suffered so much, and for so many years, and now I was a refugee again. He must answer for it.

We trusted Father Caddaric to find us as we journeyed toward the coast. He had many ways of doing it. Priest or wizard—or both—he was comfortable in the real world as well as the magical one. Animals and birds carried messages to him, and, as I knew myself, animals and birds could carry messages to me. Sooner or later we would hear from him and know where we were to go next.

The message came in a strange way. We were alone on a path that sloped gently upward through an open field, when a crow swooped down low over us and dropped a stone at my feet. "Here's a lucky stone for you, *Gwenore*," it said—in King Harry's voice. "Or maybe it's not lucky. Why don't you ask that stupid dog?"

"King Harry!" I exclaimed.

In a messy flutter of black feathers, he landed at my feet and instantly changed into the cat. "Pick up the stone," he said. "A wretch like you can use all the luck it carries."

Brennan and Tom heard him, too, and both backed away a full step. I picked up the stone, small and white, with a black ring around it. It felt warm. But I suspected that King Harry was not likely to give away a lucky stone, so I tossed it to one side.

"I have seen stones like this before," I said. "They are common enough on beaches."

"Ungrateful creature," King Harry said calmly. "But I'll tell you the news, if you pay the price."

"What price, cat?"

"I'm weary of sleeping outside in the cold, and I'm lonely without my old friend, Umma. He was the best man I ever knew. Take me with you and I'll serve you—but get rid of that dog."

"That—cat—is one of the Fair Folk, Gwenore,"

Brennan said warningly. "Take him in and you will regret it."

"And what might *you* know of the Fair Folk, madam?" King Harry asked Brennan.

"I know that they have no need of human companions," Brennan said. "Or the simple comforts that humans might offer. The Fair Folk keep their own company and they sleep in palaces."

The cat examined one paw, pretending great interest in it. "We're not always of the same mind, my family and I," he said. "They have made accusations and allegations about this and that, so for the present it is best that I make my own way. Take me with you, Gwenore. I am a reliable messenger, and while I can't be of much help to you here, I will be able to help you when you reach the Middle Passage. Unless, of course, that crazy old priest decides to accompany you."

"What Middle Passage?" I demanded. "What are you talking about?"

The cat looked as if he was smiling. "It's the place where the old gods rule, separate from the lands belonging to the new ones. I know you will blunder in there before you are done—you are the sort of human who can't pass by a mystery or a maze—and you will need me then, as well as the priest."

"What is he talking about, Gwenore?" Brennan asked.

"Ignore his babbling," I said. "King Harry is a pest, but he is a useful messenger. We can't leave him behind. Umma took him in and he fared very well for years." It was hard to say Umma's name, and I had to swallow to keep from sobbing. "You can go with us, King Harry, but my dog will always come before you. Now, tell me your news."

"Father Caddaric waits a day and a half ahead, according to my feathered brethren. Your mother has sent word to London that she wants to hire someone who knows how to build a castle in the Eastern desert way, one with high stone towers. She has money—a great deal of it, and probably stolen. But what does that matter, eh?"

"She can't build a castle," I said. "The king won't allow it. He knows that any castle he does not authorize is a threat to him."

"She says that King Henry will not live forever, and his son Richard has no interest in what goes on in England."

I did not know much about those things, and there were matters more urgent to me. "Is anyone looking for us?"

"The physician Hiram wonders where *you* are. He knows that you were present when his wife lived through the childbirth he had meant to be fatal. He would like to throw you into the cellar with Margarite, and he daydreams about two fires burning in the town square. But Margarite's friends are circling back for her now, and Simon has a brave plan."

"Will they succeed?" I asked eagerly.

King Harry sighed. "That's in the future. Consult your looking glass."

"Gwenore, we have to keep moving," Tom cautioned.

"King Harry, you'll travel easier if you fly," I said. "The path is rocky."

"Someone could carry me on his shoulder," the cat said meaningfully, looking at Tom.

I almost expected Tom to refuse; there was a time when he had not been the sort to involve himself with Fair Folk. But he had been cured by a goddess in a pool. He held out his hands and said, "Bird or cat, you can ride on my shoulder, until I tire of you. Then you walk or fly."

Their friendship was forged at that moment. Striker growled. Bird or cat, he had no use for either.

The following day brought a heavy rainstorm, and we found shelter under an overhanging cliff. Striker, happy to rest for a while in Brennan's lap, fell asleep almost instantly, but King Harry was restless, turning in nervous circles, and muttering under his breath. Finally he shook himself into feathers.

"The rain will stop in a moment or two, and then I will search out news of the Blessingwood ladies and the priest. And—think of this!— perhaps Gwenore's witch mother has been murdered. It is such a hope that keeps us all young and alive." He ruffled his wings and cocked one eye at me. "Do you agree, Singer?"

I nodded.

"What did he call you?" Tom asked, ready to laugh.

"Singer," I said. I felt strangely uneasy. Who was I to be called by that name, when he had been one of the players, perhaps even a gleeman, a professional musician? We had not spoken of the years we were separated, and his life during that time was as much a mystery to me as Brennan's was. Most of the time we had walked quickly, in silence, as fugitives do. And everyone knows that secrets are extremely valuable—

or dangerous—especially when they concern ourselves.
"I don't remember that you were interested in music,"
Brennan said.

"I learned when I lived in a convent, and then I had lessons in singing and playing many instruments from Julienne, at Blessingwood. Lessons in music, medicine, gardening, and surgery." I looked straight ahead, hoping that they would not think I was boasting.

There was a small silence, and then Tom asked, "What were they preparing you for, marriage to a rich man?"

I could not help laughing. "No, never. They knew I could not marry, even though they didn't know the reason why. As long as my mother lives, I will not be safe, nor will anyone with me be safe. Look! The rain seems to be stopping, just as King Harry said. Let's move on now."

"Then what were the women preparing you for?" Tom persisted. He had never been one to let matters drop.

I shook my head. "I do not know. To be one of the Blessingwood women, perhaps. They had told me that I was welcome there forever." Suddenly, I began to weep and I could not stop. "It's all gone," I said. "That wonderful place. The house and the baths and the blacksmith shop and the stables and the gardens and orchards. And Umma!"

I held out my arms for Striker and he leaped up to nuzzle my neck.

"Let's walk on," Brennan said, and she touched my shoulder sympathetically. "One day, girl, all this will be made right."

But I did not believe her.

◀ ◀ ◀

King Harry returned to us late in the afternoon and settled on the branch of an oak. "The news is good. Sarah and Simon rescued Margarite in the middle of the night by tunneling into her cellar room. All five of them were taken out of the village by the farmer to whom they had given their cows and horses. They will travel to the western coast by night and take the first ship to Ireland. Eventually you will see them there—if you go." He settled his feathers, stretched his neck, and turned his head from side to side. "I regret to tell you, Gwenore, that your mother has not been murdered after all. There is no real justice in the human world, in spite of all the babblings on and on about your three gods, that father and son and family ghost, who are expected to deliver the good people to paradise and send the evil people to hell."

"What?" exclaimed Brennan indignantly. "Be careful of what you say, crow, lest you be struck dead where you perch."

The crow laughed. "I've been cursed before, by uglier women than you, Brennan."

"Let's keep going," Tom said. "We can bicker tonight, when we find a dry place to stay."

The crow perched on his shoulder, briskly shook himself into the form of the cat, and said, "It's straight ahead now. There's a fine inn, with an innkeeper who is wise enough to put out a dish of milk every night for the Fair Folk. We keep watch over her and make sure that only the best people find their way to her, people who can pay and don't drink too much ale. An hour's brisk walk will take you there. Then it's a good meal for me, nothing for that stupid dog, and a fine night's sleep by the fire."

To make sure Tom moved fast enough to suit him, he dug in his claws, and Tom laughed instead of cursing the creature.

Brennan shook her head. "I don't know what's to become of that boy. I think your pagan goddess put a spell on him." Tom had told her of his magical healing in the underground bath.

"No, the goddess just healed him," I said. "And it was beautiful to watch, Brennan."

Brennan crossed herself and shook her head again.

The inn was all that King Harry had promised. Brennan and I had adjoining rooms, and mine had a small nook next to the fire for Striker. Tom and King Harry chose the loft over the stable, even though there was another room available for them. "It will be easier to keep watch from there," Tom said.

"I'm going to teach him to play a pleasant dice game I learned from Umma," the cat said. "It's one that he learned in a far-off place where the heathen eat small white dogs. Of course, I always win."

Striker showed his teeth over my shoulder as I carried him toward the stairs and our room.

"Those two," Brennan muttered behind me. "The cat—or crow or whatever he is—will corrupt our Tom, and then what?"

"What indeed?" I asked. I was grateful for the company of King Harry. He was a comforting reminder of my days at Blessingwood.

That night I dreamed of the four circling swans again. They were reflected in a beautiful calm lake set in a green field, and they circled overhead again and again. But in my dream, I could hear children crying. There was something I was supposed to know about them, but I could not discern it. I woke suddenly, and without waking Brennan, I took my looking glass from my pack and carried it close to the fire.

On the back, the silver swans were circling. I turned it over and bent close to the glass. "Show me," I whispered.

But it did not show me the swans. It showed me the cave again, and a dark and terrible land where black horses ran at me, threatening me with their silver hooves, and I tried to take refuge behind a great stone altar sprinkled with drops of blood.

Drops that looked like my birthmark.

The looking glass showed only my face after that, and on the silver back, the swans were gone and all I saw was the animal I could never identify.

Brennan turned over in her sleep and mumbled something. I put my looking glass back in my pack and crawled into the bed, but I did not sleep again.

What was I supposed to understand about the swans—and the crying children?

We had a fine breakfast in the morning, and the innkeeper gave both Striker and King Harry small bowls of meat and milk. Apparently she did not hear King Harry when he complained of having to eat on the floor, because she did not even glance at him.

We left immediately, and we had not walked more than an hour when Father Caddaric stepped out from behind a hedgerow and greeted us. His pet crow shot out of his sleeve and cried, "There you are, you scoundrel!"

King Harry flashed into a crow. "*Vespers!* You liar! You mewling crybaby! Don't think I haven't heard what you have been telling the family."

"It was only *half* of the truth," Vespers shouted back. "If I had told our parents all of it, they would have thrown themselves into the sea for the shame of it."

King Harry's feathers smoothed back into place. "Oh, that. Mother has been throwing herself into the sea since Roman times. The water spirits throw her back, because who can listen to so much nagging? And Father hasn't been near water for a thousand years."

"There! There!" Vespers shouted. "See? That's why you have been disinherited and must walk the roads with . . . with . . . cast-off humans like these!"

"Be quiet," Father Caddaric said wearily. "No one cares at all about your bickering. What news do you have, Pip?"

"*Pip?*" Tom muttered, gawking at King Harry.

King Harry shouted something unintelligible, then settled down to report that the women who had made a home for me were safe now and on the road to the coast. "They will join us in Ireland."

"Yes," Father Caddaric said, and he would have said more, but I cried, "No! I'm not going until you tell me why

I should. Why are all these people running away because of me? What happened that I should be born with this!" I held up my wrist to show the mark. "What happened that everyone around me is always in danger? That Umma is dead?"

The priest made a gesture, as if to indicate that he would have no part of a discussion with me. I grabbed his arm.

"Tell me! Tell me what you know and tell me now."

He shook his head. "There is nothing to tell."

"Liar! You *are* lying. You told me you were sorry that you had given me a dangerous life. *Why* did you do it? *What* did you do to me?"

He looked around, as if my shouting might have attracted attention, but no human was near us, only a flock of curious sheep. "Do you want your friends to be caught?" he asked. "Learn to be quiet unless that is your intention."

"It is not and you know it." I dragged him away from the others and lowered my voice. "I have a right to know. I was told that you did something, that you are an enchanter, and that I had a right to question you."

"I am an enchanter?" he repeated angrily. "An *enchanter*? Who told you such a thing?"

"Someone who *was* enchanted—by someone like you," I said. "Tell me, or if I am caught, I will tell my captors what you are, and you will burn for it."

"It could be true," Brennan said from behind me. She drew closer. "I had heard many things about you, priest, and 'enchanter' was the worst. But if you were not burned for that, then you might be hanged because of that woman and your daughter."

"What?" I exclaimed, startled. "Brennan! Was he one of

those priests who gathers tithes to spend on a wife instead of the poor?" I did not believe it, of course, but I was more than willing to apply extra pressure to the old man in order to find out what I needed to know.

But then I saw his face and suddenly I read his mind, clearly. He had a daughter, a plump young woman with a small child and a good husband. Nearby. Too close for safety if they were found out.

"Enough, Brennan," I said quietly. "He will tell me what I need to know now, *for the sake of his grandchild.*"

Father Caddaric wiped his hand over his face, as if rubbing away water. Or the memory of tears shed long before. "Your words remind me of your mother." Then he shook his head. "I cannot tell you here. You would not believe me."

"Then where?" I cried.

"He's talking about the Middle Passage," King Harry said grimly. "That is a dark shadow of this world, and dark curses can be made there. I have seen your mark. You are like others who have suffered entire lifetimes because of these curses, which are called 'blessings' by the ignorant who think that sacrifice is some sort of virtue."

"She's not going to any *Middle Passage*," Tom said, and he stepped between the priest and me. "Tell us everything here and now."

Father Caddaric met his unblinking stare. "I will not tell you. I will tell no one but Gwenore, and only in one place, where she can see and believe. It is more important than you. More important than anything you have ever imagined or dreamed for yourself. And it is not yours to know."

I spoke up quickly. "I will go with Father Caddaric,

Tom. You take Brennan to the coast. I will find you in Ireland. *I will.*"

He would have spoken again, but Brennan stopped him. "Come, Tom," she said quietly. "This is right. I know it is. Trust me that we can leave Gwenore with Father Caddaric. If he brought her to this dangerous place, then let him explain it to her. And he will protect her as he has protected her before."

Tom looked down at his feet for a moment, and then he said, "I will do what you want, Gwenore. Brennan and I will look for you in Ireland."

King Harry flapped to my shoulder. "I'll go with Singer," he said. "To keep her out of trouble."

Vespers leaned forward from Father Caddaric's shoulder and aimed a quick peck at his brother's eye and missed. "Go with your friends, *Pip.* This is work for those who have not been disgraced before the Fair Folk's council."

King Harry let out a squawk and was about to shout a reply when Father Caddaric held up his hand for silence. "Tom, learn to listen carefully, and the Fair Folk will give you news of us. Good-bye, Brennan. We shall meet again. Good-bye, Tom. Keep your wits about you in the next days." He walked off then, clearly expecting me to follow.

I smiled as sincerely as I could. "Don't worry," I told my friends. "I have Striker for company, and the crows to give me news of you, and Father Caddaric will keep me safe."

"He put you in danger in the first place," Tom said angrily.

"Tom, don't," I said. "My mother did that. Somehow, everything starts with her."

"I hope it doesn't end with her, too, because of *him*."

I stood on my toes and kissed Tom's face quickly. "I will see you when I know what I am," I said. I kissed Brennan, too, and ran after Father Caddaric, who had not waited, but was disappearing over a hill, with the crow perched on his shoulder.

"Well, that was enough to make anybody sick," King Harry called out as he leaped out of the brush beside me, his tail frizzed out. "I hate fond farewells."

"I don't imagine that anybody has ever felt fondly toward you," I said. And then I was sorry. "I know Umma loved you."

But he had changed back into a crow, and he flew away without a word. I hugged Striker close and told him, "I need someone to teach me to be kind."

He did not disagree.

Father Caddaric seemed weary as the day went on, and since he would not call for a rest, I did. He leaned back against a tree and fell asleep almost immediately. Striker curled in my lap, with his chin resting across my arm, and slept, too. King Harry sat down and stared at his brother, who was sitting in his usual place, Father Caddaric's shoulder.

"Don't start arguing," I said, suspecting them of the worst.

King Harry shrugged and Vespers groomed himself.

"Tell me about the Middle Passage," I said to them.

"You'll see soon enough," King Harry said. "It's full of creatures from other times, some even older than the times that brought forth my family. And there are tales there that tell themselves, whether you want to listen or not. You'll be miserable if you stay long, because it will remind you too much of your life here. There is no place safe from creatures that cause pain for pleasure, Gwenore, just as there is no place without beauty."

I scowled. "If there is a Middle Passage, is there a Lower Passage?"

"You don't want to see the Lower Passage," the cat said with a faint shudder. "It's like your hell, filled with the spirits of fighting men—knights and tribal warriors, men of all colors and sizes, wearing every kind of clothing that you could imagine, and some with no clothes at all. It smells of blood and fear—and goblins. I have no power there. None of the Fair Folk do."

I felt sorry for King Harry, because he was trembling now, so I reached out and stroked him. He rose and moved out of reach haughtily.

"Then if there is a Middle Passage and a Lower Passage, there must be—"

"A Higher Passage," Vespers said.

I waited but he said nothing more. "Then tell me about it," I urged.

"Seeing heaven is better than hearing about it," Vespers said, and he closed his eyes and tucked his head under his wing. Obviously he planned to stop the conversation by sleeping.

"Let it be," King Harry said. "It's a place of lakes and skies and strings of pearls and swans, and the likes of you will never see it. Nor will I." He heaved a great sigh then, and added, "But I have been told that there are dogs in that heaven, although I don't believe it."

He, too, slept abruptly, and I suspected that it was as much to shut me out as it was because he was weary.

In a while, Father Caddaric got to his feet, rubbed his hands, and said, "Let us go on. The path ahead is difficult, and we must cover a long way before dark falls."

We walked deep into the mountains, following a path next to a river that coursed through a ravine. The sky overhead was thick with dark clouds, and more than once we heard thunder. The wind was sharp and cold, and I bundled Striker under my cloak. King Harry huddled close to Father Caddaric's neck, and Vespers tucked himself inside the priest's sleeve. Lightning flashed.

Suddenly a black dog sprang out of a hole in the ground. He was heavy-bodied, with a broad, savage face, and he was so large that his head could have reached as high as my shoulder. Striker stuck his head out of my cloak and withdrew it again immediately. He trembled violently.

The black dog growled deep in his throat and stepped forward.

"Father Caddaric," I said softly, "we must turn back. This is a war dog, the kind that the knights took into battle with them."

King Harry turned into a cat, leaped high into the air, and landed on the dog's back, digging in his claws. "Damn your eyes, fleabag!" he shouted. "How dare you set upon your own kin!"

Instantly, the dog turned into a cat and the two of them

wrestled and rolled on the path, yowling and cursing in languages I had never heard. Then they were hawks, soaring above us, circling each other, calling out in high cries. The hawks dropped to the ground and turned into wolves, and one wolf followed the other toward a dolmen, a passage grave marked by two great, rough stones capped with a third. They circled the dolmen and came back, then tumbled over and over as badgers and sprang apart as griffins. A dragon rose up on its strong back legs, balancing itself against its tail, and he shot smoke and fire at another dragon sidling toward him, its eyes aflame.

I held my breath, prepared to turn and run. But one cat dropped to the ground at the feet of a dragon, and called out, "Singer, this is my cousin, Keir."

The dragon shimmered and faded away, leaving behind a small gray cat with a notch in his left ear. I stared at him.

Vespers pushed out of Father Caddaric's sleeve. "We have no time to play games, Keir. We are going into the Middle Passage."

The gray cat's hair stood on end. "Think twice, cousins. No humans are worth a journey as hazardous as that."

"Are you going with us?" Father Caddaric demanded. "If you are not, then be on your way."

"I'll wait on the other side of the Passage," the gray cat said. "Although I do not expect to see you coming out, not any of you."

Father Caddaric turned to look straight at me. "Are you sure you want to go on?"

I hesitated. "Can't you tell me what happened? Why do I have to see this place?"

"I want to be done with your questions for all time," he said. "For that, I must show you where your mother was, and *what* she was, and what she did, to bring about her plans. And I want you to understand what I did to stop her."

I nearly choked on my bitterness. "What you did to stop her? From what? I wish you had stopped her from the harm she did me."

"There was worse harm she could have done, if she had had her way," Father Caddaric said. "You are not the only person alive in this world, Gwenore. You are not the center of the universe."

He turned away from me and walked toward the dolmen, and I followed, silent now. The gray cat disappeared into a hole in the ground beneath the capstone, and Vespers crept back into the priest's sleeve.

"Are you still willing to go?" King Harry asked.

I hesitated for only a moment, and then I said, "Yes." I did not see that I had a choice, unless I wanted to spend the rest of my life running away without knowing the reason for it.

So I followed the cat, who followed the priest, and ahead of us loomed the ancient stones marking the grave of someone no one remembered.

Below the stones was the opening of a cave, deep and dark. The air around us turned cold as we approached. Then, when we were only ten steps away, I heard thunder, but not from the air above. Instead, it came from the cave.

King Harry hesitated, then changed into a crow and flapped to Father Caddaric's shoulder. "Let me hide in your other sleeve," he begged.

"Coward!" shouted Vespers from his own safe place.

Father Caddaric let King Harry into his sleeve. "Quiet now, sons of the Fae. If you know prayers, say them. If you do not, make them up. This is a time for Believers."

And so we entered the cave.

9

IN THE LAND BELOW DARK

The damp floor of the cave sloped gradually, but not into complete darkness, as I had feared. Instead, there were cracks and fissures in the rock ceiling that let in light, and after a while, light shone from the far end. For a moment, I thought we were returning to the surface, but the floor still sloped down. I hesitated, and Father Caddaric turned and said, "You cannot stop here. It is not allowed."

"Not allowed by whom?" I asked, startled. "Who makes the rules here?"

Father Caddaric's laugh was more like a bark. "Who rules? The lands in the Middle Passage show the truth about the lands above it. The one who rules is the one who is strongest, cruelest, and richest. Walk on, Gwenore. We cannot loiter—we might attract attention."

I followed him, and shortly we stepped out into broad sunlight, in a place that looked so different from any other I had ever seen that I thought for an instant that we had walked into another world. I stopped again, amazed. "There is a sun here?"

"There is only one sun," Father Caddaric said impatiently. "At least, there is only one that we know of. Who can say what there might be in the skies above us. Come along. It's not safe to hesitate."

We walked through a broad meadow of tall, ribbonlike grass mixed with flowers I did not recognize, bright yellow blossoms tipped with green spikes. The grass rippled as if in a warm wind, as water in a pond ripples, showing a silver underside, but I felt no wind on my face. The blades hummed, but the sound was not musical, and it grated on my nerves, rather like an out-of-tune harp.

Across the meadow, a white unicorn stepped out from under a spreading tree that bore small orange fruit. She stared at me for a long moment, as I stared at her, and then she backed out of sight again. When I gasped, shrill laughter rang out from the grass at my feet.

I bent to see where the sound came from. The grass rustled and was still. From behind me, a small voice said, "Give our regards to Keir." The shrill laughter sounded again, all around. Striker growled, and the creatures in the grass mimicked him until he stopped.

"Where are you going, Gwenore?" the voices called. "How long will you stay with us? Are you certain that you should be here? We have lords and ladies—and witches and sheriffs—too."

"Don't listen to them," Father Caddaric told me. "They'll waste our time with nonsense. The meadow is full of the Fair Folk. They run in and out like mice, and they are twice as annoying." Then he added thoughtfully, "Although some of them can be quite cruel."

Both crows stuck their heads out of his sleeves, glared up at him, and withdrew again. "Annoying?" one of them muttered. "Cruel?"

Father Caddaric ploughed through the long grass toward a rocky hillside. I heard the thunder of hooves, and the ground shook beneath my feet. Several great, black horses charged down the hill, their silver hooves flashing. These were the horses from my dreams! Their eyes blazed red and their mouths foamed.

"Look out!" I screamed at Father Caddaric, but he strode on, directly into the horses' path. At the last moment, the great beasts parted and galloped past us, their mouths open, their eyes flaming. I was too terrified to move.

"They are like children!" Father Caddaric shouted back at me. "Like ignorant bullies. They want attention. But if you give it to them, you'll never be rid of them. Pretend that you don't see them and they will give up their games."

I looked back at the horses and saw that they had stopped and were watching me, suddenly dejected, almost as if they had understood what the priest said. Indeed, they truly were like children, whose game had been spoiled by a parent. One snorted when he saw me watching, tossed his head and stamped one foot. But then he turned his back, and I could not tell if his sudden interest in grazing was real or pretended.

"How much farther are we going?" I called out to the priest.

"Farther," he answered. "Much farther. A question with an easy answer isn't worth asking."

I did not understand him, but I seldom did, so I said

nothing and followed him. I was tired. The pack on my back seemed heavier now, and even little Striker seemed to gain weight as we walked. But I could not put him down in that place, where unseen creatures still teased us in the grass. There were great birds flying high over us, too, and though I could not identify them for certain, I suspected that they were vultures of some kind. That was one more reason to keep Striker safe in my arms. This Middle Passage was full of threats. Sometimes I thought I heard distant voices, laughter and shouts that were almost human, but I could not be sure, and so I hurried a little faster.

We crossed through a woodland, where the trunks of the trees were as smooth as glass, and I saw my reflection in them, over and over. There were no birds or tree spirits here, and I was not surprised. The woods seemed unhealthy, and I suspected that if I touched one of the trees, my fingers would be injured somehow.

We moved into another meadow, but the grass was thinner here, and the soil was studded with sharp pebbles. I saw, in the center, what appeared to be the vine-choked ruins of a stone wall, but I could not guess what had stood there. I had seen ruins like that in England and Wales, the remains of old fortresses or farms. For a moment, I thought I heard the echoes of men shouting, but the wind blew harder and I could not be certain.

Ahead of Father Caddaric, a white bull rushed out from behind a rocky outcropping and skidded to a stop, only a few steps from the priest. Father Caddaric shook his staff at the bull and shouted, "Go home! I've warned you before. Go home and don't look back!"

I did not think that treating the bull like a dog would result in much, even though the bull was wearing a studded black collar, as if he belonged to someone. The bull lowered his head and swung it threateningly toward me. His horns were long, curved, and sharp. I held my breath.

"Go!" Father Caddaric shouted again.

The bull shimmered and faded, and a small, crooked man stood there. He was no taller than a three-year-old child, but Father Caddaric must have considered him dangerous, because he raised his staff again and would have brought it down on the small man's head if the creature had not turned and run.

"Who was that?" I asked.

"Someone very nasty, who considers himself a king since his father died so—hmm—unexpectedly. Now hurry, because we're wasting time with these creatures," the priest said. "If you keep your head down and act as if you know where you're going, they are not so inclined to pester you—you might have important friends here, for all they know. Otherwise, you may be trapped in one of their games, and that is as good a way as any in this place to end up sorry and bleeding."

The Fair Folk in the grass screamed with laughter, and small pebbles flew at me, stinging me even through my clothes. "Act as if you know where you're going, Gwenore!" one of them cried, mimicking the priest. "Not that it will do you any good here."

Tired no longer, I ran until Father Caddaric finally stopped. "There," he said, and he pointed ahead to a flat black rock, shaped like a table.

"What is it?" I asked. I was afraid to draw nearer to it. The long grass around me was suddenly silent and still, and I wondered if the mean-spirited creatures had run away. In fright?

"This is the place where your mother lay when I called up the enchantment that will bind you for the rest of time," the priest said.

He gestured to me to draw closer to it, and I did, even though his words had disturbed me. No grass grew close to the stone. Instead, the ground was blackened and blighted, as if it had been set on fire long before. Or as if it had been poisoned somehow. Now clouds blew across the sun and cast shadows over the stone and dead ground. I shivered inside my cloak.

"Your mother sought me out," Father Caddaric said bitterly. "She expected to give birth to a son, one who would achieve for her the power and high station she wanted. But no mother can enchant her own child, and so she made me a devil's bargain. She had learned of my daughter, and she promised to keep her a secret if I would make certain that her unborn son had all the powers necessary to become a warrior king. She wanted him to be determined and ruthless and cold, with the cunning of a sharp blade. She wanted him to be immortal, even though the only ones who can be immortal are those whose lives have been so hard that they do not care if they live or die."

"But she did not have a son," I said. "She had me."

"I knew she was carrying a girl child." The old priest sighed. "But I lied to her. 'You will have the king you want,'

I told her. And I gave you gifts that could conquer her, not empower her. She realized what I had done the moment you were born, when she saw your birthmark. It was not the lightning bolt I had promised. It was the drop of blood that would be forever offered in sacrifice to those who need it."

Father Caddaric pointed to symbols carved on the rock. "These are your heritage, Gwenore. I carved them after your mother left, so that there would be a record of what was done that day. So that there would be an accounting for *you*, if you ever came here, but I hoped that you would not."

"What do you mean?" I drew close and examined the first carving. "This is only a plain circle. What can it say about me?"

"That is the sun, and it brings healing. You are a healer of flesh and blood. This was not of your mother's choosing. She enjoyed the pain and suffering of others, especially if she inflicted it on them herself. She expected her son to be the same."

I had been trained to be a healer, not a destroyer. How my mother would hate that. "Then this is the moon?" I asked, touching a crescent.

"You are a healer of minds and spirits," he said. "Your mother did not ask for that for her child, either. She was too selfish to care if anyone's soul cried out."

I thought of what I had been taught, by nuns and by Julienne. There was nothing that healed minds and spirits better than music. So once again, my destiny had been fulfilled by the people who had given me the safe shelter my mother had denied me.

"Here is a cross," I said, running my finger over another carving.

"For peace," he said. "At least, that was the meaning of it ten thousand years ago. Now the meaning has been perverted in the minds of some, but not in yours. You can tell the difference between responsibility and cowardice. Your mother wanted a son who would not know anything but brute force."

"And this?" I asked, pointing to what seemed to be a carving of a blade.

"It is a sword, for bravery, and it is the reason your mother came here. It gives victory over armies and kingdoms. It gives power. She wanted power more than anything else."

Yes, I thought, that is what she would want, for the son she did not have. I did not see what it had to do with me, however. I did not feel powerful. I pointed to the last symbol, an eye. "What is this?"

"Wisdom, which you will have one day when you are older. Now look at the end of the table. You'll see all the symbols combined into one."

I bent over to look closely. "But it only looks like a drop of blood. There is even some color, a dye. . . ."

"The red color is blood, of course. No rain can wash it away. Tears cannot dissolve it. Fire will not burn it off."

I stared at him. My birthmark stung, and Striker whimpered, as if he felt the heat of it on his flank. "I don't understand any of this," I said. "How did you decide on these symbols?"

"The eye is for a priest, a heretic, who taught me the wisest thing I learned about the Creator—that the Creator does not speak . . . or write. He *creates*. My friend was burned to death. The cross is for the man I walked with once, who saw war, sickened of it, and spoke against it until the war lovers killed him. The sword is for the bravest man I ever saw, because he refused to take up his sword except to defend the helpless, and so he died by it. The sun is for the blood of a physician who saved my life in the midst of battle. He died of his own wounds that he did not take time to tend. The moon is for my mother, who could heal with one touch or one whisper."

I pulled my hand away and tucked it next to Striker. "Then you cursed me with their deaths."

"No, I gave you everything they had that was taken from them. Your mother wanted only battle skill and ambition for the son she thought she would have. I told her she would know that my spells had worked if her son was born with the sign of a lightning bolt on his wrist. But I gave you a drop of blood on your wrist so that you would remember forever that you are here to save others, that you are here to sacrifice your time and fortune for those in need. When you were born, and your mother saw the mark, she sent men to kill me. But she cannot touch me."

"Why not?" I asked.

"Have you already forgotten what I said, Gwenore? She cannot kill me because I do not care if I live or die. That is the power I have over your mother."

"And what of your daughter?"

He sighed. "I confessed to her before your mother reached her. She despises me."

"Is this all there is?"

"Is it not enough?" he asked.

"Too much," I said. "But I don't want any more surprises in my life."

He was silent too long. Finally he said, "Every child inherits something from the mother, but I do not know what Rhiamon unknowingly passed on to you. It is for you to discover one day, perhaps when you face her again."

"I will never face her again, not if I can avoid it," I said fervently. "I want no gift from her." Then I asked, "Who used this altar before you?"

"Who can say?" he said. "There were other carvings on it, but too old to decipher. The Fair Folk are liars, and so their wild tales about the altar cannot be believed. But it goes back to the first days of the world, and it is said that it will be the last stone left at the end of the world."

I shuddered then and moved away from it. "Why did you enchant me, priest? I do not want your burdens."

"I am not interested in what you want or do not want," he said. "You are the weapon I chose to stand against your mother and all who are like her. Now I am done. You know your gifts, all but one. Use them or not. No one can give you love or generosity or honesty. Those we earn through lessons we are forced to learn."

He began walking away from me, so I called out, "What am I to do now?"

"Whatever you want," he said. The crows, silent so long

in his sleeves, peered out at me and muttered between themselves.

"Will I see you again?" I cried.

"In Ireland." He stopped and looked back. "When the battle begins. We shall see how you choose to fight it." He looked up for a moment, and then he looked back at me. "There is one more thing, Gwenore."

"What is that?"

"You will not die."

"In the battle you were talking about?"

He shook his head. "No. That is not what I mean."

And then he was gone, slipping between trees and becoming part of the mist that clung to the branches of the forest. I called out to him again and again, but he did not answer, so I made my way back through the meadow alone, terrified of what he had said, unable to understand it, and wondering how one can never die.

Voices giggled at my feet. "Never die, Gwenore!" they cried, laughing. "Like us, you can never die." The unicorn left the shelter of her tree to stare at me with elegant disapproval. The black horses charged me again and again, until I ducked back inside the cave. I, who had been told that I could never die, was afraid they would trample me and leave me crippled until the end of time.

Ridiculous! All this has been lies, I told myself. Everyone knew that Father Caddaric was mad. And even worse, I might be dreaming all of this. Or I could have gone mad, too. No one lives forever!

Just as I told myself that the place I had just left was not as dangerous as I had feared, I realized that something was following me. I whirled around, but saw nothing. Under my cloak, Striker growled and stiffened. He knew something was there, too.

"Who is there?" I shouted.

Thunder roared around me, as it had when I passed through it before. Lightning flickered overhead. Striker trembled then, and I patted his small head, trying to console both of us. Something was there, right behind us, but I did not know what.

I hurried out of the cave into the cold twilight. Keir, the gray cat, was waiting, as he had promised. "Hurry!" he cried when he saw me. "You are only a short reach from one of the shadow dragons, and he'll kill you."

Unless I am able to live forever, I thought bitterly.

I ran until I was breathless, with the cat scampering beside me. "You must travel by night now," he said. "Your name has been shouted everywhere in Wales. You are charged with the death of Sir Richard, and you must not be found. Your mother is offering your weight in gold as a reward."

"Where shall I go?" I asked. I was frightened again, alone in a part of Wales that I did not know.

"Why, you'll go to Ireland, of course," Keir said. He sat down before me, his gray tail curled around his feet. "Your friends will be there. And the old priest will go there, sooner or later. Where else can you go?"

I looked around me. "I don't know," I said. "It's growing dark, cat. Will you walk with me for a while?"

"Not I," he said. "I am tied by spells to the farm where

I live, and I cannot go more than an hour's walk from the barn. Hurry, before the night patrols find you. Go down this path, until you reach the river, and buy passage on a boat."

"What boat?" I asked. But he was gone.

A chilly wind blew around me, rustling in the trees. I was hungry, and I was sure that Striker must be hungry, too, but I did not waste time by taking food from my pack then. I hurried down the path until I reached the riverbank, barely visible in the dark. There was a small shack teetering on the edge of the water, and a boat rocking in the shallows.

I knocked on the door of the shack, and after a moment, a gray-haired woman opened it, holding a small lamp in one hand. "Who are you?" she asked.

"I am Mary," I said. "Do you know a boatman here who will take me down the river?"

She raised up the lamp and stared at me for a long moment, and then she said, "No, you are not called Mary. You are the Gwenore everyone searches for. I will take you to the river. You cannot wait long enough for my son to return."

I stepped back, ready to turn and run from her.

"I hate your mother, Gwenore," she said. "I hate her, for reasons I choose not to tell. If her spies learn that you are here, they will find and kill you. I will take you down the river to the coast, and from there, you must find your own way."

She put out the lamp and closed the door to the hut behind her, then helped me into the boat. Striker poked his head out from under my cloak, but she did not comment. I thought that she was a woman who had not smiled for many years.

We were nearer to the coast than I had thought, and we reached it soon. She guided her small boat to the foot of a ladder that led up the side of a stone quay, and as she steadied the craft, I reached into my deepest pocket for coins to pay her.

"I want nothing," she said quietly. "I consider this a small payment against the great debt your evil mother owes me. May the goddess bless you, Gwenore."

I climbed the ladder awkwardly, one-handed, holding Striker so tightly that he squeaked in protest, and when I reached the top, the little boat was already gone. No one was on the quay, but several larger boats were tied up there. On the shore, I saw a fire burning, and I started toward it. Perhaps the owner of one of the boats would be there, and I could arrange passage somewhere, even to Ireland.

Or perhaps someone there would turn me in to one of the patrols. I stopped and crouched down behind a stack of odorous hides waiting for shipment.

Footsteps came down the quay, scraping on the uneven stones. "I smell that dog," King Harry said loudly.

Someone hushed him. I stood up and saw Simon only a few steps away.

"I thought you were in Ireland!" I cried. "I thought you were with the Blessingwood women."

"That was our plan," he said. "But I was uneasy about you, so I returned. You were easy to find. I mentioned 'Singer' to birds along the way, and before long King Harry presented himself."

"I know when I am needed," the cat said proudly as he draped himself around Simon's neck. "And the priest's sleeve was boring, fit only for my idiot brother. Now let us find suitable passage for ourselves. I have a relative who works for a fisherman's wife, and he has a boat good enough to get us across. Let me make the arrangements." King Harry, as a crow, flapped off into the dark.

Simon and I sat on the pile of hides. "Have you eaten?" he asked.

"I brought food," I said, opening my pack. "I haven't had time to eat it, or to feed Striker."

My dog waited impatiently while I broke off bits of dried beef for him. I ate bread and cheese. Simon took pleasure in telling me that he had dined well at an inn, on hot mutton stew and fresh bread.

"Have you heard anything from the Fair Folk about anyone?" I said with my mouth full.

"The women are as well as they were when I left them, except for Julienne," he said. "King Harry's messages do not always make sense, so the best I could understand was that they are well situated in Ireland now, and waiting to see you. But Julienne's age is costing her much now, so I was told, and there is little to be done for her."

I was grieved to hear that, for Julienne was especially dear to me. Without her, I would have no magic in my music. But Simon also must be grieving for her, for he had been her student, too, during those long afternoons in her quiet room.

"How did you come to live at Blessingwood?" I asked. I had wondered many times, but he had never seemed to welcome curiosity.

"My mother died when I was born, and my father cast

me out when I was small. When Umma escaped from the prison in the desert lands, he found me there and brought me back to England with him. Blessingwood was my home after that. Now. Are you satisfied, Singer?"

"Yes." That was not true, but what he had told me would do until we had time to rest in a peaceful place.

"And do you know about your birthmark now?" he asked.

"I do not know anything that makes sense to me," I said. "So I have decided not to think about it anymore. Father Caddaric is probably mad—or he is someone who gets attention by making everything seem mysterious to everyone else. And he hates my mother. That alone would give someone reason to lose one's wits and make up tales about curses and enchantments."

King Harry was back, a cat now, leading a thin man who carried a lighted lantern. "Do you want passage across?" the man asked quietly.

"Can you take us?" Simon asked.

"My brother-in-law will be here shortly, and the tide will turn before dawn. We will take you then. My wife was once done a great and painful wrong when she was in the service of the witch Rhiamon, and this favor for you will ease her memories. Is that the way of it, cat?"

"That is the way of it," King Harry said. "Her anger will be cooled and she will sleep well again."

The man crossed himself and stepped into a boat beside the quay. "Get in," he said gruffly.

I looked behind me into the dark and wondered if I would see Wales—or even England—again.

"You will not, Gwenore," King Harry said, answering my thought.

"Then I am leaving behind my troubles," I said quietly.

"No," King Harry said. "They will follow you, strong and cruel."

"I thought that you could not see into the future," I said. "You do not know what will happen next."

"I know that liars lie and killers kill—and the ones who want revenge will seek it until they die. That is the way of the world."

Simon grunted disapproval. "Quiet, cat, or I'll wring your neck and throw you overboard. And *that* is the way of the world."

King Harry turned into a crow and perched on the railing, grooming his wings. Occasionally he muttered to himself angrily, and once I thought I heard him say, "Vespers, that wretch!" I could not help but smile.

And so we crossed the water to Ireland, and I nearly forgot King Harry's warning.

10

tHe DReam cHiLDReN

We reached Ireland, but not easily and not in the place our boatmen had intended. In the morning after our escape, a wild storm caught us, and we were driven blindly ahead of it, helpless and lost in the Irish Sea. Over and over again, I was certain that we would die on those cold waves.

During the next night, more by accident than by the intent of the men, our boat reached a shallow cove where we could be put on land. The storm was spent, but the sky was so overcast that the moon and stars could not light our way. A great fire burned on a high hill, and the boatmen had used it as a beacon and brought us to a rocky beach. Simon and I scrambled ashore gratefully. As we ran out of reach of the lapping water, the boat left, and when we turned to look, it was out of sight already between the black night and the black sea.

"Where shall we go?" I asked Simon. I was cold, my clothes were wet, and the wind was as sharp as a blade.

"Let's climb to where the fire burns and see who is there," Simon said. "They might be friendly enough to ask us to sit with them and dry out."

"And they might attack us on sight," I said.

"Then we won't let them see us unless we've watched them for a while and they seem trustworthy," Simon said. King Harry drew close to Simon's neck and settled down, muttering and rearranging his feathers.

Simon strode across the rough, rocky beach, and I stumbled behind, shivering and exhausted. Once or twice Striker whimpered, but I reassured him with a pat. How long until dawn? Where would we find ourselves when daylight came at last? And would we be welcomed by people willing to be friends, or attacked?

The fire was closer than I thought. We crouched among stone outcroppings and studied the scene cautiously. No one was there, but the fire seemed to have been freshly fed with good dry logs that burned briskly, crackling and sending up showers of sparks. It invited approach.

"I don't see anyone nearby," Simon whispered.

"The fire must be for you," King Harry told us. "The Fair Folk may have built it. Or perhaps some of the local witches set it. They would have heard that you were coming, Gwenore. You are not a secret from anyone, although I cannot understand why you are of such interest."

Simon brushed King Harry off his shoulder irritably, and the crow turned into a cat before he landed lightly on the ground. "Why do you say things like that about her?" Simon demanded of him.

"Why not?" King Harry retorted. "Should I lie? Everybody knows about her, thanks to my babbling relatives. 'Gwenore, dear Gwenore,' they all call out. 'Gwenore, sing to us! Gwenore, play your harp! Gwenore, heal us! Gwenore, fight for us! Gwenore—'"

Striker barked sharply, and King Harry fell silent. But around us in the dark, faint, high voices laughed. I saw the shimmering in the air that meant fairies were near, more of King Harry's distant relatives, probably.

"I'll sit by the fire and see if I draw attention from anyone around here," Simon said. He did not see the fairies. "If it's safe, you come out. We can dry our clothes here, take time to eat, and then get as much rest as we can before dawn."

I watched as he made his way between the rocks, with King Harry slipping behind him, looking in every direction, as if for enemies. When Simon reached the fire, he called out, "Hello? Is someone here?" Only the fairies answered him, and for a moment I caught glimpses of their pale, pointed faces among the rocks. *"We're here, Simon. Do you like the fire? Hello, Simon! Hello, hello, Simon! Look over here!"*

Simon could not hear them, either. I suspected that they were teasing him to entertain me. He sat down, pulled off his wet coat, and tossed it over a rock near the fire. King Harry jumped up on it and groomed himself irritably, lashing his tail from side to side. He had heard the fairies, and he was not entertained. Simon leaned over and began tugging on one of his boots.

Oh, Simon, don't pull off your boots! I thought. You will need them on your feet if you have to run.

But he only shook a stone from his boot and then pulled it back on. For a while longer, he sat very still, as if listening, and occasionally he looked into the dark beyond the fire. Finally he took off his wet boots, and only then did he call to me to join him. The fire was hot, and I sat down gratefully. Striker crawled out of my cloak and stretched, then looked around. The warmth and flickering light seemed to suit him very well. He wagged his tail and sat close to me.

"The logs don't burn down to ash," Simon said suddenly. "Look, Singer. This really is a fairy fire."

"I thought fairy fires didn't give off heat," I said.

"They do if you want heat," King Harry said. "And I do." He curled up by the fire, looked into it, and blinked.

Simon and I opened our packs and took out food. "Do you want something to eat, cat?" Simon asked King Harry.

"I wouldn't touch anything *you* have in your ragged old pack, thank you," King Harry said crossly, and he closed his eyes and slept.

But Striker begged cold meat from Simon in a most charming way, holding his head to one side and wagging his tail, and when I took out my bread, he gave me only a quick look and returned to Simon. When we were done, Simon lay down facing the fire and seemed to fall asleep. Striker returned to me and curled in my lap. Was I to be the guardian over us, then?

No. The dark around me was filled with quivering figures, small and tall, murmuring my name. "Gwenore, we watch over you. Do not fear the dark." "Gwenore, the land of Lir is only a dream away, a song away, a sigh away. The children are waiting for you. The children need you."

Lir? Was this not Ireland? What children were waiting for me?

Dawn would come, I told myself, and all things would become clear then. I lay down close to the hot fire and slept, too, while the Fair Folk sang songs that sounded more like echoes of music from dreams than anything that had ever been real. I had known beings like them all my life. Now there were more of them—or I was more aware of them—and they comforted me.

As for this land of Lir they spoke of—I would discover it soon enough, if it was to be my destiny.

Thick fog came with morning, and so we were no better off than we had been in the dark. The fairy voices were silent now, and King Harry was grumpy and disagreeable. I asked him to fly off and see if he could find a safe-looking village or farm, but he flatly refused, declaring that while his brother, Vespers, might be stupid enough to fly in fog, he would not. We would have to wait.

And so we did. The fire burned on without consuming the logs, so I knew the Fair Folk had taken good care of us. Then, slowly, the fog thinned and blew away, and we found ourselves sitting in a circle of tall gray stones, surrounded by woods dripping with moisture. Two saddled horses were tethered to the tree nearest us, and they watched us calmly, as if they knew us very well.

"That lunatic old priest sent someone—or something—with them," King Harry said. "I don't like horses, but the beasts will know where we are to go next, so let us mount now. The sooner we leave, the sooner our journey will be over."

"The saddlebags look full," I said as I approached one of the horses. "I hope there is food—and dry clothing."

We found both. First we changed clothes, our backs turned to each other. I would have preferred men's clothing, but my new tunic and gown were made of heavy wool, and they were good enough. I pulled the hood up to hide my white hair and asked, "Where are we going?" even though I knew that neither King Harry nor Simon could answer.

But the horses knew where to go, for without our guidance, they carried us along a narrow path through the woods, over several shallow streams, across a great, sloping, rocky place that was barren of all growing things, and then into another deep wood. Simon sent King Harry off as the crow, to fly high above and tell us what he saw. True to himself alone, as always, King Harry did not bother to come back to us. Now we were left without a way to communicate with Father Caddaric.

And we did not know where the Blessingwood women, Brennan, and Tom were—or even if they were still alive.

Late in the day, when we were about to stop to eat the last of our food, Simon exclaimed, "Look! There's the sea again. I thought we were moving inland."

"We were," I said slowly, apprehensively. I had a good sense of direction, and I was certain that we had been moving steadily west. But here we were, facing a distant view of the sea when we should have been looking at mountains. Somehow we had become lost.

A castle stood on a cliff over the sea, and spread out

below it were a small village and a number of farms with neat fields edged by stone walls.

"What is this place?" I wondered aloud.

The horses trotted toward a narrow road that led into the village, and we turned a curve and saw, ahead of us, a fine wagon pulled by great, strong, white horses with elaborate red harnesses that dangled jingling golden bells. The four blond children in the wagon turned to look back at us, and the boy who seemed to be the largest shouted at the driver to stop. The old man obeyed.

Our horses drew abreast of the wagon and stopped by themselves, as if they knew they should.

"Who are you?" the tall boy demanded. His voice carried authority for one so young, but I did not laugh.

"I am Mary Singer," I said. "And this is my brother, Simon. Who are you?"

The boy said, "We are Lir's children, Mary Singer."

"Who is Lir?" Simon asked. I could tell by his voice that he, too, was amused at the boy's tone.

"'*Who is Lir?*'" exclaimed the boy incredulously. "Our father is the king of Lir, and so he is called Lir, of course, as were our grandfather and great-grandfather. That is our castle on the cliff. Don't you know where you are?"

Simon and I exchanged glances. "No, we are lost," I said.

"How did you come to be lost in so small a place?" the boy asked. "No one is ever lost in Lir. It is impossible."

"Our boat was wrecked on the shore," Simon lied hastily. "We have lost track of our aunts, and we have come to look for them."

"On horses that belong to my father?" the boy asked.

He lifted his chin angrily. "Those *are* our horses. Don't try to deny it."

"We don't deny it," I said. "We found them, and we thought we might find our aunts faster if we rode."

The boy seemed disbelieving, but the other boy, at least three years younger, said, "I like these people, Connor." His two sisters nodded.

"We never see anyone new," the elder girl said. "Invite them to come home with us."

But the elder boy was not so hospitable. "You say *aunts*. How many aunts have you lost?"

"Two," I said quickly, before Simon could say anything. "And their servants. There are four servants, three maids and a young man."

"And *all six* disappeared in the water?"

"No, we lost track of them in the dark and fog once we reached land," Simon said. "We heard them calling, so we know they must be alive and well. We just can't find them."

The children thought this over. The girls whispered to one another, and then the elder one whispered at length to her big brother. He listened, frowning, and finally he nodded.

"Come home with us and meet our father," he said. "He will decide what to do with you. And if your aunts and their servants are anywhere in Lir, he will find them for you."

He tapped the old driver on the shoulder, and the white horses leaned into their jingling harnesses and pulled the wagon away. We followed in silence for a few moments, and then Simon leaned toward me and whispered, "Are you sure we should do this?"

"No," I said. "I am not sure of anything. But I don't

know what else we can do except follow them."

"King Lir," Simon said. "I have never heard of him."

The younger girl looked back at us, smiled, and waved. Were these the children that the Fair Folk talked about? The ones I dreamed about? "I think we are supposed to go with them," I told Simon. "Everything might be unfolding just as it should."

"I'd feel better if that wretched cat were with us. Sometimes he is smarter than he looks."

I wished King Harry was with us, too, if only because he served as a rather undependable source of communication with Father Caddaric. At that moment, it seemed that Simon and I were cut off from everyone.

Part of the castle was new, made of smooth plastered stone in the style brought back from the Holy War, instead of the old earthen works and wooden palisades. Several towers rose above the walls, and the walls sat sturdily on the site of an earlier fort, now only a great mound of earth grown over with grass. A road led straight up to the massive gates, and that surprised me. The castles in our own land were never so approachable. They were surrounded by moats or traps, or by water on three sides, with a cliff on the fourth, and drawbridges to control what little traffic there was. The towers should have had arrow slits, but they did not. No guards were posted on the walls.

We rode through the gatehouse and I looked up, expecting to see a murder hole overhead, where boiling water—or oil or molten lead—could be poured down on intruders, but there was no such place. The ceiling of the gatehouse was painted blue, with clouds and flying birds.

We entered the keep. Long trestle tables were set up in the square, and several dozen people sat there, eating their late-day meal. The children were greeted familiarly by all. The elder boy answered to Connor, and his younger brother was Troy. Fionna was the tall girl, Darbie, the small. All four had pale blond hair and large dark eyes. They were as slender as Fair Folk, and as beautiful. I was certain now that they were the children of my dreams, the children I had seen in my looking glass.

Darbie, lifted out of the wagon by her big brother, ran to me. "May I hold your dog? I have a dog, too, but he is too big to pick up."

I held Striker down to her, and he was glad enough for the exchange, for he was tired of bouncing on a horse and more than glad to be petted by a pretty child. Wearily, I slid down to the ground, and the other girl, Fionna, asked me if I was well.

"Very well," I said, although I was exhausted and wanted nothing more than a hot meal, a bath, and a good bed.

"While you're waiting for my father, I'll have a servant bring food for the two of you in the small sitting room inside," she said, gracious and hospitable for such a young girl.

"Your mother taught you well," I blurted without thinking.

She looked away from me. "My mother died when Darbie was born," she said quietly. "Now, if you and your friend will follow me, I will show you where you can rest.

My sister will bring your dog. You can leave your cloaks and packs on the bench here, by the door."

She led us into a small sitting room paneled in wood and richly furnished with cushioned chairs and a square table sitting on a scarlet wool carpet. Darbie ran in with Striker and whispered, "If you want me to take him for a walk later, I will." Her big sister sent her on her way, and then she supervised the maid who brought in a tray heaped with food and a pitcher of milk.

The woman did not make eye contact with me, and I should have taken more note of that, but I was tired and hungry, and so I was a fool.

We were made comfortable at the table and then left alone, the heavy door closing firmly behind Fionna.

"I'm starving for something besides dried meat and stale bread," Simon said as he reached for a small meat pie.

And then we heard a bolt slide into place with a loud *clack* that froze me where I sat.

"She has locked us in!" Simon and I said at the same moment.

He dropped the pie on the table, and we both leaped up and ran for the door, but it was bolted shut from the outside. We hammered on it with our fists and demanded that Fionna come back and release us, but no one came or answered us.

Simon leaned his forehead against the door and said, "Why didn't I see this coming? I know better than to accept the hospitality of strangers."

"They are only children," I said. "They look so innocent. Who would not trust them?"

"It would not be the first time that fools like us have been led to their deaths by children," he said. He sighed and looked back at the table. "The food might be poisoned, so we should not eat it."

"If only we had King Harry with us," I said. "He might have stayed outside the room, and now he could help us."

Simon crossed to the single small window in the room, but it was stained glass, and nothing outside could be seen through it.

"Does it open?" I asked.

"No. I could break it, but it's too small for us to get through, and probably we'd be caught. We'll have to wait."

The food brought to us did not need knives or spoons to eat, so none had been provided. If they had, they could have been used for weapons. Now I had nothing except the small knife I always carried in my belt, the knife Simon had made for me. I pulled it out. And Simon, seeing what I had done, nodded and pulled out a long, thin knife hidden in his boot.

"I wish the door opened inward," he said. "We could block it with the table and chairs."

"We would be trapping ourselves," I said. "We have no other place to go. Somehow we must slip past whoever opens the door."

"What if it's the girl—what's her name?—and she tries to stop you?" he asked. "How far are you willing to go?"

"It won't be Fionna," I said with more certainty than I felt. "Someone else will come. The father—this King Lir— perhaps. Now that Fionna has trapped us, her work is done."

And so we waited. Striker, sensing my concern, sat beside me on the floor, and sometimes he cocked his head as if he heard some small sound somewhere. But Simon and I heard nothing.

Finally the bolt was thrown back. We stepped closer together, prepared for anything. The door flew open as if shoved by someone very strong, and in came a tall, heavy man with a long red beard and a mane of thick red hair. He wore a simple tunic, but it was purple with a thin line of gold stitching around the hem, and so I knew that this must be the children's father, King Lir.

He filled the doorway. There was no way to dart around him, into whatever freedom there might be behind him. He glared first at me, then at Simon.

And then down at Striker.

"Ah!" he said. He bent down to pick up the dog, but Striker bravely bared his teeth. The giant king laughed and straightened up. "So that is the little rat that my Darbie wants me to buy," he said in a voice so big that it filled the small room. "How much will you take for him, Mary Singer?"

"He is not for sale," I said, hoping that my voice did not shake.

"Put away your knives," King Lir said to us. "The two of you look foolish standing there with your toys. I'm not going to hurt you."

But Simon and I held our knives at the ready.

King Lir sighed. "All right. Play soldier if it makes you feel better. But let us discuss that dog. Darbie wants him, and she will take good care of him. Connor tells me that you have lost your aunts and their servants. I will find them for you and trade the dog for them. What say you to that, Mary Singer?"

The answer was obvious. Of course I must trade my dog for the Blessingwood women, Brennan, and Tom. But the words would not come. Striker, teeth bared, guarded me from this giant, and he was willing to give his life. How could I outsmart this red devil? There must be a way.

King Lir bellowed laughter. "How are you going to live your life, girl, if you cannot resolve a simple philosophical problem like this? Do you think this is the only one you will face?"

Now I understood this bully. Now I understood everything. I shoved my knife back in its place and picked up my dog. "I will have them *all*," I said loudly. "Aunts, servants, and dog. And *you* will not stop me."

He laughed harder, bending backward and shaking his head. Simon, uncertain, still held his knife while he watched the man laugh.

But Striker could not wait any longer. He leaped up, snarling.

King Lir caught him in the air. "Ho, look at this killer dog!" he shouted, and he folded Striker between one thick arm and his side, hugging him tight. "Bite me and I'll bite you back," he told Striker sternly.

My dog stopped snarling as if he understood every word.

King Lir looked down at him approvingly, and then he looked at Simon and me. "Now if I can deal with the two of you that easily, I will be satisfied with this day. Sit down and tell me the real reason you are here."

He took one of the chairs and held Striker on his lap. Simon and I joined him at the table cautiously. "Speak!" King Lir shouted. "I have other tasks at hand today, and all of them are more important than you."

Simon looked at me, and I understood that I was to be responsible for our story. And why not? I was Singer, who put her own poems to music, poems of adventure and exploration and even love.

"We came to Ireland . . ." I began.

"This is Lir, not Ireland," he said, scowling.

Now I was surprised. "Is this not the island of Ireland?"

"It is an island," he said. "And Ireland shares it with us, but only because we allow it. But we are Lir!"

I understood that his pride would keep him from hearing anything I said if I did not mend his wrath. "We wanted to find Ireland," I began again. "Our aunts have a brother there, and when their husbands died, they needed to find a new home. So we set out with our servants and we were caught in a terrible storm. In the darkest night anyone could imagine, we were cast up on land. The boat and boatmen disappeared under the waves, but we knew our aunts lived, because we could hear them calling. And calling." I dropped my voice sadly and covered my eyes with one hand. "It broke my heart. We must believe that they live—but where are they?"

I looked up and saw him studying me closely. "There was a great storm. That I believe. And I also believe that you are looking for someone. But I warn you that your missing companions had better be old women and a few servants, and not a company of armed knights. We do not tolerate knights in this land." He paused for a dramatic moment, and I realized that he was as good a storyteller as I was. "We kill them when we find them," he added with relish.

In spite of myself, I shuddered. I heard Simon's quick intake of breath. Had the king found his sword in his pack outside the door?

"We search for old women and servants," I said. "Please believe us. Can you help us?"

"Why should I?" he demanded. "What can you do for me in exchange, if you will not trade me your little rat?"

"I am a healer and a gardener. I can read and write. I am a poet. I can play every musical instrument you can name, and I fashion my own music, too. And my brother, Simon, is a blacksmith. He can make anything from farm tools to fine metalwork for your castle."

"What if I do not want or need any of those services?"

I sat up a little straighter. "Then we will leave. I am sorry that you are not willing to help us. But your children are charming and beautiful, and I will sing of them wherever I go."

"You will *not!*" he shouted. Striker let out a squeak of alarm and struggled in the king's arms.

I realized my terrible mistake and apologized instantly. "I did not mean to threaten your children's safety," I said. "I meant only to honor their manners and beauty. But if you do not want them spoken of outside the kingdom of Lir, I will never mention their names." And then, my senses somewhat restored, I added, "Nor will I ever mention this kingdom."

I had guessed correctly, for that was what he wanted. I could read it in his mind. But he blustered and said, "I care not whether you tell outsiders of Lir or not. After all, some may have heard of us—and our strong opposition to intruders. But only a devil would mention young children outside of the circle of safety provided by their families."

"You are right," I said. "Now, Your Majesty, are we agreed that Simon and I should leave here immediately and search for our aunts outside your kingdom?"

He searched my face for some hint of hidden meaning, but I was careful that he was shut out of my secrets. "You say you play instruments and sing?" he asked. "You say you are a healer?"

"I am."

He rubbed his jaw. "Then I will make a bargain with you, Mary Singer. Heal my jaw, and your brother will be free to leave to find your aunts."

"What about me?" I asked. "Will I be free to leave?"

"I will offer you employment instead. Remain here, to teach my children to sing and play the harp, as their mother would have if she had lived. When your brother has found your aunts, he can find someone to carry word over the border to you, and you can join them then."

"Would you keep me as a slave?" I asked, for that was what he had meant. If I was not free to leave when I wanted to go, then I was a slave, a prisoner.

He paused, and then said, "Yes, you will be a slave. But only until your aunts are found."

I had no choice but to trust him. "What is wrong with your jaw? I cannot promise to heal you if you do not tell me first what is wrong."

"I have a broken tooth that needs pulling," he said, and he could not hide his wince.

My spirit sank. I had watched Margarite pull teeth a hundred times. I had even watched her clean the rot out of a tooth with a metal burr and fill the hole with gold or a mixture of silver and quicksilver, something she had learned from Umma. I had the proper tools in my pack. But I had never done anything more than extract loose baby teeth from squirming children.

"Let me see," I said. "Please sit down and open your mouth."

He handed Striker to Simon and sat down. I bent to peer into his mouth and saw the offending molar immediately. It was broken in half, and the gum around it was swollen and blackened. I restrained myself from gasping in alarm. He must have been in agony.

"I can pull your tooth—if you are as brave as you look," I said.

His chest expanded and I expected him to roar at me again. But instead, he exhaled and said, "I am brave enough, Mary Singer. But what of the fever I can feel in it?"

"I can mix a concoction of herbs to draw off the fever," I said, more certain of myself now.

He rose suddenly and faced Simon. "What have you to say about all this, Simon?"

Simon glanced at me, and then he said, "I choose to take my sister with me when I leave. She is not a slave."

"No," I said. "No, Simon. Let me stay. When you have found our aunts, send word to me and I will join you wherever you are."

"I will send her to you with an escort of armed men," King Lir told Simon. "I pledge this."

Simon looked into my eyes for a long moment, read my wishes, and then he said, "I will go."

"I will send a good lad with you, and when you are successful, he will return to tell your sister," the king said. He rubbed his jaw again. "And now, Mary Singer, let us do what needs to be done to end my pain."

I drew a deep breath. "Do not worry, Simon. I will see you soon enough." I watched him leave, and then I said, "Please let me have my travel pack, your highness. It contains my instruments and the medicines I will use to draw the fever out of your jaw. I even have something that will ease your pain."

"I need nothing to ease my pain, Mary Singer," he growled. "But you had better be as good a physician as you say you are, for if anything happens to me, your brother will receive your head in a bag and none of your family will leave this island alive. Do you understand me?"

I knew that he was afraid that I would hurt him, but I said, "I understand you completely. As soon as I have my pack, I will apply a drop or two of a healing mixture to your jaw to soothe the inflammation, and then you must sit very still, because that is a big tooth and it will not come out without a struggle, I fear. You are ready for this?"

"I am ready!" he said, and he shouted for a maid to bring in my pack.

He made himself comfortable and opened his mouth. I rubbed three drops of opium into his gums and waited. Briefly.

He slept, snoring, while I inserted a wooden block to hold open his mouth, and then I grabbed his tooth with my pliers, prayed that I would pull it cleanly the first time I tried, and twisted my wrist the way Margarite had shown me.

King Lir awoke later, after I had removed the wooden block and was applying a bitter-tasting concoction to the inflammation in his jaw.

"Phaw!" he shouted, pushing me away. "What a foul taste! When does the tooth come out, Mary Singer? How long must I sit here?"

I handed him the broken, decayed snag that had hurt him for so long. "Here is your tooth," I said. "But it is an ugly thing, so perhaps you do not want to wear it on a gold chain around your neck."

He laughed, spraying blood on both of us, and took the tooth with him when he left the room. He staggered a little, still under the effects of the opium he did not know he had been given.

"What do you think of that, Striker?" I asked my little dog. But he was bored, and he only yawned.

I would not see Simon for far more than a year, and the Blessingwood women, Brennan, and Tom were better hidden than we had imagined. And in the meantime, I served as music teacher and healer for the beautiful children of Lir and their royal household, along with Striker and the truly impossible King Harry, who had returned as a stray cat and charmed Darbie into adopting him.

This was a good year, and I learned to love the land and the people in it. Everyone was friendly, and the children were welcomed everywhere, so we visited all the homes and farms, shared meals with the owners, and returned to the castle with gifts of sweetmeats, cakes, and toys.

King Lir allowed me to consult with all the other physicians, and we exchanged knowledge of instruments and herbs. And one day I healed the young son of the kingdom's most talented weaver. He paid me with new clothing, made of white linen, silk, and wool, and his brother, the very best cobbler, made white shoes for me, sewn with pearls and silver beads.

I should have been happy. I *was* happy! But at night I longed for my friends, and when King Harry joined me in my room, I pressed him for news. He rarely had any, and sometimes I wondered if his life with Darbie had spoiled him so much that he did not want to leave this place.

Then everything changed. The king went on a long journey after that year, and in some months, he returned with a new wife—and I was forced to flee for my life again.

11

WHite WOLf RISINǴ

another summer was at an end. Three of the children of Lir and I took advantage of the good weather to move our classroom outside, to a grassy hill in sight of the castle. Servants had carried several musical instruments and food for us, and they spread carpets and pillows over the grass. They were supposed to return to the castle, but they remained behind, secluded behind a low hedge, to listen to the children sing. In the year and more that the king had been traveling in England, his children had developed voices like angels, and I was eager for him to return and hear them.

I could not have imagined better students. Connor, too, had been a fine student, but his father had taken him to England with him, to put him in the service of a rich nobleman while the boy learned the skills he would need when it was his turn to be king of Lir. Connor would not return for ten years—long after I was gone (I hoped)—and after that he would begin to assume some of the royal duties. Perhaps he might even bring a wife with him, although Fionna had confided that her father once said that he would not want his son to marry an English woman, because there was the danger of Lir's becoming too attractive to the superior English armies. Every small kingdom, even one as well hidden within mountain ranges as Lir, worried about attack. The world was an evil place. All of us looked forward to the return of the king, for his presence gave us a sense of security that the elderly chancellor could not, even though I was sure he tried to fill the king's place.

King Harry, bored with flutes, harps, and drums, slept on one corner of a blanket, while Striker slept on another, his back turned to the cat. They had never made friends, and if King Harry had not been such a fine source of news, I would have ignored him as completely as Striker did.

Long before, King Harry had reported to me that Simon had not found the Blessingwood women, but the cat had heard news of Brennan and Tom that might—or might not—be true. The Fair Folk regarded truth as a kind of coinage, to be spent or saved according to whims of their own.

I was sorry to learn that all my friends were not together. But King Harry said that everyone was well except for Julienne, and she was no worse than she had been before. The Blessingwood women had established themselves at a small convent hidden in a remote forest, where they had been welcomed for their skills. The exact location was concealed behind layers of veils put in place by Father Caddaric, and not even the Fair Folk could penetrate them. I hoped that King Harry's relatives were truthful about Julienne, at least.

Brennan and Tom, as mother and son, labored on a large farm as free workers and lived in a hut, separate from the slaves. Simon had found work at a forge, in a village not far over the border of Lir. Secretly, he made weapons, King Harry reported with a smile.

"Why could we not all live together somewhere?" I had asked King Harry. "Was there not a place for us in all of Ireland? It would take only a short time for your relatives to tell everyone where we could meet safely. Why didn't Father Caddaric arrange something like that for us?"

"There is no safe place because you would cause too much talk," King Harry had said. "It's your fault, Gwenore. You with that white hair and birthmark—and your evil little white dog. And, of course, Tom and Brennan might be identified if they were with you. Do you want them dead? Just how selfish are you? As for the Blessingwood women, they are old. Leave them alone. They have a good life where they are, and you have a good life here. You may be a slave, but you live as well as if you were a blood relative of the king's. Your clothing—white linen and wool and even white silk, if you please!—is the best to be had. Your shoes are white and sewn with pearls. The gold necklace you wear is worth more than you would be worth if the king were to sell you."

"Did King Lir ever send out anyone to search for the Blessingwood women?" I had asked, attempting to drag the conversation back to what was important.

"Don't be silly," King Harry had said. "He does not plan to let you go. You are his most useful slave. You are raising his children in place of their mother. Why should he find your missing aunts? He never intended to do that."

◁ ◁ ◁

But that day on the hill, I had almost forgotten the cat's dire view of my future, and I relaxed in the warm sun, enjoying the children and their music. Suddenly, King Harry woke from a sound sleep, startled, as if he had heard something. His hair stood on end. I had heard nothing except the singing and the calling of a few gulls that had flown inland.

Then King Harry pretended to yawn and stretch, but I could see that he was eager to run off in search of something. After a moment or two, he did. Darbie called, "Goldie!" after him, but he never had answered to the name she had given him. He disappeared into the nearby woods without a backward glance at us.

"He wants to hunt," I told her. "Cats are like that." But my heart was beating too quickly. King Harry was looking for his relatives, the Fair Folk. Had they appeared as gulls? He must have heard them calling. I would have to wait until he returned to discover if they bore important messages, or only more nonsense regarding his family's incessant quarrels and disagreements that seemed no closer to resolution than they had when I had first met him.

Fionna was practicing a difficult piece on her harp. She had written words for a song to welcome home her father when he came. Troy, interrupting her, banged on his drum and said, "That's too sad! When he comes, let us have a marching song, with flutes and drums. Lots of drums."

"He's not coming back from a war," Fionna complained. "Papa wouldn't like your spending so much time with the boys in the stables, talking about fighting, fighting, fighting. We, in Lir, don't fight."

"We might someday," Darbie said suddenly, surprising me.

I looked at her quickly. The tone of her voice worried me.

She avoided my gaze.

"Why did you say that?" I asked.

She looked down and pleated her silk skirt between her small fingers.

"Darbie, you must tell me," I said.

"I dream things," she said vaguely, avoiding my eyes.

"What sort of things?" I asked.

Her face turned red and she began weeping. I gathered her into my arms and tried to comfort her, but she would not be soothed.

"What is it?" I said. "It's safe to tell me."

She shook her head. "You will be angry with me."

"I promise I will not," I said. "Shall we walk over near the woods and you can tell me privately?"

"I want to hear, too!" Troy shouted. "She shouldn't have secrets from the rest of us."

"Practice on your drum," I said. "Maybe Fionna will play her flute for you to keep time to." I picked Darbie up and started toward the edge of the woods. Striker jumped up and followed.

"Now," I said, when we had reached the shade of a great beech tree. "Tell me what worries you so."

She still would not look at me. But finally she said, "It was not a dream. I went into your room. I took out your looking glass. . . ."

She faltered. I had to struggle to keep my face expressionless. She had looked into it? What might she have seen, besides her own reflection?

"And what did you see, Darbie?" I asked, when I could be sure that my voice would not give me away.

"I saw men fighting on the hills around the castle," she said. "I saw your brother...."

"You saw Simon?"

She nodded. "I saw him fall, with blood on his chest, and he did not get up. And Papa was asleep in his bed and I could not wake him. And then I was high in the air and could not reach him. And the terrible woman—the terrible, black-haired woman ..."

"What terrible woman?" I asked urgently. But I already knew, even before she said the name. Oh, yes, I knew.

"She was called Rhiamon."

My mother. I hugged Darbie close. What could I say? That my mother might find me and injure (oh, not kill!) Simon, and men would be fighting around King Lir's castle?

"Are you sure you weren't asleep?" I asked her softly.

She shook her head. "And on the back of the looking glass, I saw a wolf with hair like yours—white."

I pressed my cheek against her hair. "What was the wolf doing?" I asked.

"It was running and running," she said.

"Ah, well," I said, desperately searching my mind for a story that could explain this. "The wolf was running to protect you and your family. Don't fear anything. As long as the white wolf guards you, you have nothing to fear. Now tell me, did you like seeing yourself in the mirror? Did you find out how pretty you are?"

She nodded and smiled a little. "I am as pretty as Fionna," she said.

I loved small Darbie as I would a child of my own, or a precious little sister. As much as I resented being kept in slavery by her father, her presence made my captivity almost worth it. She, her sister, and her brothers were like my own kin now. I would do anything for them.

But I could not stay here. Not unless there was real danger for them and they needed me for protection. And the only way I could discover that was to wait until King Harry returned.

He did not come back. I called the servants and asked them to take the blankets and cushions back to the castle. The children, Striker, and I dawdled behind, enjoying the last of the warm afternoon. I watched the skies for crows and the grass for the shiver of light that meant fairies were near. The grass was still, and no wind stirred the leaves on the trees. The landscape held no enchantment then.

The children had their supper late, and then their personal servants helped them to bed. I sat alone in the small sitting room that had been given to me as the castle's musician. I had left the window open so that King Harry could come in, and at dusk, he did, fluttering inside and alighting on the sill.

"What have you learned?" I asked quickly.

"The worst news of all," he said. He turned into the cat

and jumped down to the carpet. Striker, who had been sleeping, woke to wag his tail once before he remembered that he hated the cat.

"Are you hungry?" I asked King Harry. "I'll give you something to eat while you talk."

"I ate with Vespers," he said. "Some sort of dried stuff that he refused to identify, so I suppose he was ashamed of it. But he sends news from the priest. And from a hundred birds between here and London. King Lir has married your mother."

"What?" I gasped.

"How is that for news to gripe one's soul?" he asked. "I will repeat it to make sure you understand. *King Lir has married your evil mother.* He left Connor with the boy's sponsor, which is good, because your mother was already planning how she might poison him. And she still has plans for that, but the priest has set Vespers to warning the Fair Folk all around to destroy the boy's food and drink if they contain poison. And to kill the poisoner. Well, it wasn't exactly the priest who decided that. My brother is quite competent in his own right."

"And!" I prompted.

"And King Lir and his new wife have set forth for home. They will travel to the west coast slowly, so that *she* can be entertained royally along the way. And then they will set sail for Lir in a fine ship with golden sails."

I closed my eyes for a moment. Then I asked, "How long do I have?"

"Long enough to escape—and a little more," he said.

"I cannot leave the children," I said. "I must find a way to protect them. If my mother wanted to poison Connor, she surely will want to kill Troy. And probably the girls, too. She will want to bear her own heir to the kingdom. All she's ever wanted was a son."

Even the cat sighed at that. "True," he said. "But if she sees you—even grown now and with white hair—she will go mad and forget her newest plans. She could destroy the entire kingdom before she is done."

"Did the priest tell you what I should do?" I asked.

"Run, of course," he said. "We have sent messages to Simon and Julienne. They can usually hear Fair Folk. The women and Tom will all meet at Simon's forge near the border, to wait for you."

"And then what?" I asked. "Where can we go?"

"The priest has a plan," he said. "He would not tell me. But he is meeting with other priests, explorer priests. You may well be on your way to a new land, Gwenore. Who can tell?"

I sighed. "The plan will not work. It would leave the children in danger. I cannot do that."

"You cannot take them with you!" he cried. "Do you know what would happen to you—to everyone—if you stole the children of a king? You would not find shelter anywhere in the world. Explorer priests go many places, but Rhiamon has black magic of the worst kind, and it can go anywhere. If only you—"

"I have to keep them safe," I said.

"*If only you had worked to develop your skills!*" he shouted.

"I hate being interrupted, Gwenore!" He fluttered into the shape of a crow. "And I hate flying in the dark!" he complained. "But I will go out and send word to Father Caddaric. We shall see what he has to say about this."

"Don't leave me alone without news for very long," I begged as he jumped to the windowsill. "I cannot bear not hearing from you."

He looked back at me with one bright, black eye. "If you long for news, go to the great oak at the edge of the forest. There is an owl living there who is only half mad, and sometimes he hears messages from the creatures that live underground. If they tell him enough, he lets them go instead of eating them."

With a cackle of laughter, he flew off into the dark.

Striker jumped into my lap and leaned hard against me, to comfort me. His muzzle was turning gray. His eyes were clouded. My beloved little companion was growing old. He looked into my eyes, and I wept over him. Why could not life be simple and safe?

Why?

My heart broke a thousand times every day. The children of Lir! I must help them somehow. But what small magic I had did not extend to enterprises as great as that. I had no magic teacher, and my mind's eye seemed to be blind. The mirror offered me nothing when I begged for help. I even took out Elaine's tapestry and hoped that it would show me something that could help. But the figures on it did not move.

One day I went alone to the oak at the edge of the forest. There was an owl there, just as King Harry had said, and he was awake, as if he had been waiting for me.

"I need help," I said. "I need news of the people I love."

"I have no news," he said. "But I don't exactly remember eating a possible messenger, either, so it may not have come. But what other help do you need? You have that look about you of the ones who should know how to help themselves but prefer to let others do it for them."

"My magic is not strong enough. I want to save the children, but I only know how to run and hide. That is all I have ever done."

"Shame on you, Gwenore," he said. "You always had the changing magic. You were born with that gift. Why did you never use it?"

I had no idea what he was talking about, and I told him so.

"You can change a creature into something else," he said. "If you try hard enough, that is. But better yet, you have the gift to prolong life. Instead of sniveling over your little dog—and believe me when I say that he is *not* too big to eat—you could extend his life by half again as long as he was meant to live."

How had he learned that about me when I did not know it myself? "You're a liar," I said flatly. "If I had been given the gift of prolonging life, Father Caddaric would have told me about it."

The owl laughed. "You are very amusing, Gwenore. You have the sign of life on your wrist. The drop of blood! That is life! How stupid are you? And the nuns taught you to write, so you can write in blood. And they taught you to sing, so you can sing the blood into a spell. *Sign, blood, sing, spell!* What more do you want, *Singer?*"

He fluttered his wings, and I was afraid he would fly away before I was done with him. "Wait!" I said.

"Sign, blood, sing, spell!" he shouted as he flew off. "And you didn't ask about the other gift, Gwenore."

My birthmark burned. I looked down at it and saw that it leaked fresh blood. It had never done that before.

I touched a drop of blood with my finger, then, remembering the signs on the stone in the Middle Passage, I used my blood to draw a sword on the back of my hand. "Make me a warrior," I sang softly, with my eyes closed. "Make me tireless and strong. Cast away my enemies. Raise up my friends."

But if there was a change in me, I did not feel it. Another drop of blood leaked out of my birthmark, and, after a moment's hesitation, I drew a sun. If I could not do one thing, then perhaps I could do another.

"By the sign of the sun," I whispered, barely able to sing now, "my Striker is young. I decree it happening, I proclaim it *done.*"

That time the air around me shivered, and I heard Fair Folk chattering excitedly. "Gwenore, Gwenore!" they cried. "Our Lady Gwenore, the Singer!"

I walked home, refusing to allow myself the slightest touch of doubt. I did not fear failure as I pushed open the door of my room. I knew what I would find. I knew it!

Striker was lying on my bed, alert, tail wagging.

The gray was gone from his muzzle. His eyes were as bright and clear as they had been when both he and I were young together. I picked him up and held him so tightly that he protested with a squeak.

So, I thought, now I know something the priest would not tell me. What harm would there have been in his letting me know that I could lengthen life? Was there no end to his deceit?

"I need you by my side while I learn more about my gift," I told my dog.

But there was something else that the owl had said. Now I remembered. I could change one creature into another? That was frightening, and not something I would want to try. Extending life—that was good. Healing? That was good. But did not every creature want to live out its own life?

I went to sleep that night, wondering why Father Caddaric had given me such a strange gift. And what good it really was.

But he had not given me that gift, after all. It was bred into me from my wicked mother, she who could turn living babes into blue corpses. She had done it. And here, in this castle, were other children who were in her way.

One morning, the chancellor told the children that their father was bringing home a new wife, a new mother for them, in four days. Messengers had been sent in relays from England to bring him the news.

He came in while the children and I were breaking our

fast, and from the expression on his face, I knew he was sorry to bring them these tidings. But the news of the marriage was not the end of it.

While the three children still sat in their chairs, stunned, the chancellor told me that I would have to leave the kingdom immediately.

"No, no!" Darbie cried. "She cannot leave us!"

"Why does she have to go?" cried Fionna.

"What will we do without her?" demanded Troy.

The chancellor, elderly and frail, sat down suddenly as if his legs had given out from beneath him. His face was white; his age-spotted hands trembled. From inside his robe, he withdrew a rolled paper and, while we waited, he smoothed it out on the table so that he could read it.

The king's strong writing was on it, and even upside down, I recognized "Mary Singer."

"'The new queen,'" the chancellor read, "'desires to be all things to my children. She will be their mother as well as their fond teacher and nurse. From her they will learn all the noble manners that suit their station, and, because she already loves them, she will be jealous of anyone seeking to displace her. Therefore, the slave called Mary Singer must depart the castle and the kingdom forthwith. I commission you to present her with her Writ of Freedom, ten gold pieces, and suitable clothing and food for a journey. Send a man to escort her to the border and watch to see that she takes to the road swiftly, so that the queen will not be distressed by the accidental sight of one who might cause her pain and unhappiness.'"

The old man looked up at me and said, "I will send you on a horse with a suitable guard to take you to the village nearest to the other side of the border. He would not object to that."

"There is no need," I said, my mouth so dry that I could barely speak. "I can take care of myself."

Was this a blessing? I could not yet tell. I had been waiting to hear news of the king, and I planned to run away immediately. But I had not expected that I would be made to leave. However, at least I would not be an escaped slave.

"What is this woman's name?" Fionna asked worriedly. "This woman who has married our father?"

"Rhiamon," the chancellor said, pursing his lips as if the name tasted bad—and indeed it did. "But you will address her as Your Majesty, of course. Perhaps in the future, she will allow you to call her Mother."

"I will never call her Mother," Darbie shouted. "I would rather be dead than call a strange woman Mother."

My blood turned to ice. I knew the future in an instant. Darbie would be the first one my mother would kill, because she would be the most rebellious.

The chancellor left, after murmuring a few ineffectual words that helped no one, not even himself. The children immediately began babbling their assurances to me. Their papa would not dismiss me. There had been a mistake. They would explain to him how important I was to them. They would make everything right, if only I would stay and give them a chance to make it clear to him—and to their new stepmother—that I was a necessary part of the household.

I could not listen anymore. They had no idea how much danger they were in, nor how much worse it would be if my mother caught a glimpse of me and recognized me. I got up and told them that I would see them later, outside on the hill, and we would have our music lesson there.

In my room, I spent a while staring into my looking glass, willing it to show me the future. I needed to make plans, but I could not do it unless I knew what I would be facing. But I saw nothing in the glass except my own face. Striker whimpered as he watched me.

King Harry flapped in through the open window, shook his feathers, and dropped to the floor as a cat. "She caught us all by surprise," he said.

"What do you mean?"

"Your mother has a few new skills," he said sourly. "She has learned to surround herself and anyone with her with a veil of forgetfulness. The Fair Folk don't remember seeing her, so they can't report her movements. At least, they can't so far. Clever, isn't she? But there is a goblin who hates her, and he is preparing a spell to dissolve the veil. We'll know when she is close, he promises. He does not often do favors for the Fair Folk, but he and your mother had a falling out when last she traveled through his fell, and now he wants nothing more than her downfall."

"She is four days away, according to the chancellor," I said.

"That was not true even when it was written," he said. "The king wanted to surprise the children. He and the evil one will be here tomorrow."

Now the mirror I held was flooded with images. King Harry jumped back from it in surprise.

I saw my mother standing at the prow of a ship, looking toward Lir's castle on the cliff. I saw her paging through a small, ancient book of poisons. I saw her servants searching the woods for me, but the owl had created a false dream wall around me, and so they passed Striker and me by. Striker, me—*and Simon and Tom!*

"They are coming?" I asked King Harry. "Simon and Tom are coming here?"

"As soon as Vespers got hold of himself and sorted it all out, we sent relatives to Simon to warn him, and they confessed that they knew how to find Tom. The young men are coming to help you."

"What about the woman with Tom? Brennan? And the Blessingwood women? Where are they?"

"They, also, will come to your aid, but they will not cross into Lir, not yet—not until you have drawn your blade and used it."

I stared at him. "Drawn my blade?"

"Gwenore, did you think you could save the children without spilling blood? But that is not to happen yet. Not yet. More fearful things come first, but I cannot describe them, because I do not know. Ask your mirror."

But the mirror now showed only my face, pale, with heavy white hair pulled back from it, and my dark blue eyes staring back at me.

I looked like a young witch. I looked more like a witch than my mother ever had.

12

BLack witch, white witch

During the night, King Harry came into my room, switching his tail and scowling. I had left a lamp burning because I was unable to sleep, and the dim, flickering light consoled me. King Harry blew it out with one irritated puff.

"Why don't you invite your mother's spies inside for a cup of cider? You don't lock your door—"

"I have no lock! The king would not allow it!"

King Harry sighed and sat on the bed, where he contemplated Striker contemptuously. "He looked much better as an old dog, and I certainly felt safer around his dull old teeth."

Striker displayed his sharp white teeth.

"Why are you here? Do you have news?" I asked.

"News of a sort," he said. "The Red Goblin sent word across the water that he has melted your mother's veil of forgetfulness, so everyone will know when she approaches shore. But I hope you will be gone by then. I doubt if she could recognize you only by sight, for you have changed much, Gwenore. But she has other senses. And she never believed in her black heart that you had died."

"What of Father Caddaric?" I asked. "Where is he?"

King Harry sighed. "My cousin reports that he is residing in a monastery on the western coast of Ireland, and he is completing his plans to travel with the explorer priests. You and your friends will be included in the journey, of course. But whether he will come to your aid here, to rescue the children, I cannot say. I suspect that he would think you are a fool."

"How many times must I say that I will not leave the children behind when I go? No matter what happens to me afterward, they must be kept safe until my mother can be dealt with."

"And how many times does anyone have to tell you that you cannot kidnap a king's children? Why not plan to kill your mother as soon as she arrives? That would be easier. And it's a plan that would bring cheers all over the world."

He was right. But I did not know how I could kill her. She was my mother! And my own magic was not the right sort. There was a weakness to it, or perhaps "weakness" was not the correct word. There was a *difference* to it, one that prevented me from dwelling for very long on ways that could cause physical harm to people. And, even though I knew better, part of me still hoped that one day my witch mother would love me, and we could be truly mother and daughter.

I sighed from my heart. "Perhaps I might change her into something else, if it is true that I have that power."

"What creature could she become that would not be as

dangerous as she is now?" King Harry asked in his practical way. "Even as an insect, she would be the kind that could sting you and leave you lying on your back, stone dead, while she scuttled off laughing to rob your bedchamber of everything, including your night pot."

I shook my head. It was hopeless. My mother was powerful and magical. No one could get rid of her—or change her—not even the daughter who had wanted to love her for so long.

"I will stay here and guard the children," I said. "But the others should go with the explorers—the Blessingwood women, Brennan, Simon, and Tom."

King Harry sighed mightily and then studied one paw. "The Fair Folk—at least those who are sober and intelligent (and I can count *them* on one paw)—say that a great battle is coming, too soon for anyone to escape from it. And it will be all *your* fault, of course."

"There is *always* a great battle coming," I said. "That's all people do—just as they always find someone to blame, especially someone who was only trying to help. Wars, killing, blame . . . that's what people do."

"It is the same with us," he said, and he sounded almost cheerful. "Except that we don't kill one another. Humans really are so dreadfully crude." And with that, he was gone.

I lay awake for a long time, wishing I might have a prophetic dream that would tell me what I should do next. But when I finally slept, it was to dream of playing with Striker and the children of Lir near the beautiful small lake that the children had shown me once.

In the morning, the chancellor presented me with my Writ of Freedom and a small sack of gold pieces while we stood by the table in the small dining room. He made a ceremony of it, for the children's benefit, but they were unhappy and agitated instead of satisfied. As soon as the chancellor left the room, the children jumped up and clustered around me.

"You won't really go, will you?" Darbie begged. "Can't you hide in the stables or in the attics for a few days, until everyone forgets about you?"

Poor little girl. My mother would remember every detail she had heard of the young musician who was caring for the king's helpless children, and she would be madly jealous. "They won't forget about me," I said. "Probably the servants have all been warned to watch that I don't return. They would surely catch me if I tried to hide in the castle."

"Then hide in the woods!" Troy cried. "There are places in the woods that Connor and I found, old gamekeepers' huts. And remember the hidden lake we showed you? There is an old cottage there! There are even caves on the side of the cliff. We know them all! I'll show you. . . ."

I shook my head. Whatever my plans would be, I could not tell the children. My mother would read their innocent minds in an instant. "I must leave—but I promise that I will keep in touch with you. I'll send you messages, once I find someone I can trust. And you can send messages to me."

They did not smile. Their dark eyes were somber and frightened, and their minds were jumbled with unhappy thoughts and worries. But even the worst of their worries did not approach the true danger they were in. And the closer my mother got to them, the greater the danger. She would have her own heir, one way or another, with no young competitors around to distract the king. Or have a share of his gold one day when he was dead.

What could I tell them to keep them safe? Be careful about the food they ate? I could not predict which poison my mother might use. Do not put on garments that look or smell strange? She could poison clothing, too, so that the wearer died within hours. Be cautious about letting strangers approach them? My mother was capable of hiring someone to harm them, even someone they knew. She was very rich, and even richer now that she was a queen at last.

But—would she do such obvious things? The court physicians could easily detect poison. No strangers would ever be allowed to approach the children too closely. She would be caught, and no matter how besotted the king was with her, he would see her dead immediately if she harmed his children.

No, my mother would use what she had used on Sir Richard's wife, the gift of changing a person into something else. The living and unborn babies had been turned into dead babies, without her touching the mother. Here in Lir, living children would turn into dead children, blue and silent, probably while they were tucked up in their beds. And she would look innocent and grief-stricken. The deaths would be blamed on the many sudden illnesses that afflicted the young, illnesses often carried by travelers in ways no one understood. The king might kill everyone who accompanied him on his travels, to punish the ones who had caused his children to sicken and die, but he would not harm his new wife. His new *grieving* wife.

"I must finish packing," I told the children. "But before I do that, I will tell you a great secret that you must not repeat. If you need to let me know something quickly, look for a crow and tell him."

"Are crows magic?" Fionna asked eagerly. She had always loved stories about magical creatures.

"Some are. They listen to humans talk, and they repeat the words to other humans," I said. Surely they had already heard stories of crows that learned to mimic musical instruments and even the sounds of tools that workmen used. "Eventually I'll hear whatever you want me to hear."

"Papa said that he saw a crow once that made the sound of the soldiers' trumpets and drums, and he called out a whole army at the wrong time," Troy said. "You are sure that crows can repeat words?"

"Yes, I have heard them. But don't talk to crows when anyone else is listening." (Especially your new stepmother, I wanted to add.) "You might have to go into the woods. Tell a crow to find me, and offer him a bit of food to pay him for carrying your message."

They wanted to believe me. They wanted to believe that something magical could reunite us safely. And talking to crows would lighten their hearts.

Oh, those sweet children! So much pain was waiting for them.

What they did not know and could not know was that
Darbie's cat, Goldie—King Harry—would report to me regularly on the children—and my mother.

I left soon after, riding with a stableman who had been given
the task of seeing me over the border into Ireland. He did
not speak to me during the next hours, and I could think of
nothing to say to him, either. Striker and I were comfortable
enough on the broad back of a placid old mare, and I would
have liked to keep her. But I knew I would be refused.

At the boundary of Lir, we first crossed between giant
stone pillars that had been carved with strange symbols so
long before that the symbols were barely visible, and then we
passed over an old stone bridge. Lounging against the far side
of the bridge, on the Irish side, a dozen grotesque trolls
watched us and picked their yellow teeth with the tips of
their daggers. One, who might have been the leader, shouted, "Pay your toll! Pay your toll!" He wore clothes so soiled
that I could not tell what color they might have been, and
his beard was tangled and greasy. His nose and ears sprouted
hair, but his head was bald and wrinkled.

There were no trolls in Lir, but no one had told me that
I would see them so soon once we left that lovely land. They
stared at me insolently and nudged one another with their
elbows. While they were only half as tall as I, there was something about their ugliness that made them seem huge and
dangerous. Of course, they *were* dangerous. I had been frightened of trolls all my life, and for a long time I could not
understand why most of the people around me in Wales

could not see them, too. Brennan never could. Sometimes I had thought that Tom might see them, but I was afraid to ask. If he did not know that such creatures existed, it was better that he never learn.

At Blessingwood, there had been no trolls, either. I should have asked why not. Was it because the goodness of those women raised up a barrier to creatures such as trolls?

The man with me threw a handful of silver coins on the ground, to pay our toll, and the trolls scrambled to pick them up, quarreling among themselves and even striking one another. One, the smallest, made some sort of sneering remark in a language I did not understand, and the others fell on him and beat him until he could no longer get up. They ignored his noisy groans and weeping, and they returned to bickering with enthusiasm.

"Norse trolls," the man said disgustedly. "The Norse invaders brought them. They've killed off most of the Irish trolls."

We reached the village quickly, down a short stretch of road that looked as if it was not used often. Grass grew over most of it, and in many places the brambles nearly covered it. Apparently the trolls behaved here as the knights did in England, demanding tolls from travelers. News of that would get around soon enough and discourage anyone from wanting to journey from one land to another.

Or had King Lir so discouraged travelers that no one was even curious about his land?

The village looked quiet enough, with only a small stone church at the end of it, so small that it could not have held more than twenty people standing crushed together. Next to it, a graveyard lay near chestnut trees and one enormous willow. There were no shops in the village, and no guild signs hung outside any of the doorways. A few peddlers' carts sat before houses where people showed their wares—baked goods and fruit, mostly—and one small table displayed knitted goods. Even though it must have been market day, there were no more than a dozen people walking around. A half-dozen children played a game with sticks and a wooden ball, running back and forth on the narrow street, where a mother sow and her babies rooted around in the dirt.

The man helped me down and unloaded my packs, which he dropped on the ground without a word. Then he caught up the mare's reins and led her away, still without a word. I wondered if he knew why he had brought me here, or if he envied me for having been made free.

I turned to face the village. Striker wanted down to walk, but I was worried about what might be loose around there. Striker was no match for large, angry watchdogs—or for an annoyed mother sow, either.

I saw immediately that there was no inn, one more proof that they did not have travelers here, even though they were close to the borders of Lir. But then, in all of Lir there was not a single inn. What better way to discourage anyone from wanting to spend time in a country? Or ever return.

I would have to go from door to door in the village to find a place that would let me rent a room or even a bed. This was not something I looked forward to, in part because none of the children had looked directly at me. Children usually are the easiest ones to befriend, and in a place where the children will not approach someone, the adults are certain to be suspicious and perhaps even hostile.

But first, I had to find the blacksmith's shop, because that was where I would find Simon. It was not difficult. I heard the ring of a hammer on metal while the smithy was still out of sight. I hurried a little, hoping to see Simon, and Striker must have understood that we were about to find a friend, because his tail wagged.

Simon and an old man stood at the forge, concentrating on their work. I paused, trying to decide how to approach them. But Striker took the lead, and began barking imperiously.

Simon turned around, and when he saw us, he laughed. "It's my sister, Mary!" he said, loud enough for the people on the street to hear. Everyone within earshot turned to watch, and now most were smiling. Simon must be well liked here, I thought.

Simon ran to embrace me, and he whispered in my ear, "I told everyone that you were walking here from a convent two days' journey away."

"Brother," I said in firm tones, "you need a haircut and a good scrubbing."

The old man laughed at that, and came over to be introduced to me. He liked Striker on sight, and Striker allowed himself to be patted on the head by a grimy, broad hand.

"My landlady will make room for you," Simon told me. "I'm afraid it's only a corner in the storeroom, but I made sure the bed has clean straw. And when you are rested, tomorrow or the next day, we can make our journey east."

"I don't want to lose him," the old man told me. "He's the best helper I've ever had. But he told me about the death of your father, so the little brothers and sisters at home will need both of you now."

Little of my hair showed under my headdress, but he looked curiously at it, and I knew he wondered why it was white.

"I was very ill once when I was a child," I said, before he asked. "My hair turned white then."

"Ah well," he said in as philosophical a tone as he could manage. "No one will be wanting to marry a woman who looks old while she's still young, so it's good that your brother is willing to take care of you."

Simon blurted out a laugh, but then he said, "My sister can take care of herself. She is a fine healer, trained by one of the best in all England, and if you let her, she will take out that tooth that bothers you and get rid of the wart on your foot."

Now the old man looked at me differently, with a kind of respect that not many spinsters ever got. "If Simon swears by you, then I'll believe it," he said.

That night, after Simon had poured many mugs of wine down the old man's throat, I easily pulled his rotten front tooth and burned off the wart that covered his heel. When he sobered up a little, I told him that he must spend at least one day sitting in a chair with his foot propped up. He yelled that he could not because he was needed, but Simon assured him that he would stay until the old fellow was ready to work again.

That did not disrupt our plans. The extra day would give me time in the woods, to consult with whatever Fair Folk would consent to help me. And I needed time with my looking glass. There was a way to get the future from it, I was certain. I needed to know the future so that I could create my part in it.

In the dark storeroom, Simon told me his plans. We would journey eastward for half a day, and then turn south. Along the road, we would receive messages from Father Caddaric about our destination. "Before the month is out, we will be on our way to another land," Simon said.

"I cannot go," I said. I told him that I would not abandon the children to my mother, and I asked him for his help. "If you do not want to go back with me, at least share any ideas you might have that will help me rescue them. My mother is powerful, and she will want them dead. She will have arrived in the castle by now. I cannot rest until I find a way to protect them from her." I hesitated only a moment before I added, "Or get rid of her."

In the dark, I sensed that he was staring at me. "The children are not your responsibility."

"All children belong to all of us," I argued. "We all have the responsibility to make sure they are not harmed."

He sighed. "Let me think on this overnight," he said. "We can send a message to the priest—a crow has moved into the attic and he seems reliable enough. The priest may think of something."

"There isn't much time," I warned Simon. "My mother will destroy the children as quickly as possible."

"Let me think on it," he repeated.

◀ ◀ ◀

Halfway through the night, while I still lay awake, I heard a harp playing nearby. Or at least I thought I did. I sat up in order to hear better, and the sound died away abruptly, leaving a kind of ringing in the air, an unpleasant sound that was more physical sensation than anything else. It repulsed me.

"Is someone there?" I asked softly.

"I've caught you!" a voice shrieked. "I've fooled you and I've caught you, Gwenore! You are mine now, and this time I will finish what was begun so long ago. I will finish it, Gwenore! Finish it!"

My mother's voice filled the storeroom. The room swam with purple and dark green lights, pouring forth from the mouth of a creature that sat on a roof beam over my head. I had no idea what it was, but I guessed that it was something very like a troll, something my mother had taken over in order to give me her message.

My knife, in its ornate silver belt, was folded by my side, but a knife would not protect me from a creature like this. Striker pressed against me, whimpering, and I pulled him against my chest. The beast overhead coughed up a ball of light that tore toward us, and I raised up my left hand protectively.

The ball of light veered away and blew out like a harmless candle flame.

"The blood drop!" the beast screamed. "The blood drop!"

For a moment, I did not understand. And then I knew that the beast meant my birthmark. I raised up on my knees

and thrust my wrist at him, so that he had to look at the scarlet drop on my skin.

Abruptly he was gone, leaving behind a stench so evil
that I had to hold my breath for a few moments.

Was this a spy for my mother? Had he just found me, or
had he been waiting for such a vulnerable moment?

He had spoken in my mother's voice, and I believed
now that she not only knew I was still alive, but she might
even know where I was. But did she know that I had been
the one who taught music to the children of Lir, her
stepchildren?

I spent the rest of the night sitting there, holding my dog
in my lap, and waiting for dawn. When it came at last, I took
the looking glass out of my pack, held it before my face, and
said, "Do not hide from me now. I command you to show
me who sent that beast."

My mother's face swam in the glass, surrounded by
wisps of purple and green color. She smiled.

"Does she see me?" I demanded of the glass. "Answer
me, I command you!"

"She does not," a quiet voice answered. I could have
sworn that I had heard the voice before, perhaps in the convent, perhaps somewhere in my terrible childhood. "But the
imp will tell her, as soon as he reaches her. And then she will
be certain that you still live. The reward for this information
will be so great that you will never see the imp again, for he
will have his own castle soon enough, and an army of his
own. What your mother will do with the information has yet
to be seen for certain. But I can show you this much."

With that, the colors in the mirror swam and then steadied, and I saw my mother wringing the necks of four swans, skinning them when they were barely dead, and throwing the skins over images of the children of Lir, drawn in sand. The swans flew away into the dawn sky, leaving behind three small bodies floating facedown near the shore below the castle in Lir—and one in England, drowned in a pool below a waterfall. Their wet blond hair stirred in the water.

"I will stop her!" I cried.

"No one can stop her," the gentle voice said. "The deed is already done, after a ceremony welcoming your mother to the kingdom of Lir, yesterday afternoon."

"They are dead already?" I cried. "Dead even now?" I rose up, leaving Striker at my feet, and raised both my fists. "I will destroy her for this!"

"Think of the children first," the voice said. "Your passion blinds you. Think of the children first!"

In the mirror, I watched four white swans circle a black lake, calling for me. Only they did not call me Mary Singer. They called, "Gwenore!"

I knew that lake. The children had led me there for a secret picnic. I knew exactly where it was—across the border in Lir.

Dawn broke, and I dressed and hurried out of the storeroom to find Simon. We must return to Lir—and to the black lake deep in the woods. But when I found him dousing his hair in a bucket of water behind the shop, he refused to go with me.

"We must wait for the others," he said. "I will send the crow for them. But we must wait. We cannot fight all of Lir alone. And we *will* be fighting the entire kingdom. *You* may be sure of your mother's guilt in this, but her new husband will never believe it. If you cause her harm, the king will turn on you in a moment."

"I don't care about him!" I cried. "I want to find the children."

"And do what?" he asked. "She has killed them. And changed them."

"And I will change them back!"

"We wait," he said. "Even if I have to tell the blacksmith that you have gone mad with grief and so I tied you up and gagged you to keep you from frightening the villagers. I will do it, Singer! I will! We need help with this."

She had destroyed the children in so short a time. I wept as I returned to the storeroom. She must have planned it before she ever arrived.

Four dead children so soon?

Four swans circling over a lake.

I took out my looking glass and watched them. Now I saw clearly. Now when it was too late, I saw the four swans circling the lake I recognized. Each one wore a golden crown. Little princes and princesses, dead at the hands of my mother.

"Why did you not show me in time?" I asked savagely.

The glass would not answer. And a drop of blood fell from my wrist, spattering the glass, staining the white swans, circling while they wept and sang my name.

13

the face in the mirror

Soon after daybreak, Simon's landlady fed me bread and cheese for breakfast, bringing it to the storeroom where I still lay in bed. She stared curiously at my hair, for it was not covered then, and I felt her pity for me. Poor freak of a girl, she thought. What good can happen to her?

Oh, lady, it is worse than you know, I thought.

I shared my food with Striker and waited for Simon to return from an errand he would not explain. He had sent the messenger crow to Father Caddaric during the night, and he said he would speak to others that morning. "You can't send too many crows with messages," he had said, "because they can be such liars."

"Some are not crows," I told him. "Some are Fair Folk."

"They are liars, too," he said. "Like your friend, King Harry." And with that, he was gone.

I had not slept much the night before, and I could not nap now, for I was thinking of the children flying endlessly over the lake, calling my name. And my mother! My mother! Was she gloating, there in the palace where everyone was mourning the lost children?

What would King Lir think when he received the news that Connor, too, had drowned? Would he not suspect her of having a connection to all the tragedy?

No, she was too clever for that, my dark witch mother. She had become more dangerous than ever. The secret, buried hope I had always held that one day she might be a true mother to me had been torn out, as if it were my beating heart, and now I was her enemy. I wanted nothing from her now—nothing but revenge for what she had done to King Lir's children.

Time and again I took out the looking glass and stared into it, seeing only my own reflection, the pale face and white hair, the haunted blue eyes. The glass refused to show me the children again. I asked to see Simon, and it refused that, also. And when I asked to see the Blessingwood women and Brennan, the light in the glass shimmered violently, showing all the colors and shapes I could imagine, but not one picture I could understand. Were the reflections distorted because of me, because I could not calm my mind enough to see what was true?

I turned it over. There was a white wolf on the back, looking out at me.

Why did I have such a useless thing as a magical looking glass that revealed nothing until it was too late to stop it? It was almost as if the glass had found a way to capture my worst fears and then show them to me, but without resolution or result, just the fears, playing again and again before me, like a festival players' performance that had no final act.

I repacked my bags, taking great care with my small store of surgical instruments and medicines. I had sharpened my scalpels and my knife, and I had made sure that the lid of every pot was fastened down tightly and every little bag of herbs tied securely. All of my clothing was white, unfortunately, and since I no longer had the help of a maid to keep my garments clean, I would be a sorry sight before long.

A small, elderly hen trotted into the storeroom, eyed Striker cautiously, and then said, "Gwenore, King Harry sends his respects—well, no, he did not exactly send respects, but he sent a kind of greeting—"

Striker barked in alarm. Neither of us had ever known a talking hen, and this one surprised us.

"Where did you see him?" I asked.

"On the other side of the village," she said. She sat down and fluffed her feathers. " 'You should go talk to Gwenore yourself,' I told King Harry, but he said, 'If you're lucky, she'll be so grateful that she'll make you young again,' and so I am here, Gwenore, to give you his message and ask that you make me young again, for I am afraid that old hens go to the stewing pot in this part of the world instead of being treated with the respect they—"

"What is the message?" I interrupted. I had known hens before, and they were friendly, clucking creatures, but this one seemed to have stored up a whole book of comments and could make them all.

"King Harry said that the women—and he said you would know which women—were even now coming quickly on horseback and should reach you in good time. And he said that the old priest was a devil, so he was coming with something called a Vespers and would arrive before moonrise, with someone named Tom. Or perhaps it was Tim—or perhaps Tom was arriving with the women. Or perhaps the whole thing was the other way around." She stopped and peered at me. "Does what I say make sense? I often don't make much sense anymore."

"It makes a kind of sense," I admitted.

"Then will you make me young again before the woman comes with the ax and cuts off my head? Once I could have prevented it, of course, but these last years—or perhaps I mean these last ages—have been hard ones."

The idea of her losing her head horrified me. I had eaten chicken in my life, but I had not realized that any of them ever gave their fate a thought. But then I remembered that this was one of the Fair Folk, and so she would know her fate well enough.

"I will try," I said, trying to calm myself enough so that I could make a song and change her back to her youth. "Let us be very quiet for a few minutes, so that I can think."

The hen agreed, and I closed my eyes, struggling to think of a song that would turn back the days and months for her. A ray of sunlight poured through the small window and warmed my face, and I suddenly remembered what it was that I had never really forgotten—none of us are truly what we appear to be. We are the stuff of stars and suns, all of us. Our friends and our enemies, and all those whom we do not know, are the stuff of stars.

I nudged Striker out of my lap and picked up the hen, smoothing her feathers gently, and when her heart did not beat so hard, I sang, "How were you caught here, Fairy one,

Fair one, how did you lose your way? Taste and hear sunlight,
Fairy one, Fair one, and turn once to go home to stay."

She stretched herself up in my lap, circled one time, and
the sunlight fell on her, and while I watched, she became a
young bird again, a wild and free one, and with one high cry,
she flew up and out the window.

What a strange gift I have, I marveled. It is almost like
the eternal life that is talked of in the church, a life I never
believed could be true.

But if it is not true, I thought, then where did I learn
the words?

Simon was back. The roll of leather he carried over his
shoulder contained objects that were heavy, and when he set
it down on the earthen floor, it clanked.

"What have you there?" I asked.

"Weapons," he said. "I have been making them since I
came here and hiding them until we needed them." He knelt
and unrolled the bundle, showing me two swords, two short
pikes, and several iron hammers. He picked up one of the
hammers and swung it over his head with both hands. "This
will stop a man fast enough," he said, grinning. "But a pike
will be a better weapon for you, because you don't have the
long arms of a man."

"I want a sword," I said, reaching for one.

"You will not get one," he said, pushing away my hand.
"You've had no training, and a sword in the hands of someone without training is more dangerous to him than to
his enemy. Umma taught me, and he was a master."

Just hearing Umma's name caused my eyes to burn with tears. There were evil people in the world, more than I had even suspected during those weeks when I was a prisoner in the castle cellar. That had been so many years before that it seemed almost another world. Then I had thought that only Sir Richard and my mother were capable of bringing on disaster, but after I ran away, I discovered evil everywhere. Sometimes it was small and petty; sometimes it destroyed homes and lives. Sometimes it even cursed children.

"King Harry is in the village," I told Simon, who only shrugged and replied, "It wouldn't have been possible to lose him. Not that I wanted to do that, you understand, because he has his uses."

"Uses?" King Harry cried from the doorway. "How dare you speak of using me?" He strolled in, lashing his tail, gave Striker a look that might have crushed the spirit of a different kind of dog, and sat down by me.

"I wish you could see those old women rushing along on horseback," he said. "One might think that you are important, Gwenore."

"They come because of the children," I told him sourly. "Do you bring news, or are you now only someone who sends me hens who need refurbishing?"

"I bring news," he said. He sprang up to the rafters as a crow and looked down at me. "Vespers sends word that there is a clear path over the border a few leagues east of here. There was a strange fog in that valley this morning, a fog that causes heavy sleep. The guardian trolls will not wake until tomorrow, so if the old women reach here in time—and if you stir yourselves—you can meet in a place I will show you and cross into Lir together. For whatever good you think it will do. Your mother traveled here with a sorcerer who pretends to be her personal scribe, and he has powers that strengthen hers. It will not be easy to release the children from their curse." He preened his feathers for a moment and then said, "The Fair Folk are making wagers on you, Gwenore. Would you like to know the odds?"

"I will win all that I desire to win," I said. "I will take all that I desire to take. And I will *kill* anyone or anything that tries to stop me."

Simon's laugh was short, like a bark. "Believe her, for I have seen her new powers."

"Liar," King Harry said.

Simon picked up a small rock from the earthen floor and threw it at King Harry, who ducked just in time. He flapped out the window and we heard him cawing furiously, probably to some of his relatives.

"I don't know what good he is," Simon said.

"He will take us to the meeting place at the pass," I said. "No matter how he behaves, he will do it to honor Umma's memory, for he loved him."

"Who did not love him?" Simon said, and his voice broke.

We were apprehensive as we left the village, for we had no idea what lay ahead of us. We bade good-bye to the blacksmith, who gave Simon a small silver coin as a reward for being a good worker, and then we turned toward the mountains ahead. Occasionally we caught a glimpse of King

Harry, flying ahead of us, and once we saw him with several other crows, apparently having some sort of meeting. But he did not drop down to report to us, and so we assumed that he was gossiping with friends or relatives.

In late afternoon, we stopped by the bank of a stream to eat and rest. Clouds were blowing across the sky, covering the sun, and I felt for rain in the air, but there was none. We would need to find shelter of some kind for the night, if our friends had not joined us by then.

"Where is King Harry?" Simon asked irritably and he sorted through his pack for another chunk of the bread our landlady had given him. "Where is the pass? Where are our friends?"

"Be patient," I told him, even though I was not.

A sudden crack of thunder startled both of us. A bolt of lightning seemed to rise up from the ground not ten steps from us, shattering a stone the size of a sheep. Smoke rose from the pieces of stone, and out of the smoke slithered a snake no longer than my forearm. It raised its head and forked its tongue into the air, tasting it.

"Ah, Gwenore, so it *is* you," the snake said. "I have heard that you are fond of harp music." Its laugh was one of the most unpleasant sounds I had ever heard.

Simon had grabbed Striker and both of us jumped to our feet in alarm.

I did not dare admit that I was Gwenore, because I had no idea who this snake was or where it had come from. "What do you want?" I asked it.

The snake eased its way between the sharp edges of the

broken stone until it reached my feet. "Pick me up," it said in a coaxing tone. "I will not harm you. Pick me up from the cold ground."

I backed up a step. "I will not. Tell me what you want."

The snake edged closer. "I want to see if it is true that you have the powers you claim to have."

What powers had I claimed? That I could bring youth to old creatures through my songs. That I could sense rain and read minds—sometimes. That I could occasionally tell the future, but not well enough to be of use. That I could heal, but most of my healing gifts did not involve any of the magical arts.

"What power do you want me to use on you?" I asked, trying to avoid answering the snake directly.

It laughed, a strange, dry sound that caused Striker to whine nervously. "Can you not change one creature into another—the way your mother does?"

I gasped. My mother changed living creatures into dead creatures. And she changed children into swans. I could do neither, nor did I want to do those things. But how much should I tell the snake?

"Is that what you want, snake?" I asked. "To be turned into something different from what you are?"

"Singer," Simon warned quietly. "Be careful."

"Singer?" asked the snake. "I like that. Sing me a song that will change me into a beautiful woman."

Was this one of my mother's tricks? I backed up another step, and the snake slithered forward, laughing again.

"I want to be beautiful," it said. "Like you. Like your

mother. But not light or dark. Not one of the extremes. Give me red hair, like the Blessingwood woman you loved so much. Do it now, and I will show you the mountain pass and bring your friends to you."

"Singer," Simon warned again.

Instantly, I pulled my knife from my belt and plunged it downward, intending to pierce the snake. But it flashed away and disappeared into the tall grass nearby.

"Was that something sent by your mother to test you, to see if you are Gwenore?" Simon asked.

I had no clear way of knowing. "Let's move on," I said. "This place is evil now. We need to get help from the Fair Folk."

I had not sensed them around us for a long time. The presence of trolls in a land often discourages Fair Folk from staying long. Now, as we walked, I strained my eyes to see the shimmer in the air that announced their presence.

At last I saw it, in the trees ahead of us. Tree spirits were not closely related to the Fair Folk, but they were friends of mine, and far more trustworthy than the relatives of King Harry and Vespers.

I motioned Simon to stay behind me and I stopped under a tree to look up. Was that a narrow, pale face above me? Did I see cobwebs woven into braided hair, and a necklace of tiny green berries?

"Can you help me?" I asked. "I am Gwenore."

"I knew you as Singer," the voice said. The narrow face grew more visible and beautiful. "Do you remember me, from the apple orchard at Blessingwood? Some of us have been following you for a long time."

I nearly wept with relief. The tree spirits at Blessingwood were dear to all of us. "Simon and I need to find the pass to Lir," I said. "And we need to find the Blessingwood women, and Brennan and Tom. And an old priest called Caddaric. Can you help?"

The tree spirit floated down to a branch almost at eye level. "You must cross through the pass tonight, while the trolls sleep," it said. "I will show you the way with spirit lights, if you wish."

"I can't go without our friends," I said. "I need them."

"The priest, a woman, and a young man already wait at the pass for you," the tree spirit said. "The Blessingwood women are coming, but one is ill, and the physician cannot heal her, so they travel slowly for her sake."

"Julienne," I whispered. She had been so frail, and now she was coming to help children she had never met, because I had asked.

"When will they arrive?" I asked.

"Perhaps at moonrise. You must hurry now, for your mother is gathering her dark forces, and her sorcerer is trying to find you."

"Was he the snake?"

"Yes. You are much changed, Gwenore, and he could not recognize you from your mother's description. And she has not been able to see you in dreams or any other way, for you have many friends in the spirit world, and they veil you as much as they can."

I reached out to touch the tree spirit, but my hand went

through its arm, as if I had attempted to touch mist. It laughed a little, and raised one hand to shower me with crystal flowers that melted as they touched me. "Luck and blessings and good visions upon you, Gwenore," it said. "I will send a friend to keep you company." And then it drifted upward and disappeared into the leaves. "If ever you should need us, only call out, and we shall come." The leaves sighed gently behind the tree spirit.

"You have strange friends," Simon said.

"And apparently I will soon be having a new one," I said. "But let us not wait for surprises, because we can't be sure we won't have more bad ones, too. Which direction shall we walk now?"

At that moment, a young deer stepped daintily out from the edge of the nearby forest, and she said, "I will show you the quickest way to the pass, Gwenore. Follow me."

Simon and I picked up our belongings, and I tucked Striker under my arm. "What do we call you?" I asked the deer as I walked behind her.

She looked back over her shoulder at me. "You may call me Damisi," she said. "I am your guard for the rest of your journey."

"A young doe is a guard?" Simon asked skeptically under his breath.

"I am a warrior," she said calmly, and she walked on. I noticed then that she had a narrow leather collar not much wider than my little finger around her neck, and a small medallion hung from it.

"What is that around your neck?" I asked as I walked.

"It is my mother's true blessing," she said.

I dropped back several steps. Her words stung me. Her mother had blessed her? I was on my way to battle my mother. In fact, I thought, my own mother would kill me if she could.

The sun went down as we entered the mountain pass, and immediately a hundred spirit lights formed around us among the trees, like small lamps, illuminating our way gently. They hung in the air, pale globes of soft light that provided just enough help to keep us from stumbling but not so much brightness that anyone in the distance might notice. Half a dozen clustered around Damisi's head, and I wondered if they were speaking together in voices I could not hear.

Finally, Damisi said, "The priest, a woman with a scarred face, and a young man wait nearby. A messenger has brought them news of four old women coming, too."

"Are they all well?" I asked urgently.

"Three are well, one is ill," she said calmly. "Come along. We cannot slow down now. There is danger in the woods."

"What danger?" Simon asked. He withdrew the sword he was carrying under his cloak.

"A sorcerer is probing the twilight, looking for news of Gwenore," Damisi said. "But the Fair Folk are spinning lies for him, like cobwebs to catch him, and he is busy unraveling the lies, instead of continuing on to look for the truth. This will keep him occupied for a while, but then he will learn that he has been tricked, and he will catch you if he can find you, Gwenore."

"He cannot catch me," I said firmly, but I was afraid that

he might. I was growing tired, and as my strength left me, so did my courage.

Suddenly I heard a shout of laughter, and ahead of Damisi, I saw Tom running toward us. "I thought you'd never get here, Gwenore!" he shouted. "What kept you so long?"

He was so healthy now, so strong, and even as I threw my free arm around him, I remembered the healing ceremony in the underground bath. Striker barked a welcome, for he surely remembered the time he and Tom had worked with the band of players, traveling all over England for years.

"We came as soon as we could," Simon said gruffly.

"Where is Brennan?" I asked Tom, but even as I asked, I saw her coming. She was a little stouter, but her smile was the same as it always was, full of warmth and love for me. She hugged me so hard that Striker complained, and she hugged and kissed him, too, although she complained that he needed a bath.

Last to come forward was Father Caddaric. He did not seem happy to see me, but instead he was scowling. "We have no time for sentimental nonsense," he said. "All of us must push forward to cross the pass tonight. There are trolls nearby, and they sleep for now, but we cannot take chances on the spell keeping them from waking."

"We must wait for the Blessingwood women," I said.

"I sent Vespers to watch over them," he said. "They will arrive safely or they will not, but your role in the future of the children of Lir has been set. Do you want to find the lost children? Because if you do, we have no time to lose. They are despairing, and if they are not rescued soon, I fear that they will drown themselves."

"*Drown* themselves," Brennan echoed. "How can this be?"

"My mother married their father and then she turned them into swans to get rid of them. I must find a way to undo what she has done."

"If I can be a part of rescuing them from her enchantment," Brennan said, "then that is what I want to do, no matter what it takes. I will settle up with God on my deathbed." She touched the scar on her face. "Your mother is the source of most of the evil in my life."

We waited there, at the start of the pass through the mountains, but the Blessingwood women did not come, so Damisi told us that we must move on. "Some of the trolls are stirring in their sleep," she said.

We walked on, surrounded by spirit lights, but I looked back many times, hoping to see the women coming. "We need a crow to carry messages," I said. "He might be able to locate them and tell them exactly where we are."

"You must not hesitate now," Damisi said. "Not if you want to rescue the children. There is time enough for messages, after we reach the lake where the children are living."

I thought of their despair, and I feared that they would drown themselves if I could not find them in time. "You are right," I told Damisi.

The five of us walked on quickly, led by our guardian deer. No one spoke, for we needed all of our breath for climbing over the rough ground in the pass. Then, suddenly, we heard voices shouting behind us.

"I will claw out your good eye and spit in the bad one!" one voice cried. "I will snap your spindly spider legs."

"I will tell the family, and they will hunt you down and yank your tail out by the roots and hang it from a tree!" shouted the other.

Brennan gasped, but I said, "It's only King Harry and Vespers."

The two flew down and landed on Father Caddaric's shoulders. Vespers leaned forward and pecked at King Harry's head, and King Harry shouted, "I curse your descendants for a thousand years, you worthless bag of feathers."

"Kindly shut the hole in your head," Vespers said. He rubbed his head against Father Caddaric's beard and said, "I have news, friend."

"Speak your news and stop your racket," Father Caddaric growled. "We are on a serious journey."

"That is why we are here," King Harry said. "It's the Blessingwood women. They are not far behind, but they urge you to press on. One of them has had a vision of swans drowning themselves at the first light of dawn."

I hurried forward, stumbling over rocks until the spirit lights clustered around my knees, clearly showing me the way. Damisi was far ahead now, almost out of sight. "Hurry!" she called back to us. "You must hurry!"

We reached the far end of the pass at the time of false dawn, when the eastern sky turned to the color of pearl. As we made our way through a rough meadow, the sky turned dark again, and then the first light of the sun broke over the horizon. The sky turned the color of wild strawberries.

Far ahead of us lay the hidden lake that Connor and the others had shown me one day when we were happy. I was no longer sure that there ever had been such a time.

"I don't see swans anywhere," Simon said.

"They might not be awake yet," Brennan said. "They might be hidden by long grasses or trees. We're too far away to be sure of anything."

"Call them by name, Gwenore," Tom said suddenly. "If they hear your voice, they will answer. I'm sure of it."

The others looked to me expectantly. My mouth was dry, and I was not certain I could call loudly enough for them to hear.

"Call!" Father Caddaric shouted.

"Call, call, call!" yelled the crows.

And so I did. I called the children, one by one, beginning with Connor. Then we saw them, rising from the meadow at the far end of the lake. They flew up and began circling the lake.

Their voices would have broken the heart of anyone—except my mother. Together they sang one of the songs I had composed for them, and they circled slowly, elegantly, like the royal children they were. As the sun rose, it reflected light from their crowns. A more beautiful—and terrible—sight I have never seen.

"There they are," I said. "But what should we do now?"

Damisi nudged me gently. "You and the children have seen each other. Now you must find a way to save them. You have the power, Singer."

"You have the power, Gwenore," Father Caddaric said. "You have all the power you need to make right the wrong that has been done to them."

I looked out at the circling swans and heard them

singing. I would find a way to help them, even though I did not know that way yet, I promised myself.

Striker barked suddenly. He was looking back over my shoulder. Then we all heard what he was hearing. Horses were coming.

"It must be the Blessingwood women," Simon said. "They are here at last."

But Striker growled then, and the hair on his back stood up. "It might be someone else," I cautioned.

Father Caddaric tossed the crows up into the air. "See who is coming!" he shouted. "Hurry!" King Harry and Vespers flapped off without argument.

"We must move out of sight until we find out who the riders are," Tom said. "Over here, by the trees. Quickly."

We hid ourselves among the trees and waited. The sun rose. The swans sang and circled.

The horses drew nearer, hooves scattering rocks. There were many horses, more than the four we were expecting.

The crows were back, shouting before they landed on Father Caddaric's shoulders again. "There are knights in pursuit of the women!" King Harry cried.

"Twenty or more!" shouted Vespers.

"The women cannot escape!" King Harry cried, and he dropped to the ground as a cat. "Gwenore, do something! Those knights have the look and smell of trolls about them."

Simon pulled out his swords and tossed one to Tom. "Here, Player! I hope you know how to use this."

They ran toward the sounds of the horses, with the early morning sun on their shoulders, and King Harry scampered behind them. Vespers yelled, "Wait for me!" and rushed after his brother, having taken the form of a small fox.

But I am the white wolf, and I can do whatever must be done, I told myself. I handed Striker to Brennan for safe-keeping, dropped my pack, tore off my hood, and I ran after my friends, holding my small, sharp blade in my hand.

The birthmark on my left wrist spattered blood on my clothing as I ran.

14

the reckoning

There was a narrow place in the pass, near the end, where horses must go one by one, and the Blessingwood women were riding through that needle's eye when I first saw them. All four were there! I had feared that the trip had killed Julienne.

Tom, Simon, and I stood together, waiting for them to clear the last of the cliffs. Close behind them, also in single file, came two dozen gray knights mounted on small horses with strangely heavy legs. Even from this great a distance, I could smell the stench of the trolls.

"Those knights are not human," Simon said. "The trolls have tried to take the form of men, but they have not succeeded. They aren't as tall as we are, and I doubt if they are as strong."

"What do you make of their steeds?" Tom asked him. "They don't look like horses."

"They are creatures that they conjured up themselves," I said, certain that I was right. "They made them from wild boars, I think. If they had been horses, they would have caught our friends, because their own mounts must be exhausted by now."

We moved closer to be prepared for whatever came next.

"Umma told me once of a battle he fought in the Holy Land," Simon said slowly. "They caught their enemies at the end of a long pass by rolling boulders down on them to crush them."

"We don't have time to climb so far," Tom said, looking up at the sides of the cliff. "Although there are some rocks up there that might do the work very well."

"Call the tree spirits!" yelled King Harry. "They'll do anything for you. Call them up to help."

"They are *spirits*," I said sharply. "They have no strength in their limbs. They are not much more than mist or fog."

"They are what you want them to be," Vespers said. His foxy eyes stared furiously into mine. "Think, Gwenore!"

"The women will be here in moments," Tom warned. "See? Margarite is first. She sees us!"

I bent my head, desperate. In order to concentrate better, I clapped my hands over my eyes. "Now," I whispered to myself. "See the way it could be. Tree spirits, do you hear me? Can you hear me?"

"We hear," I heard in my mind. "What do you want of us, Gwenore?"

"Can you fight the troll knights? Are you strong enough?"

"We are not, Gwenore. But we can send down great rocks of our own making to stop them, for a while, at least. We can give the women time to reach you."

"Then do it."

"Well?" King Harry demanded. "What did they say?"

"The tree spirits will send down rocks," I said. "They will stop the trolls long enough for the women to get out of the pass."

Even as I spoke, great boulders teetered on the high cliffs hanging over the pass, and then, all at one time, they fell suddenly and terribly on the riders below. They looked real enough, and I hoped that they had some weight to them, to do as much damage to the trolls as possible.

The women barely escaped. The boulders thundered down, crashing into great chunks of rubble, blocking the troll knights. While we watched, a wall of rubble grew and grew as more boulders fell. The pass was nearly filled.

But I saw the boulders shimmer, and I knew that they were made of spirit stuff. It would all fade away when the time was up.

The women reached us, and Tom and Simon jumped forward to grab the bridles of the first two horses. Margarite and Sarah nearly fell from their saddles, but they were still strong enough to cry out greetings to us.

Behind them, Hildegard rode next to Julienne, who had sagged forward, against her horse's neck. "Help her quickly!" Hildegard called out. "I do not believe that she is conscious any longer."

Tom and Simon ran to Julienne and eased her gently off her horse. Her eyes were closed, her face so white that I was afraid she was already dead. My friends put her down on the grass and I knelt beside her.

"I am here, Julienne," I whispered. I reached out to

smooth back the hair that had escaped from her hood, and a drop of my blood fell on her forehead.

I stared down at it. The blood was from my birthmark, and it meant life.

The sun meant life.

I drew a sun on her forehead in my blood, and her eyes opened. "Mary," she whispered. "I did not think I would see you again."

"We have work to do, you and I," I murmured. "You must help me save the children of Lir."

She smiled. "I will do anything I can for you."

Their horses were exhausted, and so Father Caddaric set them free. We found a small hut near the lake, hidden among willows, where we made a bed for Julienne out of evergreen branches. Her three old friends, worn out by their travel, sat down beside her, and I told them to rest for a while.

Then the three men, Brennan, and I had a meeting. "What can you do for Julienne and the swans?" Simon demanded.

"Gwenore, you have the power," Father Caddaric said. "What do you want to do for them?"

I looked up and saw the circling, singing swans. "I want them alive as children again," I said. "This enchantment must end."

"The children are dead," Father Caddaric reminded me.

"The bodies of three of them lie on pallets made of wicker and flowers," Vespers said. "That is what the crows tell. The king is waiting to bury them until his elder son's body is brought home, and that will not be long from now. Tomorrow, perhaps."

I looked down at my birthmark. Drops of blood still seeped from it.

"I need to bring their bodies here," I said, looking up at the swans. "I think I can change them back, but I need the bodies here, so that I can write on their foreheads in my blood."

Brennan sucked in her breath. "Gwenore!"

Simon shook his head. "No one will allow any of us near the children's bodies. Bringing them here is impossible. And what of the boy who is not there yet? Would you leave him behind?"

I stared at the swans again. "No, I will not leave any of them behind." But then I added, "Not if I can help it."

"Let us do what we can," Father Caddaric said. "You can make Vespers and King Harry your agents, and send them to write on the foreheads of the bodies. Remember your gifts. You can do such a thing."

"Yes, yes, we will do it!" King Harry cried. "I grew fond of Darbie. I will do what you ask, if it will save her."

"I won't," Vespers said. He changed into a crow and flicked his feathers. "What reason would I have to do anything more for humans than I have already done?"

"Your reason will be clear enough as I wring your neck," Father Caddaric said.

"I will give all possible aid," Vespers said hastily, and he flapped up to Father Caddaric's shoulder.

"What of us, then?" Simon asked.

I looked back at the pass. "Keep me safe for as long as it takes to make the change," I said. "I have never done this— changed the dead to the living—but my mother has changed the living to the dead. If she could do evil, then I will do good."

Brennan handed Striker back to me because he was whining, but I did not hold him for long. "Take him," I said to her. "He is yours now. I want you to walk west, toward the coast. Sooner or later Father Caddaric will find you, and he will take you with him when he joins the explorer priests. If we do not see each other again, remember how much I loved you. Now go."

But Brennan refused. "I can't leave you behind."

"I will catch up if I can," I said. "That is all I can promise."

I turned away so that I would not see them leave, and I wept when I heard Striker keening for me. Then, when I was done with tears, I turned back to my friends and said, "This is what we will do."

I outlined my plan for them, argued against their objections, and finally convinced them all. I would need the strength of the Blessingwood women for what was to come, except for Julienne, who was not strong enough to lend her spiritual strength to us.

I found my pack and pulled out my looking glass. The glass was full of images. I saw my mother, dressed in black as usual, but this time she wore a large ruby on her right forefinger, and I knew when I saw it that it was a sorcerer's ring. I saw the sorcerer who gave it to her, who was as ugly as the imp on the roof beam and as evil as the snake on the ground. I saw King Lir standing before three pallets holding the bodies of his children.

I saw the body of Connor being placed aboard a ship—

on an English quay. He would not arrive in time.

I clenched my fists hard enough to dig my fingernails into my palms. I would not weep again. If I could not help Connor, so be it.

"I hear something coming through the pass!" Tom said.

"Are the boulders disappearing?" I asked urgently.

"I'll go to keep guard," Simon said, and before I could stop him, he ran back toward the pass. Tom looked as if he was about to follow, but I asked him to stay, because we needed someone with a strong sword arm to stand guard over us.

If Simon failed.

Father Caddaric brought the women out of the hut, except for Julienne. I told them what I planned to do, and I was grateful for their approval. These woman had been my teachers for so long. How good it would be to show them that I had learned from them.

I had even learned from the old priest.

I chose the symbol of the sword for King Harry and Vespers to paint on the foreheads of the children of Lir. "The sword will give strength to our work," I told them. "But you must be careful to draw it so that it can be recognized by anyone. This magic is not evil, and so it does not need to be hidden."

I showed them how to draw the sword properly, using a stick and the soft dirt at the edge of the lake. "I will shred the ends of two sticks to make brushes, and I will soak them in my blood. When you reach the children, draw the swords quickly and then fly away."

There was a shout behind me. I could not understand

Simon's words, but King Harry repeated them. "The trolls are moving through the pass!"

"We have to stop them!" Father Caddaric shouted, and we ran toward the opening of the pass. We could see Simon, standing with his sword raised. Tom sprinted forward, his own sword drawn and ready.

But then . . .

But then a troll dropped down from the cliffs behind Simon and thrust a short troll sword through his back.

He crumpled, and I knew from the way he fell that he was already dead.

"Simon!" I screamed, and I ran for him without thinking.

Father Caddaric jerked me back by one arm. "Remember your gifts!"

"I want him to be alive!" I cried, struggling to be free of his grasp.

"He was willing to die," he said. "But the children were *not* willing. Remember your duty. You were born for sacrifice and duty, Gwenore."

"Call the tree spirits!" King Harry and Vespers were shrieking. "Call them! Call them!"

I knelt on the ground and covered my eyes. "Can you hear me?" I begged.

"We hear, Gwenore."

"Can you come as knights before the trolls and drive them back?" I asked. "Can you make yourselves appear tall and strong?"

"We can, but we cannot kill, Gwenore. If the trolls

believe, then we can frighten them. If they do not believe, they will simply charge through us."

I pulled my hands away from my eyes and looked toward the pass. Most of the troll knights were on foot now, and running with them were a dozen wild boars, which scattered into the woods as soon as they were clear of the pass. The remaining mounted knights looked formidable.

"Please," I asked the tree spirit who spoke to me. "Please help."

Instantly a large company of knights in silver armor, riding white horses, poured out of the woods and charged the troll knights. They raised glittering swords and shields. A trumpet sounded from their midst, and one knight, taller than all the others, rode ahead, carrying a white banner bearing a silver moon.

The troll knights pulled up their horses, then turned and rode away. A few of the trolls on foot hesitated, shaking their swords at us, but they, too, finally fled.

The silver knights shimmered and disappeared, and the branches in the trees rustled, even though there was no wind.

"I don't believe it," Tom said. "You did that, Gwenore?"

"No. My friends, the tree spirits, did it."

I went to Simon, then, and knelt beside him. In death, his face was peaceful, almost smiling, and for a moment I thought I saw Umma kneeling on the other side of him. "Take him home with you," I whispered to my old friend. Then, tenderly, I folded Simon's hands on his chest and spread my cloak over him, covering his face. "I will see you both again," I whispered. A dozen tree spirits had gathered around us, and I stood back while they bent over my friend, singing words I almost remembered, and when they left, Simon was gone, too. I gathered up my cloak and found it warm to my touch, and when I put it on again, I felt as if I had been embraced. *Simon,* I thought.

Now I returned to the problem of making the crows ready to fly to the castle, just out of sight beyond the woods. I drew the proper symbol several times for them, until I believed that they could make the mark exactly as I showed them. The sword must have a very slight curve to the tip, and a strong horizontal line at the other end, signifying the handle.

Tom had cut two short twigs and sliced the tips into brushes. I applied my blood to them, and then we watched while the crows flew away.

"Now we must call down the swans," I said.

The Blessingwood women helped me then, calling the children by name in gentle voices, reaching up their tender hands to hold them when they finally trusted us enough to approach. Each of us held a swan, then, a wild bird with a child trapped inside.

One would stay a swan, after we were done. Connor would not reach Lir in time. The swan I carried in my arms wore a crown with a small blue stone in it, and I believed that he was the elder son. I held him against my heart and promised him that somehow I would find a way.

Then I explained that we must sit in a circle, with Tom and Father Caddaric watching over us, while we concentrated on the spell we must weave to take the children from the swans and return them to their father.

"You have forgotten your mother," Father Caddaric said calmly. "Why, Gwenore? Do you *still* think that there is a way she can be a true mother to you?"

I closed my eyes, and behind my eyelids I saw the looking glass. In it, my mother and the sorcerer watched us, there by the side of the lake, and they laughed.

Quickly, I carried the swan I held into the hut and asked Julienne if she was strong enough to sit up and hold him. She pushed herself up and held out her arms. "I know what you are going to do, Mary."

"Then tell me, for I cannot see how I can stop my mother."

She turned away her face. "Did you go to the Middle Passage? Did the priest tell you why you had been born?"

"Yes, and he has reminded me."

"Sacrifice," she whispered. "That is the way to remove evil. Sacrifice."

When I left the hut, she was weeping. Her tears told me what my duty was.

"I must be at the castle when the children awake," I told the others. Tom believed me, and perhaps even Father Caddaric did, too. But the Blessingwood women somehow knew why I was going. I could read it in their eyes.

I hurried away without looking back. I would reach the castle by the time the sun had crossed half of the sky, and then I would do what had to be done.

Damisi found me as I made my way through the woods. "The Fair Folk do not want you to go on, Gwenore," she said as she walked beside me. "They want you to forget what the old priest told you."

"If you see my dog again, tell him . . ."

But she was gone, and I was alone again. I left the woods behind and crossed the meadow where the children and I had held our music lessons so many times. Ahead, the castle waited, unguarded as usual, with white mourning banners flying from all the towers. I saw the crows overhead, flying with the sticks still in their beaks, waiting for their opportunity to write upon the foreheads of the children.

It was not a sword that I had taught them to draw. It was my small knife, made for me by my dead friend. I pulled it from my belt.

I walked into the gatehouse and looked up. There, on the ceiling, was the blue sky with white clouds and flying birds.

I stepped into the keep.

"Gwenore!" My mother stepped in front of me, her black skirts swirling, and she held out her arms, blocking me. "I knew you would come. I knew you would be that stupid."

Standing to one side and slightly behind her stood a short, fat man. I recognized in him the imp and the snake. I darted forward and slashed at him with my knife, and he fell backward, his throat cut. His blood was not red, like mine, but yellow.

My mother backed away. For the first time in my life, I saw my mother afraid of someone.

But then she smiled. "Well, well, Gwenore, where have you been that you learned to murder without conscience or hesitation?" she asked.

"I learned from you," I said.

The keep was empty except for us, and I wondered where all the people were, even while I watched my mother. I moved a step forward. She moved a step back. I laughed then, knowing that I could threaten her.

Where were the children? I could see the crows overhead, and one by one they dropped down to the eastern wall. Ah, there. The children had been laid out on the east side of the castle, almost as if they were awaiting their brother.

"I will kill you if you do not leave," my mother said. "I should have killed you when you were a child."

"You could not," I said. "You never had that power over me. You made my life so miserable that I did not care if I lived or died, and so you lost your power. But that is not all of it. You know that I cannot die. Father Caddaric made sure of it."

She darted toward me, holding out a long needle, and she meant to plunge it into my face, but I was faster. Simon had said that the little knife would not fail me, and it did not, even now. I slid the knife between her ribs, under her arm.

She laughed. I had not hurt her at all! "What games we play, Gwenore," she said. "Did you think I feared you? Did it give you hope that you could bring the brats back to life? Never. I will have my own heir, and this land will be mine, and there is nothing you can do to stop me."

I stared down at the knife and I saw that it had been

blunted. The tip was turned aside. What was she made of that my knife could not kill her?

She shook her head as she read my mind. "You showed me that you had a weapon when you killed my sorcerer. Gwenore, I am not without power. Have you forgotten?"

I had lost. If the crows restored the children, she would kill them again, as many times as necessary to ensure that one day Lir would be hers.

But then, above me on the wall, I saw Darbie standing, holding King Harry, the cat, in her arms. "Mary Singer!" she called out. "My father is coming for you."

But he was already there. My mother saw him at the same moment I did, and she said, "My lord, here you are. . . ."

But he ran at her with his fists raised above his head. She fled, but instead of running through the gatehouse where she might have had a small chance to escape into the country-side, she ran inside the castle. King Lir followed, roaring like a bull. I caught glimpses of them through the windows of the tower as they climbed the spiral steps.

And then I saw the struggle at the top. And then I watched her fall, fall, fall, until she was out of sight.

Darbie had climbed down from the wall, and now she stood beside me, holding the smirking King Harry in her arms. "Did you come back to stay, Mary Singer? Did you know that my brother and sister died? But I only slept. Did you know that Connor had died, too? Is what why you came home?"

I knelt beside her, weeping. Had my spell only worked for one? Just the one?

"Fionna always slept late," King Harry said to me. "And Troy will be along soon. He would have been here sooner, but my brother cannot write well at all."

Darbie had not heard him. She was still looking sadly at me.

I stood and picked her up. "Let us go see if your brother and sister are still sleeping," I said.

"No, Mary Singer, they are dead."

"They live, child."

King Lir found us there later, while his son and daughter were yawning and stretching on their flower pallets. "You knew *her*?" he asked.

I knew whom he meant. "She was my mother," I said.

"She was no one's mother," he said bitterly. He embraced Fionna and Troy and told them and Darbie to follow him. They glanced back at me, bewildered, and then they followed their father into the royal sitting room. The door closed behind them, shutting me out.

I went back to the keep. The people of the castle had gathered there, and they stared at me strangely. I realized then that my wrist was still bleeding, and blood had stained the left side of my clothing.

"Is it you, Mary Singer?" one of the maids asked. "Did you come back for the funerals of the children?"

"There will be only one," I said, my voice breaking. "Connor's."

Before I left the castle, I looked over the wall and saw some of the men of the castle bundling up my mother's broken body in a canvas. They had been given their instructions,

I thought. She was on her way to being buried in a hole in the woods, like rubbish.

I left wearily, as dark fell, and turned toward the hidden lake where my friends waited. Father Caddaric sat sleeping outside the hut in bright moonlight, with Vespers and King Harry roosting on his shoulders, and both crows seemed to be sleeping, too. I found my other friends gathered around Julienne, who was barely breathing, but one swan still huddled next to her, his head resting on her chest.

"I finished my work," I told them as I sat down between Margarite and Tom. "How is Julienne? Is there something I can do?"

"No, she has said that her time is up, by more than half," Margarite said. "She extended it for as long as she could, but we all must leave this world. But until she fell asleep a short time ago, she worried about the swan. The boy trapped in him was not with the others?"

"His body is crossing the sea," I said wearily. I stroked the swan's back as I spoke, but I had shed all the tears I had, so I had none left for him. "There was no way to mark his forehead. Where are the other swans?"

"They huddled together on the bank," Sarah said. "They are alive, but something is missing from them. They are almost like children's toys. The three of them seem to breathe, but nothing about them seems real. The one with Julienne will have nothing to do with them."

"They were so young to be caught up in my mother's black spell," I said. "Young and healthy, and yet three of them have no spirits now."

"Ah, if I could be a swan," Julienne said, her voice so weak that I could barely hear it. "Think of it, Gwenore. Flying . . ." She could not speak any more.

I thought about it. "Would you like to be this swan, Julienne?" I asked quietly.

"Gwenore!" Hildegard said sharply. "Even if you could . . ."

"I can," I said. "I will do it if she wants it."

Julienne opened her eyes and looked straight at me. "Let me fly," she said.

Tom touched my shoulder. "Come outside," he said, and his voice had a harsh edge to it. We woke Father Caddaric as we passed him, and he rose and followed us, limping and sighing, the crows fluttering awake on his shoulders.

"You can't change Julienne into a swan," Tom said. "That isn't possible. What if you tried and something went wrong."

"Julienne is dying," I said. "She wants to become the swan. The swan is alone now, for the others are neither swans nor humans. Probably they will not even be breathing tomorrow. And I can change Julienne. I have already changed one creature into another. And I made Striker young again."

"She has the gift," Father Caddaric told Tom. He looked curiously at me, peering in the dark. "I am surprised that you returned here after your meeting with your mother."

"Where else could I have gone?" I said.

"What happened?" Tom said. "When you came in, you said only that your work was done. We had already heard from the crows that the children were not dead after all."

"They *were* dead," Father Caddaric said.

"My mother was killed," I told Tom. He would have begun the argument about the swans again, but I was too tired for it, and what strength I had left had to be used for the good of Julienne. "The only reason I might hesitate is because of Connor. His body is on the way home. If the crows could mark his forehead, his body might live again, too, and he would leave this swan's body."

Father Caddaric nodded. "But that is not possible. Unless, of course, a worthless crow was willing to try to find the ship on the great sea, and then find the child's body, and then make the mark, and then return to me."

The crows exchanged a vicious peck or two, and then Vespers said, "I will go. I am faster."

"No, *I* will go, because I write better than you do," King Harry said.

"Both go, and if only one returns, then I will still have a companion for the rest of my days," Father Caddaric said.

"Not on your life," both crows said. "We want to be done with you and your kind. You are all mad."

We prepared two more sticks, in case only one crow succeeded in finding the ship, and I soaked the brush tips with my blood. The crows left by moonlight, and I sat down in the hut with the women of Blessingwood.

"The crows will find the boy's body, and I will release his spirit to join the body, so if you still want the change, Julienne, I will do it."

Julienne opened her eyes again and reached out one thin hand. Her skin was like softly wrinkled paper. "We have something to tell you," she whispered.

"What is it?" I asked, looking around.

"We decided that we all want to fly," Margarite said. "We are old, and for a little while we could be young again. Think of it, Mary. To fly. That is what we want."

And so that night, under a pure moon, Father Caddaric and I helped four old women into the bodies of swans. Tom watched, disbelieving until the spell was done. The women of Blessingwood were nowhere to be seen, and four swans circled the lake when the sun rose.

Father Caddaric looked up at them with satisfaction. "You have done a fine thing, Gwenore," he said. "And your birthmark is no longer bleeding."

I looked down in surprise. He was right. There was no sign of blood except the stains on my white clothing.

Vespers and King Harry dropped from the morning sky to Father Caddaric's shoulders, bickering furiously. "You bawling coward! I would not have come back except for you."

"You lie, you squeaking hatchling!"

"Peace," Father Caddaric said, and he flapped his sleeves. "Rest for a while. You've done good work, and now you can sleep."

Grumbling, they took shelter inside his sleeves, but not before attempting once again to peck out each other's eyes.

"Now where should we go?" Tom asked. "I don't want to be in Lir when the gossip starts. A dead queen. A dead sorcerer. Children who were thought to be dead who are now alive. A young woman in a white dress with bloodstains. These things cause my neck to imagine a noose around it."

"We will find Brennan and then remind the explorer priests that they promised to take us with them."

"I'm not going!" Vespers cried from inside his sleeve.

"Are, too!" King Harry cried from his.

"Not!"

So we journeyed toward the coast, three exhausted people, two bickering crows, and overhead, four beautiful swans who followed us faithfully. We found Brennan and my little Striker, and the explorer priests were more than willing to protect us, in exchange for our writing down our tales so that they could put them in books, not unlike this one.

And one beautiful morning, the strong outgoing tide carried us out on the ocean in a fine ship with good company. Overhead, four swans followed us to a new world.

a u t h o r ' s   n o t e

I took certain liberties with time, history, and mythology for this novel. For those who are curious about where I began, here are some of the books I read while I was writing *Singer*. But for those who want to see for yourselves, go to Wales, England, and Ireland, and experience the enchantment I have found over the past twenty years.

W. T. Barber. *Historic Places of Wales*. Butler and Tanner Ltd., 1984.

Norman F. Cantor, general editor. *The Encyclopedia of the Middle Ages*. Viking, 1999.

Madeleine Pelner Cosman. *Women at Work in Medieval Europe*. Facts on File, Inc., 2000.

Georges Duby, editor. *A History of Private Life*. Belknap Harvard, 1985.

Judith Herrin, editor. *A Medieval Miscellany*. Viking Studio, 1999.

Stephen Johnson. *Later Roman Britain*. Charles Scribner's Sons, 1980.

Vicki Leon. *Uppity Women of Medieval Times*. Conari Books, 1997.

Trevor Rowley. *The Norman Heritage. 1066–1200*, Routledge & Kegan Paul, 1983.

Michael Wood. *Domesday, a Search for the Roots of England*. BBC Books, 1986.

Geoffrey N. Wright. *Discovering Abbeys and Priories*. Shire Publications Ltd., 1969.

◀ ◀ ◀

j e a n   t h e s m a n is the author of many novels for teenagers. She is a member of the Authors Guild and the Society of Children's Book Writers and Illustrators, and lives in Washington State. Visit her Web site at **www.jeanthesman.com**